A French Liaison

G000057533

L J Paine

Copyright © 2017 L J Paine

All rights reserved.

ISBN:1514292440
ISBN-13: 978-1514292440

THANK YOU

With thanks to my sister in law Viv Paine for all the encouragement you've given me. Without you I would have given up on this book.

Thanks to my friend Di Cohen for your honest opinion and for your encouragement.

Thanks to all my wonderful family and friends, especially those who have patiently waited for this novel to go on sale. I know it has taken ages!

With <u>SPECIAL</u> thanks to my son in law Karl Dawkins for all your help.

And to Wendy Hall for your expert work in proof reading and editing this for me.

I feel extremely proud to have managed to write this book which has been quite a learning curve. I hope you enjoy reading it as much as I enjoyed writing.

Author's Note

This book uses a mixture of US and UK English. The narrative is in UK English, but where written items are quoted, the appropriate spelling, grammar and idiom of the character is used.

This is a fictional work. All the characters and names used along with some businesses and events are either the products of the author's imagination or used in a fictitious manor. Any actual resemblance to actual persons are purely coincidental.

CONTENTS

L J Paine

CHAPTER ONE

Florence, a very attractive curvaceous young blonde French woman was carried along with the hustle and bustle of London shoppers. Loaded with bags full of groceries in one hand, she struggled to call her friend and tell her to get the kettle on as she was only five minutes away.

She had already split one carrier bag spilling her box of tampons, toothpaste, shampoo and packet of loo roll out onto the pavement. Red-faced and in a fluster she thanked the old man who'd offered her one of his bags, and rushed off like a rocket, barging straight into a handsome young American.

"Whoa - whoa - whoa, look where you are going Ma'am!" he shouted standing in her path with his hands in the air.

Florence looked up at the tall, dark-haired handsome stranger and made her mumbled apologies, dropping her mobile phone on the pavement, causing the screen to crack.

"Merde!" she exclaimed, staring down at the broken phone.

Harvey could see the young woman was struggling and bent down to pick up her phone at the same time as she did, causing them to bang their heads together.

"Ouch, you klutz!" she shouted, holding the top of her head and looking highly annoyed.
Harvey bent down again and picked the phone up for her, placing it in her pocket as both her hands were full of shopping bags.

"Merci beaucoup. I am sorry, my arms are dropping off, these are so heavy!" Florence apologised again in a strong

French accent and walked around him, leaving him behind her.

Harvey being a true gentleman ran after her offering to help Florence carry the bags. She politely refused his help and promptly dropped another bag smashing a jar of pasta sauce all over the pavement. Harvey, frustrated by now, insisted that he help her and grabbed three of the bags, whilst she picked up the shattered pieces of glass, placing them in a bin, on a lamp post by the roadside.

"It is not far, just around the corner," Florence said, rushing along with her fringe in her eyes and her scarf which hung off her shoulders, trailing on the ground behind her. He admired her small shapely derrière pertly moving up and down in her white skinny jeans. Harvey chuckled to himself as he followed the very dizzy young blonde along the road, both of them dodging various shoppers along the way.

They arrived outside the flat, Florence clumsily dropped her bags, the heaviest almost crushing her foot, causing her to swear loudly.

She pressed the buzzer then hopped around in a full circle. Her flatmate asking in jest via the intercom "Who's there?" knowing full well that it was her ditzy friend.

The door electronically opened and Florence turned around to face the American. "Thank you, er?" expecting him to introduce himself.
Instead he just raised his eyebrows and said, "Let me take these upstairs for you Ma'am," looking at her and then at the stairs leading from the entrance hall inside.

"OK, Merci." Florence led the way. She tripped as she got

to the door and banged her head on the doorframe. "Merde!" Florence exclaimed rubbing her head.

The door opened and her tall, skinny, redheaded, English friend burst out laughing.

"What have you done now? You are so accident prone! Oh, hello!" she smiled, adjusting her hair and fluttering her eyelashes at the tall stranger. "I'm Lucy, who are you?"

Florence pushed passed with a couple of the bags, leaving Harvey in the doorway with the rest. Lucy followed into the kitchen. "Wow, where did you find him?" She giggled.

"I do not know him; he simply helped me with my bags. I dropped my phone. It is broken. Now what am I going to do? I do not know where to get it repaired," Florence said feeling in her pocket for her phone. Harvey followed them into the kitchen with the other bags.

"Shall we start again? I'm Harvey, howdy." He said with a deep Texan twang.
Lucy shook his hand.

"Oh gosh, pleased to meet you! My friend here is Flo. She's French and she's staying with me for a few weeks, then she'll be on her way back again to sunnier climes."

Lucy had a posh husky voice and a sexy laugh and was a lovely girl who was always the life and soul of a party. She welcomed Harvey, thanked him for helping Flo and invited him for lunch, cheese omelettes. He thanked Lucy but explained that he had to dash as he was late for an appointment to view a piece of art. He quickly rushed down the stairs and was gone. Lucy looked out of the window just in time to see Harvey disappear into the hustle and bustle of the crowd.

"That's a shame. We didn't even get his phone number."

CHAPTER TWO

Harvey was late and cursed himself for constantly being a gentleman and always helping a damsel in distress. He made it to the art exhibition to find that the particular painting he'd had his eye on had been sold.

"Dang it!" he cursed and stared, mesmerized by the beautiful painting hanging in the gallery. It was an acrylic created by a new artist. The young woman, stood shyly, her face partly concealed by her long blonde hair, her body was lightly draped with white organza. There was an air of innocence about the painting, which the artist had captured perfectly. He felt as if he knew her and was totally infatuated with the image before him.

He had to have it; he made his mind up that he would find out who had bought it. He continued around the gallery, admiring all the various paintings. He chose another piece of art, also a female form but very abstract and brightly coloured, a complete contrast to the delicate brush strokes of the painting he was desperate to own. He bought a couple of huge canvasses depicting typical London scenes of the Houses of Parliament and the Shard, knowing they would sell well in his gallery as Texan clients always loved English artwork. He went on to choose a water colour of a Kent country scene, and a couple of abstracts in bright oranges and yellows. His main interests had always been the human female form but today he thought he would buy a few totally different styles.

Harvey wandered around the galleries seeking more unusual paintings and found four more, this time in oils. All of them by the same established artist.

"Quite a mixture this time," he thought and whilst making

his purchases, enquired whether he could have the contact details of the artist and the buyer of the one he'd gone to the exhibition for.

Harvey was a very successful art dealer who often visited Europe on his mission to buy from top artists but also liked to include new talent in his galleries. The owner of the exhibition was happy to oblige the rich Texan, knowing that if he kept his buyer sweet he would return to buy much more art from him.

Harvey really wanted the painting and couldn't wait to call the buyer. Much to his disappointment the buyer wanted to keep it for herself. Harvey offered her an extra one thousand pounds but this wasn't enough to change her mind.

"Could I meet you for a coffee?" He asked, desperate to talk her into selling him the painting.

The buyer, Mrs Dorothy Hamilton-Smythe, was a very well to do English woman, who spoke very quietly but firmly. "I don't wish to sell Mr Dove! That is final!" She had every intention of making a deal but was calling his bluff.

Harvey wasn't prepared to give up and offered her double the price she had paid. Dorothy said she was tempted and agreed to meet him in the café in the gallery, later that afternoon.

Meanwhile Harvey shopped in Selfridges, buying a couple of Lardini suits and an Armani jacket. He enjoyed shopping in the UK for clothes. Back home in Texas his casual attire consisted of a leather Stetson, checked shirt and denim jeans. He loved the whole cowboy look. He owned several pairs of well-used cowboy boots which came in handy on the ranch he jointly owned with his father Ed. They owned several dozen horses, cattle, a few pigs, sheep, chicken and geese. Harvey would occasionally enter into a rodeo, demonstrating his excellent ability to ride Magic Boy, his favourite black stallion He and his horse would gallop at high speed from one end of the arena to the other, collecting items along the way such as flags and hoops. It was such good fun and Harvey enjoyed the sound of the audience participation as they roared and cheered him on. Since he was a young boy, Harvey had always been involved in rodeos with his father. At the age of six he entered his first rodeo on the back of one of their prize sheep. The sheep wore a harness and reins and Harvey hung on tight for as long as he could, eventually being bucked off. Half a dozen youngsters all did the same and the boy who managed to stay on the longest won a rosette. Harvey was hooked after his first competition, especially as he won first prize in all three of his races.

Harvey wandered around the shops for over an hour before returning to the art gallery. He could spend hours admiring beautiful works of art. He stood arms folded, admiring the painting of the shy blonde woman. Again, he had a strong feeling that he knew her. Just then, someone tapped him on the shoulder.

"Hello again!"

Harvey turned to see Lucy who was fluttering her long black eyelashes at him again.

"This is my painting!" Lucy said, flashing her wide smile at him. "I came to see whether I had sold any of my work. I've only exhibited half a dozen pieces, I'm a fairly new artist. I usually sculpt but I thought I would test my newly found skills in water colours and acrylics."

Harvey was impressed. "It's beautiful, I want to buy it but it's sold. I'm meeting the buyer here in around half an hour to negotiate a price with her. If I hadn't have helped your friend I would have been here in time to purchase it."

"Really!" Lucy exclaimed with excitement.

"Wow, I can always paint another, especially for you! You've already met my model... it's Flo."

Harvey looked at the painting in more depth. "I thought she was familiar. I'm surprised your friend managed to sit still long enough to model for you!"

"Ha ha, she's a bit clumsy but she's a fantastic artist herself, also a beautiful model."

Harvey stood before the painting in deep thought, running his fingers through his dark curly hair.

"Could you really re-create such beauty again?"

"Oh my goodness, yes! She's so utterly gorgeous the paintbrush knows exactly how to create her curves!"

Harvey still wasn't convinced. He needed this painting. He was in love with this image.

"Maybe we could convince Mrs Hamilton-Smythe to sell me this one, on the condition that you paint her another one?" Harvey said, thinking aloud. "It could work, I don't think I could convince her without you being there, explaining that you are the artist Lucy."

Harvey checked his watch. "I'm due to meet her in about fifteen minutes are you able to stay and have a coffee?" He asked, turning to face Lucy, who was hoping he would ask her to join him.

"Ooh yes! If you buy me a piece of their delicious carrot cake to go with it!" she replied licking her lips.

Together they made their way to the next floor to find an empty table in the café. Just as they were seated, a very important looking woman made her way over to them. She was tall, slim and attractive for her age. She wore a black pencil skirt, with a cerise blouse and black patent leather stiletto shoes. Her hair was long and black, swept back in a ponytail which was tied with a velvet bow. Upon her arm she carried a Chanel patent handbag. Her wrist was laden with jewel encrusted gold bangles and her fingers with extra-large diamond rings.

"Wow! Joan Collins look-alike," thought Lucy.
The woman held out her hand enquiring in a very posh English accent, "Mr Dove?"
Harvey stood up, shaking her hand, "Mrs Hamilton-Smythe, call me Harvey, please. This is Lucy, the artist."

He nodded his head towards her. Lucy stood and shook her hand, then sat down feeling very inadequate in her red T-shirt, baggy denim dungarees and white Nike trainers.

The waitress came over and took their order, and they made small talk about the English weather until she came back and served them.

"Right," Harvey said, looking straight at Dorothy "down to business. I will pay you whatever you want for that painting. I have it on good authority that Lucy will be able to paint another for you, of very similar quality and style, because her friend is the model."

"Are you married Mr Dove? Dorothy enquired.

Harvey looked puzzled. "What has that got to do with anything?"

"Are you married?" She asked again.

"No, I am not married or engaged, neither do I have a gal." he answered indignantly, wondering what his marital status had to do with buying a painting.

"Good, because the only way I will sell you my painting is if you agree to take a friend of mine to the charity ball I'm hosting in June," she said smiling with a crafty cat got the cream type smile.

Harvey checked his planner; he was back in London in eight weeks' time as it happened to attend a charity ball and another art exhibition in the West End.

Dorothy handed him an invitation which he recognised immediately because he had already received the same one at his father's ranch in Texas a couple of weeks earlier.

"What a coincidence! I'm already attending the very same ball. I have my invite at home in the USA. I don't have a plus one so I agree to your terms. How much will you sell the painting to me for?"

She looked at him like a Siamese cat about to eat her prey.

"You can have the painting for the same price that I paid but only after you have taken my friend to the ball."

Harvey thought it rather strange. Her friend must be some kind of freak or something, as this woman was so desperate to get her a date. What was he letting himself in for?

Lucy was intrigued but very flattered that these two people were so desperate for her artwork and just sat there drinking her coffee and savouring every mouthful of delicious cake, whilst she homed in on several different conversations going on around her. A couple behind her were having a row about the mother-in-law coming to stay, the two old ladies next to her were discussing last night's Coronation Street and an eccentric old man behind Harvey was having a complete conversation all by himself whilst Harvey and Dorothy discussed the terms and conditions of the ownership of her painting.

Dorothy Hamilton-Smythe commissioned another painting of the same model but requested that she had a purple satin drape so that she could hang the painting in her snug. Lucy and Dorothy exchanged contact details. She checked her watch, made her excuses and was gone, leaving a waft of Chanel No. 5 behind.

Harvey couldn't believe his luck. He sat there in a bit of a daze, wondering what had just happened. Most importantly he realised he would have to stick to his side of the agreement so that he would be the new owner of the painting.

Lucy watched Dorothy Hamilton-Smythe as she made her way to the lift.

"Wow, that's one classy lady! She knows what she wants and knows how to get it! Look at her!"

Harvey turned to see Dorothy disappear into the lift. "Hell yeah! She's not one to mess with is she?! I'm sitting here wondering what I've got myself into! It's just for one evening I guess, a small price to pay if I get that painting! You're very talented. I'm an art dealer and very interested in your work. Take me around and show me your other paintings."

Lucy stood. "I'm sorry Harvey, I happen to have sold all six! It's amazing! I can't believe my luck!"

Harvey smiled, "Well done. It's not luck Lucy, it's pure talent! I would still like to see your work for future reference and commissions."

He beckoned her to follow him over to the lift. They went down a floor and Lucy proudly showed him her other exhibits which Harvey was really impressed with. Whilst he stood studying each piece Lucy couldn't help admire his dark curly hair and deep brown eyes. He looked slightly Italian with his dark suntanned skin. When he smiled his eyes smiled too; he also flashed a dimple which Lucy found very endearing and sexy.

As they parted Harvey shook Lucy's hand and kissed both her cheeks. She felt his stubble on her skin and breathed in his woody musky scent.

Harvey felt slightly awkward about how pleasantly the brief closeness had affected him and left the building with a spring in his step.

When Lucy arrived back at her flat, Florence was in the shower, so Lucy kicked her shoes off and flopped onto the sofa. She sat staring at Harvey's business card and smiled like a Cheshire cat at the thought of selling all her paintings and the prospect of selling much more art to the very handsome Mr Dove.

"Things like this don't happen to people like me", she

thought, kissing the glossy card and waving it excitedly above her head.

Florence appeared in the doorway in her pink fluffy dressing gown, with a towel wrapped around her head.

"Bonjour, where have you been? Would you like some tea?" Florence asked, her head on one side, whilst wiggling her finger in her left ear, trying to tease out the water that had filled it.

Lucy stretched her arms high above her head, grinning from ear to ear, she exclaimed, "I have had the most wonderful afternoon! I sold all my paintings and two people both wanted the one I painted of you! You'll never guess what happened? That American fellow, Harvey, who helped you with your shopping bags wanted it but some rich old bird had already snapped it up anyway, she said that he could buy it on the condition that he takes her friend to a charity ball. It was all a bit strange but he was so desperate to buy it, that he actually agreed to her terms. Poor fellow, I wonder who this friend is?"

"Ooh la la! Ha ha, fancy him wanting a painting of moi. Did he know that it was me that you had painted?" Flo asked, still wiggling her finger in her ear, oblivious to her obvious natural beauty.

Lucy laughed! "Yes he did once I'd explained. He said he thought the painting looked familiar."

"I am very flattered!" Flo said flopping down next to Lucy, as she did so her arm hit the side table, causing the lamp to precariously wobble on the edge. Flo jumped up and hugged the lamp pulling a funny face, her eyes wide and her mouth tight-lipped. Both girls giggled, relieved that the lamp was safe.

"He is very good looking and quite a gentleman that Mr Dove! Do you not think Lucy?"

"Yes he is and quite charming actually, quite a catch for some lucky woman, I quite fancy the man myself."

They both decided to slip into their fluffy onesies and then opened a bottle of Prosecco to celebrate before snuggling into the soft cream cushions scattered on the big old sofa. "To art!" Lucy shouted, raising her glass into the air.

"To art!" Flo shouted, spilling half of her glass down her arm.

They both giggled again and then put on Mamma Mia, a real feel good movie. They sang their hearts out to all the Abba hits which they knew off by heart, having watched the movie on numerous occasions.

Flo was in such a happy mood that she danced around the coffee table singing "Does Your Mother Know!" Her arms and legs flying everywhere, making Lucy laugh so much that she nearly wet herself.

Both girls were the same age, twenty-six. They met many years previously, when they attended the same university both studying the same art course. They kept in touch, becoming good and trusted friends. Whenever Flo returned to England for a visit, Lucy always invited her to stay with her in the same flat they shared in their days at uni.

Lucy was the daughter of very wealthy parents. Her father Charles was a top Harley Street surgeon and her mother Maria, a lawyer. Lucy could have been misconstrued as a spoilt little rich girl as her parents paid the rent on her London flat; but she was a well-liked and very down to earth sort of girl and the reason her parents did this for her was to give her independence and financial security with high hopes that their daughter would eventually make her name as a top artist.

Florence was not so fortunate. Her mother Annette was killed outright in a car accident when she was five. Jack, her father, was a labourer and had lived and worked in France for most of his life, apart from a few months' holiday across the pond when he was a young man. Since her mother died, her father had never even considered a relationship with another woman. He was completely devastated by the death of his young wife and devoted himself to bringing up his young daughter. He was a good father and despite working extremely hard, tried to spend as much time as he could with Florence, putting money aside every month towards her education. When it was time for her to leave France and pursue a new life in England he was sad to see her leave but happy that he was able to provide enough money for university. She loved her father dearly and sobbed when she left him standing alone at the airport, vowing to telephone him every day. He looked so sad, standing in his pale blue jeans and blue jumper, his grey hair framing his weather worn features.

"Au revoir, je t'aime ma chérie" He called out waving his hand in the air, trying hard not to weep as his precious daughter disappeared from view.

She kept her promise and telephoned him every day. She couldn't wait to call him in the morning and tell him about the Yank that wanted the painting of her... HER!!! Of all people! She still couldn't believe that he'd thought she was that special! Then she remembered that her phone was broken. She would Skype her Dad instead and anyway, she would love to see her father's kind face again.

The next morning both girls were up at seven. They wolfed down a bowl of cornflakes and yoghurt, washed down with freshly squeezed orange juice. Then they both chopped some vegetables and herbs and threw everything in a casserole with some diced lamb - dinner for later.

"I need you to pose for my next commission." Lucy said admiring her French friend as she added black mascara to her incredibly long dark eyelashes.

"Sacré bleu!" Florence cried out as she poked herself in the eye with the mascara brush, causing her to rub it, spreading black all down her left cheek. "I will now have to start again!" She cursed rushing off to the bathroom to sort out her messy face and blood shot eye.

When she returned, looking stunning as usual, both girls set up for a day's work in Lucy's art studio which was situated in the back room. It was an airy light room, filled with canvasses, clay sculptures, art materials, easels, and a couple of spotlights on stands.

There was a chaise lounge with a couple of arty, hand painted scatter cushions strewn upon it. Flo sat there checking for emails on her tablet whilst Lucy set up her canvas on an easel and spread her acrylic paints out on a nearby table, deciding which colours were best for her to use. She had already taken a few photographs of the painting that Mrs Hamilton-Smythe wanted her to recreate, but she needed Flo to sit for her so that she could capture the moment.

Flo tried Skyping her father but he wasn't available, "He

must be out on an early job." She thought.

Lucy rummaged through a box of fabric in the corner and found what she was looking for. She smiled, she knew that she had a piece of purple organza in there somewhere, this was perfect for the colour drape that Mrs Hamilton-Smythe had requested for her painting.

Flo stripped off and stood draped in the purple organza.

"Perfection!" Lucy exclaimed, excited and in awe of her friend's beauty. Flo blushed and bowed her head in embarrassment, just as she had done for the original painting. "Absolute perfection!" Lucy exclaimed again.

Lucy was a fast painter, especially when she loved the subject. She got to work, sketching the outline first, then filling in the background in dark tones, finishing the main subject before lunch time.

"I can do the finer details from the photographs Flo, let's have a spot of lunch in the café along the road. My treat. Hop along and get dressed Flo." Lucy beckoned her friend towards the door. Her friend sarcastically hopped up and over, and in doing so her foot got wrapped up in the organza drape making her trip over and fall flat on her face. They both fell about in fits of laughter. Lucy always laughed when her friend was around; she was really going to miss her when she left.

Florence slipped into a long flowing red skirt and white cheesecloth blouse. Whilst slipping on her red flat shoes she thought about her father. She must take her phone with her and get it mended.

The girls sat inside the cosy café, drinking coffee and eating hot baguettes, reminiscing on their days at university and wondering where the years had gone. Flo had never had a serious relationship with anyone. She had been on a couple of dates with a couple of geeks from university but just as mates. One lad, Ethan, had taken her to the Science museum, followed by a wander around Covent Garden, where they enjoyed a plate of paella in the open café. Although she enjoyed the museum and the street artists, shops and stalls in Covent Garden, she didn't much care for her scruffy, bearded, lanky and boring escort, especially after he'd lunged at her, trying to kiss her on the lips with his fish breath. When he asked her on a second date she declined explaining that she hadn't time for a relationship. Her other date, with David, ended in disaster after Flo accidentally knocked boiling hot coffee into the lap of her admirer, scalding him in the unmentionables. She blushed at the thought of him jumping up and down in agony in the middle of the crowded restaurant! He hadn't asked her out again.

Lucy had been out with quite a few young men and had one serious relationship when she was in her early twenties. Roy was a barman and Lucy's parents staunchly disapproved. Lucy respected her parents but wasn't prepared to give up the love of her life just because her parents expected her to marry someone who lived up to their expectations. Their relationship lasted for eighteen months and ended when Lucy came home early from a night out with girlfriends to find her lover in bed with an older woman.

The sight of that raven-haired slut crying with pleasure on top of Roy devastated Lucy, leaving her with the feeling that no man could be trusted and therefore she simply enjoyed flirting with the opposite sex but had never committed her feelings for anyone since.

The café, filled with people from all ethnic backgrounds, was buzzing. It was always busy. The girls often enjoyed lunch or a glass of wine there in the evening. They sat by the window 'people watching' and laughing at some of the shapes and sizes of the different characters passing by. They saw the eccentric old lady who often came by, wearing her leopard-skin hat and coat and pushing her pink poodle in a doggy pram. They laughed and waved at the six-foot-six transvestite as he minced past arm in arm with his little old white-haired mother who was only five feet tall. Such an odd pair. They waited with baited breath to see which famous actors and actresses they could spot amongst the London crowds, playing their usual game of 'whoever spots one first wins', though there was never actually a prize to win. Totally relaxed in each other's company, Florence and Lucy could have sat there all afternoon but Lucy was keen to head back to the flat and do some more work.

"OK, I really must get going now", Lucy stood, looking at her watch.

Florence stood too, checking her watch. "I am going to look for a mobile shop and get my phone mended. I do not want to miss any calls from my father."

The girls went their separate ways, agreeing to see each other back at the flat later that day.

Florence waited in the shop whilst a very nice young man took his time to carefully put her mobile back together, checking it to make sure it was now in full working order, he pointed out that he'd added his own mobile number, giving a cheeky wink and flashing a bright white smile. As usual she blushed and shyly tried to hide behind her long hair, whilst rummaging around in her bag for her purse.

"Merci, thank you, err, thank you, how much do I owe you?"

"Seventy quid please love." The skinny young man winked again, handing back a fully working phone.

Florence thanked him again and made a hasty retreat from the shop, red faced and flustered, bumping straight into an old guy who was walking passed. He gave her a filthy look and carried on his way, leaving Florence in an even bigger fluster, calling after him her apologies which were wasted on deaf ears. She stood in a shop doorway and attempted to ring her father again. No answer.

"Unusual! He must be very busy." She thought. She imagined her father up a ladder, perhaps mending a roof, clearing someone's guttering, or maybe building a brick wall somewhere.

Back at the flat Florence checked on the progress of Lucy's painting. It was coming along nicely. She put up an easel and picked a large blank canvas.

"I am going to join you for an afternoon of creativity." she said, waving a couple of paint brushes in the air, "I am inspired by a grumpy old man."

"Eh?" Lucy looked out from behind her easel with a puzzled expression. Florence started to paint.

They painted in silence until Lucy slipped a CD into the stereo unit and selected 'Sing' from Ed Sheeran's album causing both girls to wiggle their bottoms and sing out loudly. Florence giggled like a child at the sight of Lucy's bottom jutting out from behind her easel. They both jumped out and into the middle of the room at the same time, pulling funny faces and wiggling down to the floor and back up again. Then they held hands and danced around singing at the tops of their voices.

The time passed quickly as they both concentrated on their paintings stopping for a quick boogie every now and then; both girls were beginning to feel hungry again. They had large appetites and loved their food. There was a lamb casserole cooking slowly in the oven, an easy one pot dinner. The CD had played three times over on repeat and as track one was about to start again Flo threw down her paint brush and declared starvation. "I cannot work anymore! I need food!"

They headed to the kitchen and washed their brushes, where a delicious aroma of lamb, spices and herbs came wafting from the oven.

Florence laid the kitchen table with two black slate placemats, knives, forks and wine glasses, whilst Lucy dished two large bowls of tasty lamb casserole and cut some thick crusty bread, "I have this Merlot." Florence said, clumsily plonking the bottle down in the middle of the small round table.
"Fine, just perfect, thank you!"

Lucy poured, placing the bottle on the work top in case Flo accidentally knocked it over.
They sat and ate in silence for a while, savouring every delicious mouthful. They didn't always feel the need to talk. They were always happy to just enjoy each other's company.

Florence was thinking about her father. She imagined seeing his kind face which was always tanned through spending most days working outside. He had striking blue eyes, strong cheek bones and a wide smile with a dimple in his chin. His hair was almost completely grey now, matching the colour of his eyebrows and small moustache. She reached down into her handbag and grabbed her phone. She texted him saying,

"Bonjour Père j'espère que vous êtes bien?"

then carried on eating.

Lucy was thinking about her parents and wondering what they were doing. Her father John was probably in theatre, doing major surgery, whilst her mother was at home going over paperwork for a client's case. They were always working, as a child Lucy rarely saw them. She always felt so alone and wished that she'd had a brother or sister to share her childhood with. Instead she had various nannies and childminders and attended after school clubs with other lonely children. Whatever she wanted, she got, except a normal family life. She would have given up all the gifts and luxuries her parents lavished on her to have had a happy home with siblings.

After they'd eaten they cleared the table and Flo checked her phone. Still nothing from her father. She was starting to feel a little uneasy and tried to call him. It went straight to voicemail. She left him a message saying she was concerned and that she would try to call again in the morning.

The girls showered and headed back to the café down the road for a couple of glasses of wine and a social catch up with a few friends before returning home at midnight, both tired out and falling into bed to sleep.

Both girls woke to the sun streaming through their bedroom windows. Flo sat bolt upright and checked her phone to see if there were any messages. Nothing. She clambered out of bed and slipped on her pink fluffy dressing gown, then felt around under the bed with her foot for her white velvet slippers until she stubbed her big toe on the leg of the bed.

"Ouchy, ouch!" She shouted and hopped around the bedroom holding her foot.

Lucy opened the door to see what her dappy friend had done. Whilst Flo hopped around on her left leg, holding her right foot, her dressing gown flew open revealing her shapely body, just as the window cleaner appeared in sight. He stood on his ladder with his mouth wide open. Flo didn't notice him at first but when she realized he was there she wrapped her gown around herself tightly and headed straight for the bathroom where she stayed until he had finished the windows and she heard Lucy pay him and shut the front door.

She sheepishly appeared, now washed and dressed in skinny faded denim jeans and a baggy pink T-shirt. Lucy was still in her pyjamas and had by then prepared scrambled eggs and bacon with toast.

"I am very worried about my father." Flo said, staring at her phone and willing it to ring. "I have not heard from him for days now, despite leaving texts and messages. I know that he is a very busy man this time of year but we never go more than one day without contact. I am worried that something may have happened to him. Maybe he has had an accident."

"Is there anyone you can get in touch with to find out? Don't forget your phone was broken for a day or two. I'm sure someone would have been in touch if anything has happened to him Flo." Lucy patted her hand.

Flo, stared at the phone. "I wish it would ring! Papa, ring!"

Two minutes later her phone rang. An unknown number flashed up. Flo answered. Lucy could hear a French woman's voice. Flo went white. She got up from the table and rushed into the other room to carry on talking. Lucy couldn't understand any of the one-sided conversation but she gathered that something serious had happened.

Florence came back in the kitchen. "I am sorry Lucy, but I must pack and make my way back to Auxerre. My father has had a big operation. He did not tell me because he did not want to worry me. He has had a heart attack, he needs me!" She started to shake, then burst into tears. Lucy knew how close she was to her father but could only offer her a hug as comfort. She helped Flo gather her belongings, booked a flight online, and ordered a taxi to take her to the airport. They waited in anticipation and watched the clock as the minutes slowly ticked away, Flo bouncing her handbag nervously on her shaking knees.

The taxi arrived and Flo kissed her friend on both cheeks. "Au revoir. I'll be in touch as soon as I know what is happening with my father. I will stay in France for as long as Papa needs me."

She blew her nose, making a loud honking noise. Lucy wiped a lone tear from Flo's cheek then hugged her tightly.

They both waved a solemn goodbye, the taxi disappeared and Lucy's funny French friend was gone. She prayed that everything would be all right and that her lovely Flo would be able to return again soon.

CHAPTER THREE

Harvey had taken a week out of travelling to help on the ranch. The workload was massive but always under control with good management and a large crew of ranch hands and staff.

Harvey's mother walked out on them when he was eleven. She had longed for a daughter but despite trying, Harvey remained an only child. Ella met a man at a rodeo and built a relationship with him, falling deeply in love. Then she left Ed, her husband of eleven years and her precious boy, her only child, her only son. Harvey hadn't heard from his mother since. He missed her desperately as a young boy and teenager but as the years went on he relied on the love from his father, admiring his strength and integrity.

Ed had a couple of relationships with other women. People warned him that they could be gold diggers, just after his money, but Ed being such a nice guy wasn't concerned Despite being so trustworthy the right one never came along. He was happy anyway. He had a wonderful life with his son and many close friends. He'd built up his fortune through sheer hard work. He owned one of the biggest ranches in Texas. He and Harvey had learned together the art of cider making, rearing cattle and horses and entering rodeos for fun.

At the end of a long hot day under the Dallas sun, Harvey and Ed sat in their chairs drinking beer and chatting about work. Harvey told his father about the amazing new artist he'd found. He showed him a snapshot of the painting he'd taken on his phone. Ed studied it.

"She is stunning. She reminds me of someone." His eyes studied the beautiful image trying to fathom why it was so familiar.

"She's a looker", Harvey said, gazing adoringly at the photograph.

"I can't have the painting though until I play my part of the bargain. I stupidly agreed to take someone to that charity ball coming up next month. Hell if I know what I'm getting myself into. She could look like an ogre's daughter for all I know!"

They both laughed at the thought.

"I'm prepared to take the risk. It's just for one evening and then I can have that painting! I'm not selling it on Pa."

Ed had a stupid grin on his face, imagining his son dating a green Fiona look-a-like from Shrek.

"I thought we could hang it above the fireplace?"

His father's mood changed. "Instead of your mother's painting?"

"Well… Yeah, would that be such a bad idea Pa?"

Harvey waited for his father to explode. Instead Ed got up from his chair, went into the living room, took down the painting and put his knee straight through the canvas.

Harvey looked astounded!

"Shoulda done that years ago! It's just a constant reminder of what she did to us. Get another beer son, and grab my guitar."

He threw the painting like a Frisbee, sending it twirling

through the air. It landed face down on the grass a few meters away, the golden ornate frame twisted and distorted.

They sat on the veranda and a couple of the ranch hands joined them for a beer whilst they all listened to Ed strumming country tunes on his guitar. He played the classics and sang along to Lucille and The Gambler by Kenny Rogers, John Denver's Country Roads and Always On My Mind by Willie Nelson. He also strummed his own composed tunes and everyone was happy to just soak up the gentle atmosphere.

The next morning, Harvey woke up to the sound of a shotgun. He leapt out of bed and looked out bleary-eyed to see what was going on. It was his father shooting at tin cans, lined up on the old stone wall, next to Jim, his number one ranch hand.

Harvey quickly showered and headed out to join in the fun. He hadn't shot at cans since his youth. He was thirty-seven and loved his hectic lifestyle, jetting off here and there, seeking out beautiful pieces of art, but equally he loved being back home with his father.

They fooled around for over an hour. Then went inside for some pancakes, expertly cooked by Harvey.

"When you have little 'uns of ya own Harv, make sure you take the time for them. You've ended up just like me, a friggin' workaholic! You've made your dollar now take some time out and slow down."

"Like you then, Pa?" Harvey retorted.

He reminisced about the old days but never admitted that because of his love of work he lost the love of his life, and changed the subject.

"What date is that there charity ball son?"
Harvey took the envelope out of the letter rack on the kitchen side.

"June 5th, Pa. I was gonna ask you and completely forgot all about it, until I got instructions from Dorothy Hamilton-Smythe. Now I have to take an ogre's daughter."
Ed relaxed back in his chair with his hands clasped behind his head. He looked at his son with one eyebrow raised.

"She could be a stunner for all you know!"

"Hell Pa, if she was a stunner, she woulda been snapped up already!"

Ed smiled, "Well you haven't been snapped up!"

"Neither have you, Pa."

"Touché."

Later that morning, Harvey rode his horse, Magic Boy, and met Ed over in the orchard to help him mend a broken fence. Ed's horse, Bamber, was tied up under a fruit tree where he happily munched on a couple of fallen apples laying on the ground.

They worked in the searing heat of the sun and welcomed a break to drink homemade apple cordial from a cold flask in the shade under the rows of apple trees.

Ed lifted his brown leather Stetson and wiped the sweat from his brow. Harvey studied his father. He noticed how much he'd aged. His eyes looked tired and his hair more grey than he'd ever noticed before. The hot Texan sun had made its mark in the lines on his face. His body was still lean and muscular but his back was beginning to stoop through age and hard graft. Harvey admired him and had the utmost respect for him.

After they'd fixed the fence, they rode back to the ranch to do some paperwork in the cool air conditioned office.

The phone rang and Ed answered in his husky voice.

"Ed Dove, Southern Sun Ranch. Hi Mitch... uh huh, fine... We'll be there." He scribbled some notes on a pad and put the phone down.

"We've gotta go and see some foals just born down on Mitch's ranch. He said they are beauts! He has been hangin' on 'til both the foals were born so we could view them together. You ready to go? We should be back before midnight., although I suspect as usual Mitch and Jane will suggest we stay over, so pack ya' toothbrush."

"Uh huh, we'll go in my truck if you like?"

So they packed a couple of cold cans of Coke in a cool bag and set off down the long dusty track and out of the ranch, onto the open road leading out of Dallas. They were heading towards Mitchell's cattle ranch in Austin.

On the way they laughed at Ed's ridiculous jokes and sang along to country music on the radio. They talked about rodeos and ranches and redecorating the office. They didn't stop talking until Harvey mentioned the fact that he couldn't believe Ed had taken down his mother's portrait. Then the conversation fell silent.

"Pa… You can talk about her… mother… your wife! It was hard when she walked out but we've got along without her. I used to cry myself to sleep every night when she left. I tried so hard not to and tried to cry under the bed covers so that you wouldn't hear me. It's made me strong Pa and I never went without love. You gave me all the love I needed." Harvey stared at the road ahead, afraid to look at his father's face for a reaction.

"I heard you son, every night, I heard you. I can never forgive her for that." Ed slapped the dashboard, making Harvey jump! "You didn't hear me? I cried for me but mainly I cried for you son, I cried for your loss."

Harvey sped up a little, putting his foot on the gas. "Have you never heard anything from her Pa?" Harvey asked, lifting his Stetson and scratching his head.

"Never, ever! It's like she disappeared from this earth. I wasn't worried about her though, she walked out. She left us for another man; she said she didn't mean to hurt either of us. I did hear that she emigrated to Australia but I didn't want to know. I've never looked for her. She's never asked for anything from me. When she walked out she left with a small suitcase and that was all. She even left her wedding ring. I expected to hear something by now, I kinda thought she would want a divorce… but nothing." Ed also stared at the road ahead, not wanting to glance at his son, for he knew he was not revealing the whole truth.

Harvey gripped the steering wheel. "Pa, don't get angry… I tried to find her. I didn't but I tried! I want you to know that!" He stared straight ahead, not wanting to see any anger on his father's face.

Ed slapped the dashboard again. Neither father nor son

looked at each other, they carried on the rest of their journey in silence, until they reached Mitchell's ranch and then their usual banter returned and the conversation about Ella was forgotten. They were both easy going men who didn't bear a grudge; they always said their piece and then got on with things.

They drove down the track to the ranch. Mitch was waiting for them and welcomed them both with a firm hand shake and a pat on the back. Mitch took them down to the stables and they checked over the foals.

"Healthy and handsome." Harvey said, stroking the mane of the black foal with the star on his forehead. "What say you Pa? Definitely a Lonestar."

"Yep, he'll do fine boy! Good name!"

The second foal was also strong and healthy, a fine Arabian with a healthy shiny bay coat and a long black mane.

"What do you reckon on this little filly then Pa?"

"She'll do too Harv. I think Princess Arabelle suits her, what do you think? "

Harvey agreed, the name suited her. "Fancy a beer back at the ranch fellas? Jane's just lit the grill if you wanna stay for a steak. Why not bed down for the night?" Mitch stood looking at them, hoping his old friends would agree to stay for a catch up. He hadn't seen them for about a year. Ed and Harvey both nodded and smiled at each other.

"Fine by me Pa."

It was settled. Ed rang home to let Jim know they would

head back in the morning and they all went to Mitch's ranch house. His wife Jane and daughter Hayley were laying the large dining table, situated directly outside the double doors leading into the house from the decked porch. The sun had started to go down and the large house looked homely and inviting.

Hayley flashed a wide and pretty smile when she saw Harvey's familiar face.

"Hi honey! How ya doin'? How's things in the world of Harvey's art? Haven't seen you for ages hun!"

Harvey hugged her and placed a kiss on her cheek. He was pleased to see her pretty face. She had light brown wavy shoulder length hair, which was slightly bleached by the sun. Her face was slender, with high cheek bones and her green eyes were beautifully framed with extra long eyelashes. She wore dark denim jeans with white leather cowboy boots and a white cotton blouse which was undone just enough to show a little peep of cleavage. She was a tiny young woman, just five feet tall with a slim but curvy figure. Harvey remembered the many times he had chased Hayley around the ranch on horseback, ending up sitting on a paddock fence, discussing horses and music. They had never been anything more than friends but looking at her tonight Harvey had different ideas.

"Hi Hayley! Hell, you look good honey! I'm fine, art world is fine, everything is fine and dandy honey!"

They'd both put on extra strong Texan accents which made them all laugh. Jane and Hayley put on a fine spread with rice and beans, baked potatoes, cornbread and salad to accompany the sausages, steaks, chicken and pulled pork which Mitch cooked on the grill.

The beer flowed freely and soon turned to whisky and bourbon. Mitch went inside and appeared with two guitars, handing one to Ed.

"Remember this one?" he asked as he started to strum the chords to a Kenny Rogers song.

Ed recognised it and immediately joined in singing, "in a bar in Toledo, across from the depot, on a bar stool she took off her ring."

They all joined in, "I thought I'd get closer, so I walked on over, I sat down and asked her name."

Hayley linked arms with Jane and swayed from side to side as she happily sang along with them all. Harvey couldn't help but notice how attractive she looked. He'd seen her tens of dozens of times before and had spent a lot of his childhood with her between their parents' ranches, but had never really viewed her with interest.

Ed couldn't help but notice the way his son was admiring Hayley and nudged Mitch just as a large white truck pulled into the front drive and a tall, muscular young man climbed out, slammed the door and headed up to the house.

Hayley rushed towards him. He picked her up and swung her around, kissing her passionately on the lips and smacking her bottom as he followed her up the steps to the porch where everyone was enjoying the warm summer evening.

"Guys, this is Wayne. He's my fiancé." She proudly announced holding out her left hand and showing a ring with a large diamond.

Mitch smiled, "I was just about to tell you about Hayley and

Wayne, I couldn't keep it quiet for much longer! We are all excited that he will soon be our son-in-law."

Harvey felt a sinking feeling in his gut. He hadn't noticed the ring, how could he have missed out on this gorgeous girl? He'd known her for such a long time and now it was too late to do anything about getting to know her romantically! He firmly shook Wayne's hand and introduced himself and his father Ed.

"Sorry I'm so late Mitch, Miss Jane, my plane was delayed, but I got here quick as I could. I've been working in Nashville for seven weeks, been writing an album." He shook hands with everyone else and affectionately kissed Jane on the cheek, making her blush slightly.

The evening carried on with Wayne joining in all the songs. He had the voice of a professional country singer. Hayley could not take her eyes off her man, she absolutely adored him.

They had met in a bar in Sixth Street, Austin. She was passing by with her friend Cassie and heard his dulcet tones wafting out into the street. They were both drawn in, and stood watching him perform with his guitar on the small stage surrounded by the hustle and bustle of a busy bar and restaurant. He was so very good looking and stylish, he sounded a bit like Garth Brooks and looked a bit like a dark haired rugged version of David Beckham. The bar was heaving; all the tables were taken by people of all age groups. His songs catered for the young and old as most country songs do. Wayne immediately noticed Hayley amongst the crowd and sang directly at her, trying out some of his own penned songs.

"Wait for me, when the sun goes down

Say you will meet me by the stream
We will kiss beneath the stars
And you'll step out of my dream."

Hayley melted at the thought of being held in his arms, on a starlit night…

He went on singing another of his own songs.

"Here I sit, guitar in hand
Facing the breeze, feet in the sand

Here I sit trying to write a song
Pretending I'm happy and nothing's wrong

I gaze out to sea
Thinking of you and me

Here I sit, with my jumbled mind
Trying to find the meaning
To words I cannot find

Here I sit, listening to the waves
They crash in my brain
They make me insane

I gaze out to sea
I think of you and me

I gaze out to sea
I think of you and me

The feelings are there
Can't pretend that I don't care

Oh the feelings are raw

I can't take this no more
So I gaze out to sea
And dream of you and me

What we used to have
What we used to be

I'm thinkin' 'bout you and me babe
I'm thinkin' 'bout you and me.

The audience roared and cheered and he gratefully took a bow.

When he'd finished his set, he hopped down from the stage and asked her name. From then on it was love at first sight for both of them. It wasn't many months until he went down on one knee and asked her to marry him, confidently presenting her with a huge diamond ring, which fit her finger perfectly.

He was a romantic guy, who wanted Hayley by his side as much as possible. Whenever he was away he would call or Skype her, sometimes two or three times a day, a few times he even texted her in the early hours of the morning and during the night. She had never had a boyfriend that cared about her so much, so when he proposed, she said yes straight away, even though they hadn't been together very long.

They planned to have the wedding in the fall so that they didn't have to wait too long. Her mother was excited to help plan her only daughter's wedding.

The evening proceeded with lots more singing and banter between them all. Harvey was getting very drunk and jealous, which was very unlike him.

Hayley couldn't help but notice Harvey's occasional jibes aimed at Wayne. She was intrigued as to why he was acting so out of character.

When Harvey went inside to use the bathroom, Hayley followed him. "Hey Harv, what's eatin' you tonight? Why are you giving my man a hard time? "

Harvey stood in the hallway, swaying slightly as he studied her. "You are stunning Hayley. I've never noticed so much until tonight."

He grabbed her by the waist, pulled her close and gently kissed her on the lips. She pulled away, shocked by his words and actions!

"You've had way too much to drink! I think you should go to bed Mr Dove!"

She pushed passed him and left him in the hallway feeling stupid and rejected. He went to bed without saying goodnight to anyone.

The next morning Harvey, Ed, Jane and Mitch sat down to a breakfast of eggs and bacon with plenty of coffee. Harvey and Ed, thanked them for their hospitality and headed off back to Dallas. Harvey regretted his actions from the night before but as Hayley stayed out of sight he didn't get the chance to apologise to her.

CHAPTER FOUR

Florence arrived at the busy hospital still carrying her suitcase, straight from the airport. She asked at reception where the intensive care ward was. Having no sense of direction whatsoever she ended up at the wrong end of the hospital and a very kind male nurse pointed her in the right direction. It took her a further ten minutes, going up and down in the lift, getting out at two wrong floors before she eventually arrived hot and very flustered at the intensive care unit.

She had imagined the moment she saw her father but when she came face-to-face with the frail looking man asleep before her wired up to machines, drips and bleeping equipment, she just burst into tears and walked straight back out again. She had to compose herself before entering the sterile room again. She'd never seen her father look ill. He'd always been fit and well, with not so much as a cough or cold.

She entered the room again and parked her suitcase at the end of the bed. The nurse pointed to a chair and she sat. She managed to hold back more tears and listened to the bleeps of her father's heart playing on the monitor beside his bed.

For an hour Flo sat, watching and waiting for her father's eyes to open. When they did, that familiar smile shone from his face and his eyes sparkled for a second or two.

"What are you doing here?" he asked in a very weak voice.

"I am here for you Papa. Why didn't you tell me sooner, that you were ill?" she asked, taking hold of his hand and gently kissing it.

"I didn't want to worry you my ma chérie. I didn't want to spoil your trip to London. I knew how much you were looking forward to spending time with Lucy."

A nurse came in to take Jack's blood pressure and told him that he must rest. She suggested Florence go and get a coffee and come back a little later if she wanted to.

Florence dreaded having to find a coffee machine let alone find her way back to the ward again so she just sat with her father watching him sleep, praying that he would recover.

After two and a half hours Jack woke again.

"Are you still here? You should go ma chérie. I will see you again tomorrow maybe?" He drifted off to sleep again.

Florence kissed his cheek, grabbed her suitcase and set off on her mission to find her way out of the hospital and to the car park. She lost her way a couple of times, ending up in the basement and then at the café, so she grabbed a coffee to go and eventually found herself outside the main entrance. She phoned for a taxi and made her way back to their little cottage.

As they pulled up outside the familiar welcoming little white cottage, she was overcome with gratitude for all the things her father had done for her in the past. She rummaged in her bag to find her purse and front door key. She paid the driver and headed up the path, dropping her bag and all its contents. As she bent down to put everything back in her bag, she got caught on the climbing rose growing up the side of the house which snagged a hole in her cardigan.

"Shit, shit, shit and more shit! Could it possibly get any

more SHIT!!!?" She shouted at the top of her voice, unlocking the door and slamming it behind her as she burst into tears.

Florence cried herself to sleep as she laid on the sofa in the lounge.

When she woke it was 6:00 a.m. She showered and tidied the cottage, cleaning the kitchen and the bathroom and doing the few bits of washing left in the wash basket. She checked all the post that had accumulated on the mat and found a couple of letters addressed to her. One was her usual mobile phone statement but the other was in a very posh looking gold edged envelope which she eagerly undid by running her thumb under the fold, giving herself a paper cut. She sucked her finger as she read the card inside. It was an invitation to a charity ball being held at Claridge's hotel in Mayfair. Her plus-one was a Mrs Hamilton-Smythe, who requested she call to let her know that she had received her invitation and for an explanation as to why she had been chosen to go.

"This is unreal, why the hell would Dorothy Hamilton-Smythe want anything to do with someone like me?!"

She poured a mug of coffee and took the bottle of milk from the fridge. As she poured it in her coffee, it curdled into thick creamy lumps which floated on top and smelled like strong cheese. It made her retch. She poured it down the sink wiggling her finger in the plug hole until all the lumps disappeared. She scolded her finger and had to run the cold tap to ease the burning sensation.

"Black coffee it is then!" She poured another mug of coffee and looked in the cupboards for something to eat. Her father had only the bare essentials in. She found cookies in a jar, half a box of muesli, a couple of dried up croissants in the bread crock and butter, cheese and wine in the fridge. Florence chose muesli, but then realized that without milk it would be like eating rabbit food, so she munched on a cookie.

"Off to the shop I go then!" she muttered to herself, checking for her keys and purse before setting off along the road. She walked briskly, looking at her phone screen and hoping for a signal, almost bumping into Mme Beauregard. "Bonjour Florence, comment va votre père?" she enquired, looking concerned.

Florence looked up, face-to-face with the plump old lady.

"Ooh! Excusez-moi, I am so sorry! He is very poorly. I am going to the hospital a little later. I will let him know that you asked after him. Merci."

She walked a little further and several more people enquired after Jack before she entered the little shop. Eloise, the shop owner rushed out from behind the counter and kissed Flo on both cheeks. She had a worried look on her face.

"Bonjour ma chère! I do hope Jack is doing well. I was with him when he became ill. I feel responsible. I was trying to lift some heavy plant pots when your father came in to buy some milk. He did not look well, but insisted on helping me. He held his chest and fell to the ground. He looked grey. I felt his pulse; it was very weak so I called for an ambulance. I kept checking him, I did not know what to do, so I tried to make him comfortable with a pillow and a blanket until the ambulance arrived. Thankfully he was still conscious. How is he?"

Florence hugged Eloise. She knew that it wasn't her fault

her father had a heart attack.

"Do not blame yourself Eloise. He must have had something wrong with his heart. I do not know the ins and outs of his condition; I am hoping to see the doctor when I visit him later. He looked very ill yesterday, he needed rest. I'm hoping that he will look a little better when I return."

She put some eggs, bread, milk and fruit in a basket and opened her purse to pay, spilling all her coins over the floor. She broke down and cried. Eloise picked up the money, put it back in to Flo's purse, hugged her and waived her money away, telling her "No charge, you poor thing, please tell me if there is anything I can do. I'm here if you need me, any time."

"Thank you, you are very kind Eloise."

Later, Flo drove her father's van to the hospital. She managed to make her way to the ward without getting lost. When she entered the room Jack was awake and managed a smile. He spoke slowly with a weak voice. "Ma chérie, thank you for coming to see me again. I know I'm not looking my best right now!" he chuckled. It made him cough.

Flo kissed his forehead. "You look fine Papa. I'm just going to find a doctor and ask how you are doing."

She disappeared down the corridor to the nurses' station. The doctor wasn't due for another hour but the nurses told her he had a comfortable night and had improved immensely. "It must have been because he'd seen his precious daughter," they grinned with approval.

Two weeks passed and Flo was given the go-ahead to

collect her father from hospital. She couldn't wait! She'd worked hard preparing the cottage for his return. Eloise had been to visit Jack whenever she could. She had also spent a few evenings with Flo and cooked a couple of delicious meals for them both.

Florence had forgotten all about the invitation to the ball at Claridge's. Whilst cleaning the kitchen she came across it again and read it over, still with disbelief.
She dialled the number. Florence heard a very posh English accent at the other end of the phone.

"Dorothy Hamilton-Smythe speaking."

"Bonjour Madame, it is Florence speaking. I have received your very kind invitation and would really like to know what have I done to deserve it?"

The telephone was shaking in Flo's hand as she listened with bated breath.

"Florence, my dear girl. I have a proposition for you. I would like you to be the new face for my new brand of perfume and lingerie collection called Silent Senses." Dorothy waited for a reply.

Flo was suspicious. "Ahem!" she coughed awkwardly. "Um, what sort of lingerie collection? I am not a model. I have never modelled for anything in my life before!"

Dorothy laughed. "It's all above board my dear. I'm not talking about THAT sort of lingerie. Ha ha ha. My dear girl, I'm talking about beautiful classic night dresses and underwear, French lace and beautiful delicate fabrics. If you agree to take up my invitation I will pay you a very generous wage! I am aware that you may be wary but you have nothing to fear. I have seen a painting of you and you are a truly beautiful young woman. You are just the person I need to model my collection. It would save me time and money auditioning hundreds of no hopers, when you are exactly the person I am looking for! I want a fresh new face!"

Flo was really nervous, "Oh, I do not know. Supposing that I am rubbish?"
Dorothy laughed again. "My dear, you will not be rubbish, you will be a super star! Here's the deal. You will be my guest at my charity ball at Claridge's. We shall get acquainted over a few glasses of champagne, then I will introduce you to my team. I'm sure you will be fine I have every faith in you."

Flo felt excited. Nothing like this ever happened to a girl like her. It was the sort of stuff you read about. Her hands shook so much that she dropped the phone and the back fell off. She picked it up and fixed the back on.

"Hello, are you still there?" Dorothy asked with a concerned voice.

"Yes, I am so sorry, I dropped the telephone."

"Say YES and come on a massive adventure, you only live once!"

Florence thought of her father. He had always told her to grab hold of every opportunity in life and make the most of every moment.

"Father!" Florence exclaimed. "Oh I am sorry, my father is due out of hospital today, he needs me to look after him. I do not think I can leave him."

Dorothy thought she'd almost persuaded Florence and wasn't going to give up now. "If your father needs care I will provide a nurse."

"That is extremely generous of you, I do not know if I can accept your offer. Could I have some time to think it over?"

"I will give you three days. I will telephone you to find out how your father is doing and to get an answer from you on Wednesday. Goodbye for now." Dorothy said authoritatively.

Florence looked at the phone. Dorothy had gone. "Well, well, how strange!" Flo had to tell someone. She phoned Lucy and told her the whole story.

"Wow! If you don't want to do it I will! Ha ha ha... You lucky thing... Hang on a minute! Mrs Dorothy Hamilton-Smythe? She's the rich old bird that bought your portrait. The person who agreed to let Harvey have it if he takes a friend of hers to a charity ball. The same person who wanted me to paint you again in a purple drape so that it blended in with her decor. It's all a bit weird isn't it?" Lucy said sceptically.

Flo agreed. "What do you think I should do?"
Lucy thought for a minute. "OK, if I were you I would go to the ball. If it's free champagne and posh nosh you wouldn't want to pass that up would you? Golly gosh! You can check things out and make sure everything is above board, before making a decision."
Flo thought for a minute. "Oh mon Dieu, I think I am going to faint!"

"No, no! Don't faint!" Lucy imagined her loony friend on

the end of the phone, fainting and banging her head and tried to reassure her that everything would be OK, even offering to lend her her best ball gown, handbag and shoes. Flo was very grateful as she didn't own a ball gown, let alone matching shoes or a posh handbag. She had wondered what she would wear should she decide to accept the invitation, so Lucy's offer got one hurdle out of the way.

"Merci, oh, what about my hair? What about my nails and make up?" Flo began to panic.

Lucy was very persuasive. "I'll do all that for you. Cinderella shall go to the ball." She said in jest.

Flo had taken a year career break as an art teacher and in that time visited a few European countries ending up in the UK with her best friend. She exhibited some of her paintings and sold a few at a good price, but funds were low and she needed to make a decision about whether to go back to teaching or make a career change.

Lucy carried on with the positives and had almost convinced Flo until her father came to mind again.

"Just one moment! My papa needs me. He is due out of hospital today. I am going this afternoon to bring him home and I will look after him here."

There was a knock at the front door. Flo could see the familiar outline through the glass. It was Eloise.

"I have to go. Eloise is at the door, she is coming with me to collect my father. I will call or Skype you tomorrow and let you know what I decide Lucy. Au revoir."

"Bye Flo, see you soon, give my love to your father."

Florence answered the door. Eloise kissed both her cheeks and gave her a freshly baked stick, a jar of black olives and a large wedge of Brie.

They sat and ate lunch and Flo told Eloise all about her dilemma. Eloise listened with great enthusiasm!

"This is an amazing opportunity Florence! I can look after Jack. He will be fine, trust me, I am very fond of your father."

Flo hadn't imagined for one minute that Eloise would offer to look after her father. Then she realised that perhaps Eloise had feelings for him and maybe he did for her. She hadn't noticed before, but when she put two and two together, it suddenly dawned on her. They were perfect together! Eloise was probably about ten years younger but they really got on well. They were both widowers, both enjoyed good food, both worked hard for a living and besides all that, they did look kind of cute together and Flo liked Eloise; she certainly wouldn't object to her being romantically involved with her precious papa.

Eloise was slim with short dark brown hair and brown eyes. Her trim figure had stayed that way the whole of her life mainly because she was one of those people who didn't know how to sit still for long. She had lost John, her husband and soulmate around six years previously. She had worked alongside him in their shop for over twenty years. Her husband had had cancer and it was tragic when he passed away sooner than the doctors had predicted. Eloise closed the shop for two weeks after the funeral but had only ever shut for Christmas Day since then. People in the village loved her and looked upon her as a respected member of the community.

In Flo's mind it was almost settled that she would accept Dorothy's invitation and keep an open mind about taking on the modelling role, but she needed her father's approval first.

CHAPTER FIVE

Lucy prepared for the return of her dearest friend, making sure that Florence's bed linen was freshly laundered and a box of Maltesers placed on the bedside table, they were Flo's favourite.

The buzzer went. "Hello?" Lucy spoke into the intercom.

"Bonjour c'est moi, your friend from France!" Florence answered, stating the obvious.

Lucy pressed the button and rushed down to greet her, helping her up the stairs with her suitcase and bags.

Florence dumped them in the hallway and hugged Lucy as though she hadn't seen her for years.

"How's your dad?" Lucy asked Flo, as she kissed both her cheeks.

"He is very well, thank you. He is being looked after by Eloise. She is a wonderful woman. I trust her to take good care of Papa."

Flo sat on a kitchen chair and smiled a huge smile. She was relieved that her father was OK and felt happy to be back in London.
"We should go out tonight and celebrate!"

Lucy agreed. They chatted about the upcoming ball and Lucy disappeared into her bedroom, returning with the most beautiful long black chiffon dress in her hands. It was plain, apart from the thin straps, and the sweetheart neckline which were encrusted with tiny Swarovski crystals, which twinkled and glistened in the stream of sunlight gleaming through the kitchen window.

The strappy shoes and clutch bag were Giorgio Armani and just the right size for Flo. It wasn't the first time she had borrowed Lucy's shoes. Once she'd borrowed her white stilettos and got one of the heels caught in a crack in the pavement, causing Flo to fall head first into a middle-aged man walking in her direction. He found it quite charming but Flo was embarrassed and not amused when she realised the heel was stuck firmly in the pavement and she had to hobble lopsided all the way back to the flat, leaving the broken heel behind, still embedded in the crack. When she went back the next day, it was still stuck firmly in the ground. Flo got some very strange looks when passersby stopped to watch her try to wiggle the heel free, her whole body wiggling from head to toe. One lad offered to give her a hand and managed to free it for her. It looked scratched and unrecognisable, when Flo presented it to Lucy.

"Are you absolutely sure Lucy?!" Flo asked excitedly. She pulled a funny face, her eyes wide and her mouth drooping down, making Lucy chuckle...

"Remember what I did to your white shoes?"
"Of course! Try them on later. I'm excited for you! I wish I could be a fly on the wall!" Lucy said, jumping up and down and clapping her hands together.

Dorothy had kept her word and telephoned Flo back for an answer. Flo's father had given his blessing and assured her that he would be fine.

Dorothy had arranged to take Flo out on a shopping spree to choose a dress and shoes for the ball, as well as a makeup artist and hairdresser. Much to Dorothy's disapproval and disappointment, Flo turned her down because she wanted

Lucy's help and she wanted to wear her friend's dress.

Lucy couldn't believe her nutty friend's decision!

"What? Are you mad? How could you turn down the offer of someone taking you shopping and buying you clothes? You are going to have to get used to the high life mon amie!"

Whilst the girls were in the flat in London, a plane had landed at Heathrow and a very tired Harvey was heading for passport control.
He collected his luggage and looked for his cab driver, then slept all the way to his hotel in Kent. He had a few days' business to attend to before returning to the familiar hustle and bustle of the London art galleries.
He checked into the hotel in Royal Tunbridge Wells and was shown to his suite, where he dumped his case, flopped on the bed and slept...

Harvey dreamed of Hayley. She was riding a white stallion through the orchard bareback. The sun shone through her long wavy hair which flowed behind her as she joined the rhythm of her horse. She drew up next to him and jumped down. He pulled her towards him as before, but this time she didn't pull away. She kissed him gently and firmly on his desperate lips. They were both breathless with passion. He wanted her so badly. Then she morphed into the girl in the painting. She was wearing nothing but the organza drape, which the gentle breeze teased around her beautiful naked body. He held her close, she put her arms up and around his neck. As he lifted her, she wrapped her legs around him and they kissed passionately. They wanted each other... Harvey woke up in a sweat!

He realised the time. He had slept for five hours. He felt

hungry and thirsty so showered and changed before going down to dine alone.

The restaurant was busy. Harvey ordered a Jack Daniel's and ice and was shown to a table for one. He sat in deep thought, contemplating his dream. It was so vivid. He thought about his very drunken lunge at Hayley back at Mitch's ranch. How could he have been so stupid? The girl was getting married for God's sake!

The waiter came to take his order; he chose a fillet steak with chunky chips and a side salad for his main course and cheese and biscuits to follow, instead of a dessert.

After dinner, he sat in the lounge playing a game of cards on his tablet. He couldn't concentrate and decided to send Hayley a message to apologise for his drunken behaviour the night of the cookout at her parents' ranch.

He felt much better after he'd pressed the send button. Now he could only hope that she would just put it down to him having too much to drink and that they could remain friends.

The next day he was due to meet a couple of local buyers for lunch, to discuss their stocking of his sparkling Texan Cider. He was very proud of the apples and cider produced at Southern Sun Ranch. It was just another string to his bow. He and Ed were self-taught and had learned from their mistakes, starting off by making just a few gallons and over time becoming a successful business.

Over the next couple of days Harvey did some sightseeing. He'd never visited Kent before. He found the English countryside so beautiful, with its green fields and trees, oast houses, mills and quaint cottages. Royal Tunbridge Wells couldn't be any more different from Dallas. He visited

Scotney Castle and Groombridge Place and its stunning gardens, taking dozens of photos which he forwarded to Ed.

After a few days of work and relaxation, Harvey returned the hired car, checked out of the hotel and took the train to London to resume his other business, buying art. He stared out of the window at the passing scenery and thought long and hard about his life. He was fortunate never to have to worry about where the next dollar was coming from, he was a multi-millionaire, but he was undeniably lonely. His life was slipping by without a wife and family of his own. Seeing Hayley so happy with Wayne had been a bit of a wake-up call for him.

Back in London and another hotel room, Harvey prepared for a three week stay. He unpacked his cases and bags and flicked through the television channels. He found nothing of interest, so texted Ed to tell him that he was now at the hotel in London and he would keep in touch throughout his stay.

He undressed down to his boxer shorts and looked at himself in the full-length mirror. Lean, tanned, and extremely muscular with a hairy chest, he flexed his biceps. His face was quite young for his thirty-seven years. He had a few grey hairs showing in his dark brown curls. His eyes were the darkest brown, with a cheeky twinkle. He smiled at himself, flashing a dimple in his left cheek. Having studied himself, he determined he didn't look too bad for his age. This made him wonder even more, why he hadn't found someone to settle down with yet.

He showered, put on his jeans and blue striped shirt and sat on the bed debating what to do with his time. He decided to take a walk and have a look around some art shops and visit a nearby gallery.

It was the usual London scene, people of all shapes and sizes bustling past in a rush, red buses and black taxis, traffic lights and zebra crossings, tramps sitting on the ground in front of shops begging for change. He walked past a young girl with her Jack Russell sitting in an empty shop doorway. He noticed the dog looked well, but she didn't. She looked pale, thin and dirty. He walked back to her and dropped a twenty-pound note in her black knitted cap. She sat up straight from her sad stoop and called after him. "Thank you!!!" Harvey didn't look back, he just waved his hand in the air and carried on, hoping that she would spend it on a meal and not drink or drugs.

Florence and Lucy were having lunch in their usual café and as usual were people spotting, whilst eating toasted cheese and ham sandwiches and sharing a pot of tea. Lucy thought she saw Anthony Hopkins walk by.

"Do not be ridiculous Lucy!" Florence mocked. "It was not Anthony Hopkins! It did not look anything like him!"

They laughed and carried on staring out of the window. They both set eyes on Harvey. Florence stood up and shouted, "Oh, it's him again!! Causing the entire café to turn around and look at her. She blushed bright red and sat down, knocking the table and causing the small white ceramic vase to wobble over. The water spilt out along with the single red rose which Lucy mopped up with a napkin and chuckled, thinking that it would be a great achievement if Flo could go just one day without having some sort of mishap or accident.

"He's back in the UK again. I expect he's here to buy more art and to go to Mrs Dorothy Hamilton-Smythe's ball. He has to keep his part of the agreement; otherwise he can't have the painting." Lucy said, thinking that it was time they left the café and headed back home to do some more work. "Perhaps he will buy some of your work this time Flo?"

Florence was quite excited at the thought of him buying her paintings. She couldn't wait to get back to the flat, and in her haste, got her foot wrapped around a chair leg, tripped and fell over.

"For goodness sake! You need to wear a suit of armour Florence!" Lucy exclaimed as she helped her friend up from the floor. She held her arm and firmly guided her to the door, making sure that she was all right once they were outside. Then they headed home to work.

CHAPTER SIX

Hayley woke from a deep sleep to find Wayne, propped on one elbow, staring down at her. He had stayed the night at her parent's ranch house. As Mitch and Jane were away for a few days, they had the house to themselves. The ranch hands were around and about in the day, but slept in the two small bungalows in the top paddock with their families.

She yawned and stretched her arms. "Hey honey! How long have you been looking at me like that?"

Wayne smiled and kissed her cheek. "For about half an hour, you look so beautiful when you're asleep, I can't believe you're mine. I love to watch you; you look so peaceful and innocent."

She smiled and pulled his face down over hers, gently stroking his cheeks with her hands, her lips softly caressing his. Her heart beat faster as his lips closed on hers, he slid over and on top of her. They made love over and over again Wayne wanting her more and more until she was exhausted and turned on her side away from him. Wayne pulled her arm, Hayley shrugged him off. Wayne felt rejected and forced himself on top of her. Hayley struggled as he gripped her wrists.

"What are you doing?"

"Come on honey! I want you again!"

Hayley struggled and tried to push him off, but couldn't move him. "Get off! Get off! Are you going to rape me?"

He pulled away and got out of bed storming off to the bathroom, leaving Hayley in bed upset and confused. She lay there, her mind full of mixed emotions, a single tear ran down her cheek. She heard Wayne singing in the shower and when he returned to the bedroom, he sat on the bed next to her and gently kissed her forehead.

"I'm sorry honey, I got carried away. It won't happen again. I promise you, it will never happen again. I love you so much. I don't know what came over me! I just can't get enough of you. It'll soon be time for me to go back to Nashville and I guess I'm just afraid to leave you, in case you find someone else while I'm gone."

Wayne tenderly kissed her cheek and held her hand.

"Am I forgiven my honey?"

"Don't be silly honey, I won't find anyone else. It's you I'm gonna marry!"

Hayley loved him and was prepared to put it down to pure passion and the fact they hardly ever spent intimate time together due to Wayne's singing career.

She showered and headed towards the aroma of freshly brewed coffee wafting from the kitchen.

Wayne was standing at the kitchen sink looking out across the vast open land. Hayley crept up behind him, placing her arms around his waist and hugged him tightly. He turned to face her, looking down on his tiny fiancée, he kissed the top of her head and apologised again.

"I don't know what came over me my honey."
They sat and ate a breakfast of eggs on toast, and planned a day of horse riding, then afterwards a quick trip into the city for a meeting with their wedding coordinator. Hayley

picked up her laptop and noticed that it had already been used.

"That's strange!" Hayley said looking puzzled.

Wayne looked up from his phone, "What honey?"

She pointed to her laptop. "Have you just been on this?"

Wayne nodded. "Yes, I borrowed it to check on something."

Hayley looked more puzzled. "How did you log into my Facebook account?"

"I didn't!"

"Well I know I logged out last night, before bedtime. I definitely logged out!"

"You must have thought you logged out hun. You had a long hard day yesterday." Wayne suggested, trying to reassure her.

Hayley had been very tired the night before and thought that perhaps Wayne was right. They drank another cup of coffee, and set off out of the side door towards the stables.

"Just a sec honey, I forgot something." Wayne slipped back inside the house and followed Hayley shortly after, where she was standing with Jeff and Kelvin, two of the head hands.

"Hi guys, how are you both? Lovely day for a ride. I'm taking Dandy out and Wayne can ride Zipper." Hayley said, patting her horse and kissing him on the nose.

She chatted to Jeff, putting her arm around his waist, whilst thanking him for taking care of her horse as she had been away for a couple of days.

Wayne got a bit edgy and grabbed Hayley's arm, pulling her away from Jeff. "Which one am I riding?" He asked eagerly.

Hayley rubbed her arm, thinking Wayne was a bit rough, but took him along to show him a tall, handsome stallion.

"This is Zipper, he's a bit frisky but he's such a lovely boy. If you show him who's boss, he will respect you." She brushed him and chatted to Jeff who followed them into the stable. He prepared the horse for riding and led him out into the paddock, followed by Wayne.

"How experienced a rider are you?" Jeff asked politely.

"What's that got to do with you?" Wayne snapped!

Jeff shrugged and handed Wayne the reins. Hayley mounted Dandy and watched as Wayne expertly mounted Zipper.

"Don't know what's eating Wayne today." Jeff said as he stood, pitchfork in hand, watching Hayley and Wayne ride off.

Kelvin stood next to Jeff. "There's something 'bout that guy, he ain't right... I'm not usually wrong about a person."

Hayley and Wayne rode for half an hour. The heat was becoming unbearable. Black clouds were gathering in the deep blue sky.

"Hell Hayley, looks like we're gonna have one hell of a

storm soon. What say we take shelter?"

"I'd sooner head back Wayne. We can beat the clouds if we gallop."

Hayley pulled up alongside Wayne. Just then there was a loud clap of thunder, together with a flash of lightning, which spooked both horses, causing them to bolt. Dandy threw Hayley off, she screamed as she fell to the floor, landing on her side in a cloud of dust. She looked up to see Dandy wildly ride off into the distance, leaving clouds of dust behind, followed by Wayne on Zipper. She could see he had no control and was hanging on for dear life. She sat up and cried out in pain, holding her left arm, feeling sure it was broken.

"My phone, where's my phone?!"

She felt her back pocket, it wasn't there. Trying hard not to cry Hayley managed to stand up and walk around, looking for her phone just as there was another loud thunder clap! Her phone was nowhere to be seen. She really needed help, she was in agony and just wanted to phone Jeff or Kelvin to let them know what had happened. Worried about Wayne and his lack of riding experience, Hayley wandered over to the shelter of a tree, she knew this was something you shouldn't do in a storm, but she would rather that, than stand out in the open.

Ever since childhood Hayley had been petrified of thunderstorms. She had once been caught up in a tornado at Great Aunt Molly's house and had to shelter in her Aunt's basement. It was exciting and scary for Hayley and her cousins to retreat down the rickety wooden stairs to the basement. Aunt Molly slammed shut the heavy trap door and they stayed there, huddled together, watching spooky shadows cast from the dim light of a candle, whilst listening to the wind howling above them. There were loud bangs and crashes and the sound of breaking glass. The wind moaned like a Banshee cursing them all. Suddenly the thunder got louder and louder and the wind howled like a freight train passing through. They all hugged each other, petrified, waiting for the storm to ease. It seemed like a lifetime waiting for the lull.

When the noise dwindled and when Molly felt it safe they all emerged from the basement relieved to find the house had stood up to the storm, apart from a couple of broken window panes and a few dozen missing roof tiles. Sadly the wooden house next door was razed to the ground. Hayley has never forgotten the eerie quietness that followed, broken by old Mrs James weeping at her loss, and Aunt Molly offering lost words of comfort, feeling guilty that her house was OK but her dear old neighbour was left with virtually nothing. They all helped to search amongst the wreckage for salvageable belongings for the poor little lady, until Mrs James' son arrived and took her away. She never got over the shock and died a few weeks later.

The storm continued and the sky got darker. Time went by so slowly, should she start walking back or just wait in the hope that Wayne would reach the ranch house and get help? After a while, a Land Rover could be seen in the distance. Hayley was overcome with relief. It was Jeff, Kelvin and Wayne. They pulled up next to Hayley and Wayne jumped out. He had a nasty cut on his head and was covered in dust. He held his fiancée close to him as she winced in pain and burst into tears.

"Are you OK? Are you hurt?" Wayne asked, holding her at arm's length so he could check her over.

"I think my arm is broken, how about you? What have you done to your head? What about the horses? Did you fall off? Do you know where the horses are now?" She asked, hysterically through her sobs.

Wayne pointed to the Land Rover. "Jump in my honey, let's get you to the doctor. I'm OK but should probably get checked over as well, I took a fall. The horses were just spooked by the storm; they are back in their stables now. Come on darlin', let's get you back."
On the way back the heavens opened and the rain came down so heavily that Jeff found it hard to see. The wipers could hardly cope. Hayley sat in the back with Wayne; she cradled her arm, every bump in the road made her wince.

"I couldn't find my phone! I wanted to call Jeff or Kelvin to tell them what had happened. It must have dropped out during the ride. I looked around where I fell but it wasn't there."

Wayne held her hand, "It could have dropped anywhere along the way, my honey."

Hayley remembered their appointment with the wedding coordinator. "Maybe we should cancel our appointment this afternoon?"

"Let's see how you are first. It depends on the time. You might have to have that arm of yours in plaster." Wayne said, gently squeezing her hand and trying to comfort her.

They reached the ranch house; Jeff suggested Hayley get in the front and that Wayne take her in the Land Rover to the hospital. Jeff and Kelvin hopped out and ran through the rain to the house. The vehicle sped off into the distance, returning a couple of hours later. The storm had moved away and the sun was shining. It was just before midday and Hayley was smiling as she walked inside, where Jeff and Kelvin were busy sorting some paperwork.

"Hey guys! I haven't broken my arm, I have muscle contusion." Hayley declared as she popped her head around the kitchen door. Jeff laughed at her. "In other words you badly bruised it."

Both Jeff and Kelvin thought back to Hayley as a child, always demanding a Band-Aid if she had the tiniest cut or graze and then as a teenager making a big deal if she had a headache or a slight head cold. Always overdramatic about everything, often they'd tease her calling her a hypochondriac.

"Yep, boy is it sore and black and blue... look! Just gotta rest it for a few days. I'll have to rely on you guys to groom Dandy for me."

"Nothing new then!" Kelvin was quick to reply.

"Hey! I try and do as much as I can in between work!" Hayley protested.

Hayley was a personal trainer. Four days a week, she would either visit clients at the local gym or they would come to the ranch and use her well-equipped studio. She made a good living from this, with each session lasting fifty minutes, including a ten -minute cool-down and stretch, at seventy-five dollars per session. In addition, she gave riding lessons mid-week. Loving everything in her life, Hayley now felt complete with her gorgeous fiancé.

As she'd already booked three days off to be with Wayne before he went back to Nashville, it didn't matter so much that she had to rest her arm for a few days.

Wayne followed her into the kitchen. "Shall we get lunch in town hun, before we meet the wedding coordinator?"

Hayley was really excited! The wedding was beginning to feel real. They had chosen to hold it at the ranch but needed to meet with Miss Martinez to view wedding decorations and taste cakes.

"OK, we can pop into that delicious steakhouse first. We have plenty of time. Perhaps you could drive me back up to where I came off Dandy later to see if I can find my phone?"

Jeff looked up from his paperwork. "I'm not sure about these things hun, but I think you can track a phone."

"Yes Jeff, you're right! I'll give it a go."

Hayley went to get her tablet, but Wayne stood in her way, gave her a hug and turned her around to face the door. "We can do that later honey. I'm starved, let's go out and get some lunch, otherwise we won't have time to do everything."

Hayley agreed, to track it later, "Just need to change." Which she did, into a black short skirt, white long-sleeved blouse and matching sandals before heading out to her car.

"I'll see you in the car hun. Just need the bathroom." Wayne also changed from his dusty clothes and met Hayley who was sitting in the passenger seat of her car. Wayne climbed into the driver's seat and admired Hayley's shapely legs. "You look nice Hun, good to see your legs!" He squeezed her knee, before driving off. Hayley noticed that

Wayne kept glancing at her legs and felt flattered that he liked them so much.

After a lunch of steak and salad they met Miss Martinez and tasted some luscious cake samples, deciding on a rich chocolate layer cake with fresh cream and sliced strawberries in the centre of all three layers, finished with chocolate ganache. The theme was red and white and Hayley chose red and white molded chocolate flowers for decoration. Then they were shown all sorts of themed decorations but Hayley just wanted simple red and white rose garlands, with white chair covers and red satin sashes. They decided on eight large decorative pillars with huge red vases on top, filled with roses, to line the aisle up to the gazebo where they would say their vows. The gazebo was to be decorated in white organza drapes with more garlands of red and white roses, and mini lights everywhere! Lots and lots of fairy lights. It was going to look resplendent.

Hayley came away from the meeting on a high. She had almost forgotten about the pain in her arm, she was so happy.

"I love you my handsome man", she said as they walked arm in arm back to the car.

"I love you more my honey." Wayne replied kissing his little bride-to-be on the top of her head.

Driving back to the ranch, they turned the radio up and sang happily to country music. Wayne put his hand on Hayley's leg, then moved further up to her panties. "Take them off." He said tugging at them.

"Stop it Wayne, you're driving!" Hayley laughed, thinking that he was joking. She pushed his hand away and playfully smacked it before pulling her skirt down to cover her knees.

"I'm asking you to take them off! Come on hun, it's kinda exciting don't ya think?"

"No! Not here, not now! Not while you're supposed to be concentrating on driving!"

"Come on... Play hun, play!" He said firmly, tugging at her skirt.

"No Wayne! No way!"

Wayne put his foot on the gas and sped like a lunatic along the freeway.

"Slow down Wayne, you're frightening me!" Hayley screamed as she watched the speed dial go up and up. Wayne was like someone possessed. He drove around cars and sped in front of them, almost causing several accidents.

"WAYNE! WAYNE! PLEASE! SLOW DOWN, PLEASE!" Hayley was shaking.

He laughed, looking straight ahead. Hayley was so scared, she started to cry, begging him to slow down.

Suddenly he came to his senses and slowed down. He didn't look at Hayley, he just drove.

Hayley wondered what on earth was wrong with her man. She sat next to him stiff with fear with her hands grasped tightly in her lap, frightened to move. She kept glancing at him, looking for some sort of explanation for his strange behaviour, but Wayne's face was expressionless.
Wayne drove past the turning to the ranch and down a

quiet lane and pulled over. Hayley froze. Wayne turned the radio down and sat in silence, before turning to her and looking her straight in the eye. "I'm so sorry honey. I couldn't help myself. The thought of you sitting next to me, looking so sexy, just made me want you. All the talk of the wedding and the thought of you walking down the aisle and becoming my wife, just made me want you like never before! I can't even begin to imagine how much I've frightened you. I've never felt like this about anyone before. I hope you can find it in your heart to forgive me hun."

He put his hand in his pocket and pulled out a gift wrapped box. He tenderly took her hand and placed the small package in it, then closed her fingers around it.

Hayley looked at the package, gift wrapped in pale pink with a white bow and a small silk rose.

"Undo it honey."

Hayley untied the white ribbon and carefully removed the little rose, slowly opening the box as if it were Pandora's box. Inside under a layer of pink tissue was the most stunning diamond bracelet.

"Do you like it?"

"It's exquisite. Thank you." She reached over and kissed his cheek.

Wayne held her wrist and fastened the catch on the bracelet. He looked at her before starting the engine, and turned the music back on and drove back to the ranch, happy that he had possibly smoothed things over with his fiancée. Hayley felt relieved that he hadn't wanted sex on the side of the road.

Back at the ranch house, no one was home. Jeff and Kelvin had left to finish off at the stables, so it was just Hayley and Wayne.

"Shall we just chill out tonight hun?" Wayne asked, whilst popping the top off a cold beer from the fridge. "I'll see what movies are on if you like?"

Hayley was happy to do that, it had been a long day. She was tired and bruised, and wanted to just curl up on the couch.

Wayne sipped at his beer. "I'm gonna grab a shower honey. Won't be long."

Hayley watched him through a gap in the bathroom door. He was so handsome. His body was firm, lean and muscular. His olive skin was toned and tanned; he had a couple of nasty bruises on his side from earlier. She removed the box from her bag and placed it on her bedside table, then sat staring at all the facets sparkling in the diamond bracelet on her wrist. She was one lucky girl and felt sure that he was the man she wanted to marry.

Wayne stepped into the shower and started singing one of his songs. Hayley loved his voice and listening to him took her back to the night she first heard him at the bar on Sixth Street.

The bedroom floor had Wayne's clothes strewn all over it, Hayley bent down and started to pick them up, noticing a phone under the bed. She reached under and discovered it was her own, the one she thought she had lost.

Wayne emerged from the bathroom with just a white towel

wrapped around his waist.

"Look what I found!" Hayley said waving her phone in the air. "Kinda funny. I could have sworn I'd put it in my back pocket before our ride. I never go anywhere without it."

"Well, you've found it, that's the main thing hun. It must have fallen out of your pocket before we left and you didn't realize."

Hayley thought it odd that it was under the bed, but it had probably been accidentally kicked underneath.

Wayne noticed his clothes had all been placed on the back of the chair and thought, "Thank the Lord she didn't find her phone in my pocket."

Whilst Hayley was in the shower, Wayne quickly flicked through her phone messages and then her contact list. As a result of Hayley's job she had dozens of male contacts. Wayne deleted a few numbers, Bobby, Ed, Hal, James, John, Robin and Teddy. Then he placed the phone back on the bed, put his robe on and headed for the living room to find a good movie to watch. Hayley emerged in a white bathrobe, her hair in a towel turban.

"Chick flick, horror, musical or comedy?" Wayne asked, whilst flicking through the channels.

Hayley admired her darling man as he sat on the floor in his robe and slippers. He was so strikingly handsome. How could she have felt anger towards him earlier today? She couldn't resist taking the remote from his hand and pulling him up from the floor.

"Never mind the film honey." She whispered slowly

undoing his robe and caressing his shoulders with small gentle kisses. He did the same to her, letting her bathrobe drop to the floor. He stroked her bruised arm and gently kissed it, then picked her up like a child and carried her into the bedroom. They moaned with pleasure as they kissed and stroked each other in all the right places. The evening was taken up by making love to each other in perfect harmony, each one knowing exactly what would give the other endless pleasure. They ended up falling asleep in each other's arms and woke at dawn to the sound of one of the roosters outside in the yard.

They both lay there in silence, all they could hear was the clock ticking and their heartbeats. They both felt so much in love, they fell back off to sleep until eight thirty.

The day was planned. Hayley was going to take Wayne into Austin, they were to have lunch in the bar where they'd first met and then pop in and out of the bars to watch the various singers along Sixth Street, run into the shops for some retail therapy and then just before dusk board a boat and visit the bat bridge. It was agreed that Wayne would drive because her arm was still a bit sore.

They showered and dressed. Hayley wore a long summer dress with a big bold red and yellow print. Wayne wore blue denim jeans with a white linen shirt.

Before they set off Hayley checked her phone for messages and then her work schedule for the following week once Wayne had returned to Nashville. Her usual clients were booked in for their normal sessions. She was hoping that her arm would be better by then, and thought perhaps she'd better text her clients and forewarn them in case it was still not one hundred percent. The first on her list was Bobby; he would always arrive on time for his fitness session. She scrolled down for his number. It was missing. "That's very strange!" Hayley said, running up and down her list of contacts.

"What's that hun?" Wayne asked, looking up from his phone.

"Bobby's number is missing."

"Who's Bobby?" Wayne asked, knowing full well that he was one of her many male clients.

"My client. He's my first one on Monday morning. I can't find his number!"

Wayne imagined Hayley taking a one-to-one fitness class with a man named Bobby. He pictured them getting hot and sweaty together. He believed Bobby to be young, good looking and much fitter than himself. His imagination ran wild, thinking that they got up to all sorts of things in the gym together. He could hardly contain his jealousy.

"Well who knows. Things do go wrong with phones don't they? Come on honey, let's go out now. I want to spoil you, buy you nice things. I'm looking forward to seeing the staff back at the bar, and having a nice lunch there. Can't wait to tell them we are engaged."

So Hayley grabbed her bag and shoved the phone in it, thinking that perhaps she had deleted Bobby's number by mistake. It was no big deal.

They arrived in Austin and parked. First job was to book two seats on the riverboat for the trip to see Congress Avenue Bridge, or as tourists called it, the bat bridge. Hayley had taken the trip a few times as a child. Then they walked around a few department stores, looking at household items and getting ideas for their wedding list. As they did not have a home of their own yet, they didn't have anything to put in a home and it dawned on them just how much they needed. They put together a great long list as they studied household items together.

Lunch was pleasant; Wayne was welcomed with open arms in the bar where he had a few gigs. The staff were pleased to meet Hayley and gave them a complimentary lunch. "On the house for you two guys. Good luck to you both," the owner said, offering them a bottle of Prosecco to enjoy with their meal, and hinted for Wayne to perform a couple of numbers and he was happy to oblige. Hayley felt so proud of her gorgeous man as he stood on the stage. She noticed some of the ladies admiring him as he sang.

Feeling full from a very late lunch, they popped in and out of the bars; different voices and tunes wafting out onto the street as they passed the various bars, clubs and music venues, and then in and out of shops so Wayne could buy a nice present for his girl. He watched her as she picked up a small old fashioned teddy bear, dressed in old English attire with a flat cap and round glasses. She hugged it, before placing it back on the shelf, and then carried on wandering around the shop. Wayne quickly paid for it, looking out for anything else that caught her eye. She picked up a picture frame. It was white with a shabby look to it. "I like this, do you?" She asked, holding it in front of Wayne.

"You like it, you have it, get two, get four, or six! We will need matching picture frames for all our kids. Four or five kids maybe?" Wayne laughed.

The female shopkeeper was watching and admiring the handsome young couple. "Are we expecting Ma'am?" She asked.

Hayley was a little embarrassed. "Oh... Not yet! We hope so after we get married. I'll take two of these please." she said passing the frames to the lady behind the counter. Wayne paid for them and put them in the bag with the bear, which Hayley noticed and didn't ask about. She assumed it was for her.

Time had gone by really quickly and they had to rush to board the large boat carrying many passengers who were looking forward to the trip along the river.

It was an interesting tour; the guide on his microphone pointing out various landmarks. Hayley and Wayne snuggled up closely and enjoyed the cruise. Right on time, they arrived back at the bridge, with many other boats full of tourists. The vast bridge was jam-packed full of people who were lined up from one side to the other. Watching and waiting, one or two bats flew out, followed by a few more, until thousands and thousands flew out from underneath the bridge. Such a wonderful sight! The tour guide explained "The Congress Avenue Bridge shelters the largest urban bat colony in North America. Between seven hundred and fifty thousand and one point five million bats fly out near dusk. When they do, you might experience a raindrop sensation, this is because the bats poop, so when you look up, keep your mouth shut!" Everyone laughed.

The pair of them were exhausted and enjoyed the day. It was time to head back to the ranch. Wayne opened the car door and as Hayley sat in the seat, he placed the teddy bear on her lap. "When I'm back in Nashville, think of me and hug the bear, don't hug anyone else."

Hayley thought his words were very odd, but hugged the

bear just like she had in the shop. She kissed it on the nose and said, "I shall pretend he's you."

Wayne looked pleased. As they drove back Wayne told Hayley, "After you become my wife, I don't want you working as a fitness instructor."

Rather puzzled by his remark, she laughed. "What? Don't be stupid hun it's my business, my career, I love it! What else would I do?"

"Why do you love it Hayley?" He asked in a strange voice.

"What do you mean by that? I love it because it's what I do best!"

"Do you love it because most of your clients are men?"

"What?" She asked in disbelief!

"I'll ask again... Is it because most of your clients are men?"

Hayley gulped and answered slowly, "For one, they are not mostly men, I have more female clients, and two, I am hurt to think that you think of me in that way! And another thing, I am not giving up my work! I like to keep fit, I like my clients, I like my life and my independence!"

Wayne was angry, she could see it in his face, he was gritting his teeth and squeezing the steering wheel. She didn't want another road rage episode like before and quickly thought of a way to try and calm him down.

"Honey, what if I give you a nice relaxing massage when we get home? We can talk about it when we are more relaxed. It's been a long day and we are both tired."

She placed her hand on his knee and squeezed it, then rubbed her hand up the inside of his pant leg. "Don't be angry, we've had such a wonderful day! You go back tomorrow, our time together should be happy. I'd hate to think that I make you angry."

She chose her words carefully. Wayne decided that he would drop the subject for now, but inside he knew he had to get his way.

CHAPTER SEVEN

Florence's father Jack grew stronger every day. He was happily sharing his life with his new love Eloise. She had started to stay over for the odd night or two. At first it was to make sure that Jack was comfortable and to make sure that he was OK. Then one evening Jack kissed her hand and then her cheek. Their eyes met and for the first time since he lost his wife, he felt the urge to kiss another woman on the lips. Eloise was happy to respond and shyly kissed him back. One thing lead to another and before they'd thought too much about what was inevitably going to happen, it had, and they woke up the next morning blissfully happy and next to each other in Jack's bed.

They got on really well together, enjoying a game of poker some evenings and watching movies or just sitting quietly reading. They shared the same sense of humour and spent a lot of the time laughing at the stories Jack told about things Florence had done in the past.

As a young teenager, she used to clean the vicar's house for pocket money. There was a large dark oak ornate chair in the hallway, which had lots of carvings on the arms and legs and was probably worth a fair bit. Florence moved it so she could clean the floor beneath and the arm came off in her hand. In a panic, she rushed to tell Jack, slipped on the floor and knocked herself out. This resulted in a loud crash and a bang, causing the vicar to rush down the stairs, slip and jar his back. He managed to phone Jack and an ambulance. Florence had mild concussion, the vicar had a pulled muscle and Jack mended the chair.

Another incident happened when Florence broke Mme Bonnet's teapot. She was washing up when it accidentally slipped through her hands because she had used too much washing-up liquid. In a panic she took it home and tried to glue it together with super glue. She not only stuck the spout on the wrong way around, but also glued her thumb to the handle. Luckily Jack had walked in just as Flo got stuck and helped free her very sore thumb. Then he took her shopping to replace the teapot. It cost her all her wages, only for Mme Bonnet to tell her that she really *"hated the thing anyway!"*

Eloise was fond of Flo and imagined the funny girl causing mayhem as a cleaner. She also recalled the time when Flo had visited her shop and had tried to help M. Lament, an older gentleman and regular customer. He had a small case of beer and a shopping bag. He insisted he could manage, but Flo insisted that she help him, tugging at the bag, causing M. Lament to let go and Flo to fall backwards into a tall display of canned peas and beans, which scattered all over the shop floor.

They sat in the small lounge playing cards and laughing together. Entirely happy for the first time in years.

The phone rang. It was Flo. "Bonjour Papa, comment allez-vous aujourd'hui?" she asked the usual question, how are you today? His usual reply was that he was fine. He explained that Eloise was expertly looking after him and also slipped into the conversation that Eloise was now staying with him. Florence was a little shocked at first and then asked, "Together, as a couple? A proper couple?"

"Oui."

"Merveilleux, just marvellous Papa. I am so happy for you!" Florence then blew a kiss down the telephone and hung up! She just couldn't wait to tell Lucy!

As Jack grew stronger he helped Eloise in the shop - for a couple of hours at a time at first, but then more often as he really enjoyed it, and Eloise enjoyed having him by her side. They decided that this was the right thing for them both. The customers all liked Jack and many of the ladies would go into the shop to secretly flirt with him, which he quite enjoyed. Eloise didn't mind, her takings were up thirty percent now Jack was around.

They decided that Jack wouldn't return to the building trade. He had laboured hard all his life and was happy to take things a little easy, especially since his heart attack. Eloise didn't want to appear presumptuous, but she asked him anyway. "Jack, forgive me if I am being forward but would you like to move in with me? You can work in the shop as much as you like and I can take care of you."

"Non." Jack shook his head... Eloise looked perplexed.

Jack got down on one knee. "I will only move in if you do me the honour of becoming my Mme Dubois. I am very sorry I do not have a ring yet."

Two ladies had entered the shop just as Jack had dropped to his knee. They heard him ask the question and waited excitedly in the doorway with baited breath.

Eloise was stunned and looked at the two who were smiling and nodding their heads simultaneously.

"Oui, oui, oui." She answered and rushed over to help Jack to his feet. The two ladies clapped and cheered. Jack kissed Eloise hard on the lips and laughed with joy.

That evening back at the house, Jack Skyped Florence. He started with his usual father, daughter conversation, then beckoned Eloise to come and sit next to him, so that Flo could see her face.

"We have something to tell you." Flo watched her laptop screen back in London and could see the happiness on both their smiling faces.

"We are getting married!" Jack waited for a response from his daughter.

"Congratulations Papa and Eloise! I am so happy!" Flo could be seen jumping up and down, clapping and laughing. "I am going to have a glass of something to celebrate, je vous aime tous les deux, au revoir." Flo was gone, obviously happy at her father's news.

Jack and Eloise made plans. Jack would sell his cottage and move into the flat above the shop. They would get married in the spring, just a small wedding with close friends and family. They would run the shop together and Jack would tend the pretty cottage garden at the back of the shop. Perhaps also make part of the shop as a tea room and have a few tables and chairs out in the garden. Eloise had always wanted to keep hens and suggested they buy half a dozen, if Jack would make a coop.

It was lovely to have someone special to plan a future with, something Jack had never imagined would happen again, after losing his wife all those years ago.

CHAPTER EIGHT

Back at the flat in London, Florence and Lucy danced around the kitchen, holding hands and singing to "Happy!" by Pharrell Williams.

"We need to celebrate! Shall we go to the bar? I am so happy for my papa!"

The girls were both dressed, makeup on and hair done within half an hour.

The atmosphere in the café bar had the usual happy vibes, with the regular clientele enjoying a drink and a chat together. Fred and Mo, who owned the bar, gave Flo and Lucy a free glass of Prosecco after hearing why Flo was celebrating. They turned the music up and after a couple of glasses Flo became a little tipsy, dancing in-between the tables. Lucy watched her friend and laughed, the man standing next to her at the bar laughing with her. "Whenever I see your friend, she's always smiling."

"Yes, she is, and has the ability to make everyone else around her smile."

A couple of hours later Lucy and Florence were seated at the back of the bar happily chatting to a couple of young men. The door opened and a handsome man with a familiar face entered, ordered a Jack and Coke and sat at the bar on his own. Lucy kept looking over and eventually caught his eye. She waved, but he didn't notice her, so she weaved her way through everyone and tapped him on the shoulder. "Hi, Mr Dove! What are you doing here?"

"Miss Bowes! Nice to see you again. I'm back in London buying more art. Have you anything new to show me?"

Lucy sat down on a stool next to Harvey. "I have actually and I've finished the painting for Mrs Hamilton-Smythe, so Florence is safely yours."

"Not yet she's not! I have to keep my side of the bargain and take the mystery plus one to the ball, then the painting will be mine."

"Oh gosh yes. It's soon isn't it! Florence is Dorothy's plus one, so I expect you will be seeing them both there." Lucy pointed across the room at Flo, who was deep in conversation and hadn't noticed that Lucy had left her table.

"Florence? Why is she Dorothy's plus one?" Harvey asked looking a little puzzled.

"Dorothy has offered her a modelling job. She'll be the new face for her new brand of perfume and lingerie collection. Let's face it, she is kind of stunning! So stunning, that she had both of you desperate to buy my painting of her."

Harvey nodded, "She is, she has a vintage look about her, an old-fashioned beauty. I feel as though I've seen her before, perhaps in a former life."

Lucy smiled, "Do you believe in all that? I do! I believe I was a cat in a former life. If I come back again I would prefer to come back as a cat. I would like to sleep all day and be out on the tiles all night, having a welcome cat flap allowing me back in for a hearty meal and a saucer of milk whenever I wanted to. I'd be independent and aloof, like most cats."

"I've never been a cat person myself. I prefer horses, we

buy and sell them back home. I have my own horse, 'Magic Boy'. We have this deep understanding; he feels how I feel."

Lucy looked puzzled. "He really does! He knows when I'm feeling sad or upset. He actually comforts me. I believe that horses are reflections of their owners. Besides picking up on a rider's patterns of muscular tension, the horse also picks up on the rider's emotional issues. Magic Boy sure picks up on mine! I've been doing a study on equine psychotherapy. Horses are such highly intelligent animals they now use them to stimulate children with autism. They create a spiritual connection; help with social skills, trust and self-confidence."

Lucy nodded, "Wow, that's amazing! You must have a really strong bond with him. How long have you had him?"

"He's nine. I've had him from a foal. I bought him at an auction, don't know why, he stood out from all the other horses we have dealt with, I just had to have him, a bit like your painting Lucy. I just had to have it!"

Lucy smiled. "I'm glad my friend is going to live with such a nice fellow."

"Thank you. I sometimes think my life needs a change in direction. I have always worked to the extreme. I run three businesses with my father. I'm not bragging, but I have a ranch, horses, cattle, an orchard which produces apples for cider and I buy and sell art. I'm thirty-seven years old, single and to be frank, how do you English say? Knackered most of the time."

Harvey gazed at his Jack and Coke. "To top it all I just let the girl of my dreams slip through my fingers, because I've been such a workaholic. I didn't even notice her in that way until it was too late."

Lucy patted his back in sympathy, "Gosh, it's never too late. You should take the bull by the horns and go for it! Don't miss your chance for happiness."

Harvey looked sad. "It really is too late, she's marrying the guy. She is really happy with him. He's an up-and-coming country singer, destined to be a big star. He's young, fit and good looking, with a brilliant voice. What chance have I got of winning her affections? She has never seen me in that way. We grew up together as kids and teenagers."

Lucy could see he was down. "Come to our table. Nutty Florence will cheer you up! She can cheer anyone up!"

They went and sat with Flo and the other two young men. They chatted about music, horses, art, work and what life was like growing up in France, London and America - five people from very different backgrounds, all enjoying the light banter between them.

Harvey kept noticing Flo. She was such a natural beauty and so very funny. He recalled the first day he met her when she bumped into him in such a fluster, and he helped her with her bags. There was just something about her. Lucy too, she was elegant and sophisticated, very attractive and intelligent. Two gorgeous women, yet he could only think about Hayley.

It was nearly 1:00 a.m. when they decided it was time to go home. He had enjoyed the evening and had far too many Jack and Cokes.

"Maybe I'll bump into you at the ball next week Florence?"

he said, kissing both her cheeks, then kissing Lucy's cheeks; shaking hands with the two young men, Brad and Paul. "Hope to see you guys again someday."

He made his way back to the solitude of his hotel room. Feeling completely alone, he flicked through photos on his phone. He had a few of Hayley. One was taken at the cookout. She had posed for a photograph with Jane, her mother, and looked so pretty. It just made him feel more depressed. He was drunk and not thinking straight, he typed a text to her.

"I'm missing you."

His finger hovered over the send button. Maybe Lucy was right, maybe he should try and win Hayley. "No, that's just wrong." He said out loud. His eyelids flickered as he drifted off to sleep with the phone in his hand, unbeknownst to him, he had pressed the send button.

The next morning a large parcel arrived addressed to Florence Dubois. Lucy signed for it and excitedly called out to Florence, who was taking ages in the bathroom. "Flo, hurry up! There is this amazingly huge parcel for you!"

Florence emerged with wet feet and skidded on the polished laminate floor. "Where? Oh my goodness, what could it be?" The two girls eagerly undid the parcel and lifted the lid to reveal several layers of gold tissue paper which they tore apart to find the most gorgeous dress, shoes and clutch bag!

"Oh my goodness Flo, these must have cost an absolute fortune! You lucky girl! This is the type of thing you'll be wearing from now on if you accept the job! Look at the label!" Lucy exclaimed, holding up the most exquisite slinky black lace dress.

Florence was speechless.

"Try it on, try the shoes too! You are going to look splendiferous darling." Lucy said with a Zsa Zsa Gabor accent. She helped her friend slip into the dress and zipped it up. Flo slipped on the very high heeled leather sandals and clutched the bag tightly with excitement.

"Wow, wow, wow and another WOW!" Lucy stood back and admired her, then grabbed her phone and took a photograph.

Florence was overwhelmed at the sight of herself in such a beautiful outfit. Then she remembered the offer of Lucy's dress and shoes. "But I feel bad now ma chérie." She said pulling a sad face.

"What! Why?"

Flo pointed to the bedroom door, "Because you were lending me your beautiful dress and shoes and now it looks as though I don't appreciate what you were doing for me."

Lucy hugged her, "Don't be so silly, how could you possibly want to wear mine, when you have this? It's settled, you look amazing, this is the dress for you!"

"Dorothy has got her own way then, she wanted to take me out and buy me an outfit for the ball but I refused, telling her that I was borrowing yours." Florence felt slightly annoyed that she loved the Dolce and Gabbana dress so much.

Lucy showed her the photograph she'd taken on her phone,

Flo agreed that the dress fit her perfectly and suited her better than Lucy's dress. It was settled, this was the one.

CHAPTER NINE

Hayley and Wayne arrived back at the ranch house, she was glad that she had managed to calm him down but worried about his plans for her future. She didn't want their last evening to be spoiled by having an argument. She knew exactly how to get around him and get him in a better mood.

"You get showered honey and I'll make us a drink. Then I'll give you a nice massage." She suggested, giving him a lingering kiss on the cheek.

She put the coffee on and glanced at her phone, it had been on silent, there were a couple of messages; one from Helen, a client, cancelling her appointment for next Thursday, the other from Harvey. It read, "I'm missing you." She looked a bit shocked and became a little flustered. Wayne noticed and snatched the phone from her hand. He read the words and his mood darkened even more.

"What the fuck is this? What is he doing messaging you?!"

Hayley didn't know what to say or do. "I really don't know honey! He's never messaged me before!"

Wayne grabbed hold of her and shook her. "You're hurting my arm Wayne, mind my arm!!! Ouch!"

He squeezed her tighter. She cried in pain. "Please Wayne! Please, my arm!"

He let go and flicked through her messages.

"What's this one then? A message from him apologizing for kissing you! And then this one, he misses you! Why would he send a message telling you he misses you, and when did he kiss you?"

Hayley held her arm, shaking her head, "I don't know Wayne, honey, you have to believe me, maybe he's just feeling lonely? He's just a friend, there's never been anything between us!"

Hayley thought about the last time Harvey was at the ranch and the pass he'd made. The tender kiss he'd planted on her lips and the way she had been taken back by his actions. She should have deleted his apology, but at the time forgot that it was on her phone.

He dialled Harvey's number, but Harvey was passed out on the hotel bed and had his phone on silent.

Wayne was so angry. "He's not answering!"

"He's in London, it's about two in the morning there, I expect he's sound asleep!"
Wayne picked up the two coffee mugs on the side and threw them at the wall. They smashed to pieces, splintering bone china all over the tiled kitchen floor.

Hayley couldn't believe what was happening!
"Stop it Wayne, you're doing it again! You're frightening me! Give me my phone back!"

She tried to snatch the phone back but he held it high above his head and just laughed at her.

"Please Wayne, you are really scaring me! What's got into you?!"

Wayne pushed her up against the kitchen door. He put her

phone in his back pocket. He had his hands around her neck and she froze with fear. The gorgeous man whom she was so in love with now looked unrecognisable to her. She was gasping for breath because he had his hands so tightly grasped on her wind pipe. She tried to call for help but no words were possible.

Wayne came to his senses and let go.

"Oh my God! Hayley, I am sorry, sorry, oh my God! Oh my God! I'm sorry, I am so ashamed. Here, let me get you some water."

He propped her up by holding her under one arm, he walked her to the sink and poured a glass of water, which she choked on whilst trying to take a sip. She was coughing and spluttering and trying to get her breath. Wayne frantically kissed her and stroked her hair in a complete panic! His hands shook with fear as he stroked her face and her hair, kissing the top of her head over and over.

"What have I done to you my darling? What have I done? I am sorry, oh my God, Gee honey, I am so sorry!"

He kept babbling apologies and seemed genuinely sorry. He carried her to the living room and sat her on the couch.

"Try and drink, please, please, please."

His hands were shaking uncontrollably, he spilled the water everywhere in an effort to try and get Hayley to sip from the glass. He stroked her hair, kissed her forehead, her cheeks, the top of her head, her nose and then her lips. Hayley was frozen with fear and to avoid any more conflict she kissed Wayne back; she felt like a little sparrow with a broken wing. She felt as though her whole world had been turned upside down. She lay down on the couch whilst Wayne stood over her and began to weep. As he did the tears dripped off his chin and onto her. She saw him, but didn't recognise him; her gentle man had transformed into a monster and then quickly turned into a frightened child, full of remorse.

After a while Wayne composed himself and fetched a blanket from the bedroom. He gently laid it over his very quiet fiancée. She lay there watching him, wondering what he was going to do next. He kept wiping the tears from his eyes and saying sorry over and over again. Wayne sat on the floor next to the couch where Hayley was lying. He stroked her cheek and looked her right in the eyes, in the gentlest voice he said, "I promise, I will never hurt you again. Please believe me, I promise, I love you so very much and the thought of someone else taking you away just made me see red. You have to trust me this was a one-off."

He stroked her hair, he was so gentle. Then as he kissed her lips, his tears wet her cheeks. She felt sorry for him. She knew that he loved her. She must have caused his anger because he wasn't like that. He was a good man. Her handsome darling was back in the room and she wanted to comfort him. He continued to stroke her hair and started to sob uncontrollably.

"What would I do without you? Have I ruined everything between us? Will you still marry me?"

Hayley reached out and held him close to her. She kissed him so tenderly that he knew she still loved him. He picked her up and carried her to the bathroom, where they had a hot and steamy shower together.

Afterwards Wayne sat on the bed and watched Hayley as

she dried her beautiful petite figure with a white fluffy towel. He wanted her again, he just couldn't resist her! He took the towel and gently dried her back, kissing her bruised neck, right down to her breasts. She moaned with pleasure as they made love gently and slowly. This was their last night together for a few weeks and Wayne wanted to prove to her that no one could ever give her as much pleasure as he could. He was very skilled with his hands and lips and knew exactly what she liked. Hayley soon forgot about the cruel side of him and just felt all his love.

In the morning, after a hearty breakfast, it was time for Wayne to say goodbye and head off to the airport for his trip back to Nashville. He had his bags packed and ready and he double checked his flight bag for his passport and phone. Hayley was ready to drive him to the airport and realised that he still hadn't given back her phone.

"Honey, could I have my phone now please?" She asked with a little caution in her voice.

Wayne checked it first to make sure that there were no more messages from Harvey, or any other man. Then he gave it back to her. Unbeknownst to Hayley he had already forwarded Harvey's telephone number to his own phone; he wasn't going to forget that text message! He had also erased the text and Harvey's number from Hayley's phone. It would temporarily stop her from contacting him, though he knew that Harvey was a family friend and if Hayley wanted to she could instantly get his number anyway.

"Here hun, I want you to promise me that you won't contact Harvey while I'm gone." He said handing back the phone.

Hayley looked at Wayne with puzzlement but didn't want

him to leave with any bad feelings and just nodded as she took back the phone. She had carefully chosen a white linen short sleeved shirt with a collar that hid the bruises around her neck and just to make sure she wore a pretty lace neck scarf.

Wayne admired her perfect form as she hopped and skipped down the ranch house steps to the car.

She sat in the car and watched her man walk down the steps carrying his case and bag. He was just so damned handsome. She was going to miss him.

CHAPTER TEN

Lucy told Florence to pout her lips as she added the final brush strokes of lip gloss to complete her friend's makeover.

"There! You look drop dead gorgeous! Mon amie!" Lucy said as she stood back to admire her work. "Stand up, look at you! You'll have the attention of every man at the ball!"

Flo stood up and stared at herself in the long mirror. She pouted and stood with a model's pose, then strutted up and down the hallway with a model's swagger. "Do I look like a proper model Lucy?" she asked as she stopped with her hand on her hip and the most hilarious pouting lips. She flicked her hair and did it all over again, making both girls giggle with excitement!

"Yes you do! You will make Mrs Dorothy Hamilton-Smythe, one happy woman tonight, when she shows you off as the new face of her new perfume!"

Florence pulled up her dress and turned around, showing her knickers and patting her bottom, "Not forgetting the new lingerie collection!"

"Yes of course, I'm hoping for some freebies once you are established as a super model." Lucy said, admiring her friend's pert little bottom and wishing that her own was as small and perfect.

Florence was on tenterhooks and kept pacing up and down and back and forth until the car arrived to collect her. There was a toot outside which sent her into a panic, tripping over and almost landing in the large plant pot situated by the front door.

Lucy steadied her friend, "Keep calm mon amie. You will be perfectly fine if you can just keep your cool." She kissed both her cheeks and wished her luck, wishing that she was going too so that she could keep an eye on her.

Lucy pulled back the curtain and waved frantically as Flo waited by the silver Bentley, but Flo didn't see her, she was too distracted by fear and excitement.

Dorothy Hamilton-Smythe was inside the car, looking fabulous in a deep red jewel encrusted ball gown. The chauffeur opened the car door and Dorothy welcomed Florence to sit beside her on the back seat, admiring her choice of dress which fit perfectly. Lucy had done a fabulous job of Florence's hair and makeup, but Dorothy was thinking that in future Florence would have professionals doing it all for her, when she became a proper model. For now Flo was happy to be just an ordinary girl on a huge new adventure.

"Good evening my dear Florence. You look fabulous darling! I hope you are prepared for all the attention you'll receive tonight. Everyone will be dying to meet you!" Dorothy said admiring her new model.

Florence was extremely nervous and sat with her hands and fingers tightly locked in her lap. She was aware of the very high-powered woman sitting next to her and felt very inferior, even though Dorothy was trying to put her guest at ease, the small talk was not helping.

The car pulled up outside Claridge's, one of London's poshest hotels. There was a valet waiting to open the car door for them as they stepped onto the red carpet.
The paparazzi were there in full swing, with camera flashes

coming from all directions. Famous people were everywhere. Flo couldn't believe how many faces she recognised. It all became apparent to her, this was it! This was how her future lay now that she had accepted Dorothy's very generous offer and was the new face for 'Silent Senses'. The atmosphere was like nothing Florence had ever encountered. It was electric, with the clicking of cameras and photographers and journalists all calling out famous names.

Dorothy hooked her arm in Florence's and pointed the way, smiling at everyone and waving as she passed by all the onlookers who were waiting for all the famous faces to pass. She joked, "Darling, strike a pose, as Madonna would say!" Dorothy stopped to let the photographers take photographs of the new face and figure for her collection. "Head up darling!" Dorothy eloquently whispered in Flo's ear. "Stand up straight and be important darling!"

Florence was so excited! She got her heal caught in the hem of her dress and if it hadn't have been for Dorothy holding her arm she would have tripped over and landed flat on her face, but Dorothy managed to steady her.

"Whoops, young lady you don't want to go and do that when you're on the cat walk!"

Florence blushed at the thought, knowing just how accident-prone she was, and made a mental note to take greater care.

Inside the hotel, Florence marvelled at the splendour of the entrance hall. Wide-eyed with wonder, she gazed around. It was an amazing place, with very grand and lavish furnishings, a little smaller than she had imagined it to be, but nevertheless impressive to her, as she'd never been to a hotel in Mayfair before. She spotted people from television and film and started to feel afraid. Dorothy noticed the anxious look on Florence's face.

"Darling... Are you alright? You look a little peaky. Let me get you a glass of champagne." She grabbed two glasses from a waiter passing by with a tray full of sparkling champagne.

"Here, drink this and try not to look so scared! Enjoy!" Dorothy said handing the slender glass to Flo.

The guests were all shown into the grand dining room, which was elegantly decorated in white and silver. The chairs had white satin covers and silver satin sashes, each with a white rose in the middle of each bow. In the centre of each table was a solid silver candelabrum with white roses, freesias and stephanotis embellishing each stem. Everyone had a hand written name placecard, showing where they had to sit, and a small silver gift box, tied with a white satin ribbon sitting on their side plates. The crystal glassware sparkled under the lights of the grand chandeliers. All around the room were tall pillars with huge floral displays adorning each one and with its beautiful 1930's shiny marble floor and mirrors, it looked amazing!

The head waiter showed Dorothy and Florence to their table, which was right at the far end by the stage. Florence nervously sat down, waiting to see who would be joining them.

"Are you alright now darling? Relax, relax." Dorothy held Flo's hand.

Florence looked a bit flushed. "I do not actually feel too good, if I'm honest."

"Have another sip of Dom Pérignon my dear. You'll be fine."

Just then a handsome dark haired man with a familiar face was shown to his seat, next to Florence, who looked up and smiled with relief when she realised who he was.

"Hey Florence, fancy seeing you here."

Harvey smiled, kissing the ladies on both cheeks.

"I'm very intrigued to find out who my date is, Florence is it you?"

"Darling, your date will be here in a little while, she is running slightly late."

Harvey looked around the room at all the beautiful ladies in their stunning dresses and tried to guess which one was his date. His thoughts wandered briefly to Hayley, he wished that she would suddenly appear amongst the crowd.

A tall thin distinguished man with grey hair and green eyes, walked over with a stunning red head. He introduced himself and his daughter. "Hi I'm Tom Salmon, this is my daughter Wren. We live next door to Dorothy."

Harvey was relieved that Wren wasn't an ogre, though he didn't really care that much that Wren was such a stunner. He was more attracted to Florence, even though he did think that she was a little bit ditzy.

He kissed Wren's hand and shook Tom's hand.

"Pleased to meet you both. I'm sure we'll all have a very

pleasant evening."

His date wore a cream figure-hugging high necked dress, which was cut low at the back. Her hair was extremely short, almost shaved at the sides and longer on top suiting her face with her chiselled cheekbones and ice blue eyes. She certainly stood out from the crowd.

Dorothy raised her glass of champagne. "Cheers my darlings. Enjoy! I have something important to tell you both later." she said as she looked at both Harvey and Florence.

The other three people on the table were all good friends of Dorothy's and all very rich and important people whom Florence had never heard of before.

They dined on smoked salmon and beetroot with soda bread and crème fraîche to begin. Florence was completely out of her depth and had to wait until someone else started eating before she knew which knife and fork to use. Then lobster followed, looking incredibly delicious and tasting just as good as it looked. Flo had eaten lobster before but this was exceptional. Dessert was unbelievably delicious, vanilla and mascarpone cream, malt and apricots with honeycomb wafers. All through dinner Harvey watched Florence with intrigue, noticing her smile in particular.

The evening progressed with the heads of charities on stage auctioning off some huge prizes; one being a weekend in Paris, another, a weekend break and also a game of golf for two at St Andrews. There was a case of champagne and a diamond necklace amongst the prizes. Then every table had a black velvet bag passed around for the guests to make a private donation. Luckily Florence has some cash and modestly put a ten-pound note inside, hoping that no one saw her meagre donation.

When the important part of the evening was over, there were a few speeches and introductions. Dorothy was called to the stage. She thanked everyone for their generous donations, announcing that so far that evening they had raised over a million pounds for her charity, which she had set up to help abused children. Then she proudly announced the face for her new perfume and lingerie collection, beckoning Florence to join her on stage. Harvey gallantly escorted her to the stage, where she clumsily stumbled up the steps and stood red-faced in front of everyone. They all clapped and cheered as Dorothy introduced Florence. Photographers from magazines and newspapers took more photographs whilst Florence stood up straight, holding a glass of champagne in one hand and a bottle of Silent Senses in the other.

Flo was very relieved when that part was over and she could start to relax, especially when the band started and some of the guests began to dance. She returned to her seat and sat admiring the ladies in their ball gowns. Most were exquisite, some were elegant and a few were down right outrageous. One woman had squeezed herself into a dress which was at least two sizes too small. "Seins!" Florence blurted out loud.

"Sorry?" Harvey asked, looking puzzled.

"Oops... Seins, I mean... Boobs... Sorry, the lady with the big boobs."

Flo giggled as she whispered in Harvey's ear, a little drunk after too many glasses of champagne, nodding towards the lady wearing the bright red dress "Seins." Harvey smiled, feeling a little embarrassed as the large lady looked their way and caught them staring and laughing at her.

Harvey wasn't taking much notice of Wren. He was much more attracted to Florence. He found her highly amusing and studied her closely as she chatted about her simple life in France and how much it was about to change. Her laugh was infectious and her smile was beautiful. He chuckled to himself as she blew a stray curl from her face, in doing so pulling a funny face each time and getting flustered because it would continuously hang back down again. He couldn't help but reach out and stroke her hair back up onto the top of her head. The longer he sat chatting to her the more he noticed that she had many endearing qualities. He felt as though he had known her all his life and Flo certainly seemed comfortable in his company. Harvey stood and took Flo's hand, leading her onto the dance floor. Flo was swaying a little and clung onto Harvey as they started to dance.

Dorothy was chatting to friends and turned around to spot Harvey and Flo getting a little too close on the dance floor.

"Excuse me darlings." She left her friends and hurried over.

"I need to speak to you both in private darlings."

Dorothy took both their hands and guided them into a separate room, where she closed the door behind her and sat them both down.

"What I am about to tell you both, I'm sure will come as a huge shock. I could have chosen a different time and place to tell you but under the circumstances I took a risk and chose to tell you here."

She took hold of Flo's hand. "I am your great-aunt." Then she took hold of Harvey's hand. "I am also your great-aunt."

They looked at Dorothy and then at each other, both looking totally confused.

"Hold your horses! Wait just a cotton-pickin' minute. How can you be great-aunt to both of us? We're not related?!"

Dorothy took a deep breath, "But darlings you are! You are half-brother and sister."

Florence shook her head. "Non, there is some mistake, I am an only child. My maman Annette died when I was five."

Dorothy looked sorry. "Darlings I am your mother's long lost aunt. I hadn't seen her since she was a child. I left America when I was a young woman and lost touch with the few family members that were left."

Harvey couldn't believe what she was saying. "Ella left my father when I was eleven. I tried to trace her but I couldn't find her. How can she be Florence's mother?" Then it quickly started to dawn on him!

"My mother's name wasn't Annette it was Ella! You have made a mistake!"

Dorothy had the sad facts. "I'm so sorry my darling. Your mother left America to make a new life in France with Florence's father Jack. She changed her name from Ella to Annette and also changed her last name. Look at your sister Harvey, just look at her; does she remind you of someone?"

He looked up and for a split second saw in Florence the same eyes and mouth of that in the portrait of his mother; the same portrait that had hung over the fireplace in the ranch for over thirty years. It dawned on him now, that's why he felt that he had met her before! Suddenly he felt anger and resentment towards Florence. She was the reason he had grown up without a mother.

"Dang it! It's your fault I had no momma! I used to blame myself for her leaving me and my pa. I would cry myself to sleep wondering what I had done to make my mother leave us. How could she just walk out as if I meant nothing to her? My father adored her, he was heartbroken and has never loved another woman!"

Florence got teary-eyed. "Hey, I grew up without a mother; she died when I was three. I'm sorry Harvey but your mother died in a car crash. Do not blame me; I used to cry for her every night too!"

Dorothy had stirred up a real hornets nest, but it had to be done. She couldn't keep the secret any longer. These two people were practically the only relatives she had left in the world and as she was suffering ill-health she had to bring them together somehow.

"I am so sorry that I didn't get the chance to watch you both grow up. I'm hoping to make it up to you both before I..." She hesitated and quickly changed the subject.

"Harvey, the portrait of Florence. It is now yours, it is a gift, I wouldn't... couldn't take any money for it. You understand it was just a ploy to get you here so that I could introduce you to each other."

"But how did you know that I would buy the painting?" he asked thinking about the day that he first laid eyes on it hanging in the gallery. He blushed when he thought about the erotic dream he'd had about Florence and felt sick inside.

"I found out that you were an art dealer. I found out all I could about Florence, the fact that Florence regularly stayed with Lucy and that she had painted her. I checked out everything I could via social media and all of your websites. I knew that you bought from new artists. I arranged for the owner of the gallery to suggest Lucy's paintings to you. For months I employed two private investigators to follow you both. I feel I know you both very well now." Dorothy smiled. "Darlings, family is important. I have lived almost all of my seventy-seven years without any. I am so glad that I've found you! I wanted desperately to meet you both. I know this must be a huge shock!"

Florence couldn't take it all in. "So am I really your next model or is this all just a ploy to introduce me to my half-brother?"

"Oh darling! It's for real; you are definitely my new model. This is your rags to riches story. This is my way of giving you a break in life. You deserve it darling." Dorothy said sympathetically.

Florence felt patronised. "I do not want a rags-to-riches story. I was happy with my life, my father is a very generous man, he has given me everything I need, he does not have a lot, but he gave me love! I do not want to be your next model. I want to get out of here now!"

She stormed out of the room, Dorothy following close behind leaving Harvey standing in the middle of the room, feeling dazed and confused by the whole situation.

Wren popped her head around the door. "Is everything OK?"

Harvey wasn't interested in Wren at all. He kept thinking about Hayley back in Texas. "Wren, thanks very much, I'm really sorry it has to end so abruptly, I've had some bad news and need to leave."

Harvey disappeared up the stairs to his suite. He poured a drink from the mini bar and sat on the bed, staring out of the window. Too many hotel rooms, too many lonely nights, too much hard work, even too much money! For what? His life was one big mess! Outside shining in the dark he looked at the lights in the buildings of London. All those rooms, filled with people with all sorts of problems, all different lives, different ages, families, children, mothers, fathers, brothers, sisters.

"Sister! I have a sister!" he said, sipping his Jack and Coke. The nearest he'd had to a sister was Hayley. He thought about Hayley and grabbed his phone. He flicked through his photos of horses and cattle, the ranch and the painting. He stared at the painting. Now he couldn't see Florence, he could only see his mother. Then he scrolled until he found some pictures of Hayley. His favourite picture of her was taken sitting on the fence, smiling and holding a beer in one hand. To him she was perfection, and the epitome of how a woman should be.

It was very late and Harvey fell asleep with his glass in his hand which woke him when it crashed to the floor. Luckily it bounced on the carpet but he woke to find his phone buzzing. He didn't recognise the number, but answered it. "Harvey Dove speaking."

An American voice answered. "Mr Dove. This is a warning man... Do not send messages to my girl saying that you miss her! I can be a son of a bitch and if I think you got your eye on my girl, no hang on MY FIANCÉE, I will get my revenge! In fact, I will knock you plumb into next week, you're gonna get a lickin' ah' mo kill you, you can take that to the bank."

He hung up leaving Harvey staring at his phone. At first he couldn't make out who or what he was talking about. Then he frantically scrolled through his messages and found the one saying *'I'm missing you.'* He didn't think he had sent it to Hayley but it had clearly been sent the night he had got drunk and passed out on the bed.

"Dang it!" he said, scratching his head, not knowing what to do now. If he texted or called Hayley he might get her into trouble. Wayne sounded like a nasty piece of work! Hayley's parents Mitch and Jane have obviously been fooled by his charming ways. Harvey needed to dig a bit deeper and find out more about Wayne. He didn't have long to prove himself right, their wedding was only a few months away.

He called Mitch's ranch. There was no answer. He decided not to call Wayne back on his phone but stored the number he had called him from, listing the name as PSYCHO.

CHAPTER ELEVEN

Upon returning to the ranch after dropping Wayne at the airport, Hayley wandered back in the house and poured herself an ice cold coke. Leaning against the sink, she looked across the land at the beautiful surroundings. How lucky she was to have such a good life. Jeff and Kelvin were giving work orders to the younger ranch hands. Everything was in order. She was expecting Mitch and Jane back at any moment. She skipped down the front steps to chat with the boys before opening her studio to catch up on some long overdue paperwork. She'd been thoroughly distracted the past few days with Wayne's visit and couldn't wait to start work again in the morning. "Hey guys! How all y'all doing?" she asked cheerily.

"Hey hun, we're all OK thanks. Your ma and pa back soon huh? Wayne gone now?" Kelvin asked with a smile.

"Yeah, I've just taken him to the airport." Just as she answered Kelvin there was a gust of wind which blew Hayley's scarf, showing the bruising on her neck.

"Hell Hayley! What have you done to your neck?" Jeff asked, looking shocked.

They all noticed the black and purple marks but Hayley quickly covered them by tightening her scarf and told them they must have happened when she had fallen off her horse. She turned away and scurried off to unlock her fitness studio.

The men all stood around chatting about the bruises, agreeing that they didn't look like something that could have happened from falling off a horse. They looked like strangulation marks. They all became very suspicious of

Wayne.

"Told ya there was somethin' 'bout that guy!" Kelvin frowned.

Hayley opened the door to find her studio filled with red roses. The scent filled the usual sweaty environment. There was a note with each vase saying "I love you more today than I did yesterday and I'll love you twice as much tomorrow." Her heart skipped a beat, how lovely and thoughtful of Wayne to sneak in and do this!

She opened her planner and turned to tomorrow's work page. "That's strange!" she said out loud. All of her male clients had been crossed through and the word 'cancelled' was written next to them. She flicked through the next few pages. They were all the same! A shiver ran up her spine. She thought of the time that Wayne had told her that he didn't want her to carry on working as a fitness instructor and how sinister he had been. She started to worry. He could be so wonderful and so romantic on one hand and yet so scary on the other. Her thoughts turned to anger! "How dare he!" She was glad he had gone back to Nashville, without him around she could get her head straight and decide what to do next. She sat on a bench and thought long and hard. She realised Wayne was trying to control her. She wasn't going to let him; she grabbed her phone and went to look up her clients. All the male contacts on her phone had been deleted! She started to get really scared! What should she do now? Hayley locked the door to her studio and ran back to the ranch house. She looked up Harvey's number in the household address book. It was there under Dove, next to Ed's. She dialled, nervously.

"Hey Mitch!" he answered, seeing Mitch's house number

appear on his phone.

Hayley spoke. "Hey Harv, it's me, Hayley!"
"Hun, how are you? Hey hun, I'm sorry about the text message. I understand I upset your man, he warned me off!" Harvey blurted out.

Hayley was worried and didn't understand what he meant. "What do you mean he warned you off?"

"He called me, saying he'd read my text and told me that he'd get his revenge if I contact you… About that text Hayley," Harvey felt uneasy, "I typed it and thought I fell asleep before I pressed the send button. However, it did send and I'm guessing that it got you in trouble honey. For that I'm truly sorry."

Hayley was shaking. "I'm scared Harvey. He isn't the man I thought he was, he has two sides to him and one side I don't like! He's dark, he's cruel and violent!"

Harvey didn't like the sound of that! "Have you told Mitch and Jane?"

"They've been away, they're back today, I don't want to worry them, I just needed to tell someone Harvey, I hope you don't mind? We've been friends for so long!"

"Hun, I'm flying back early, I'm heading home tomorrow. Would you like me to come to the ranch when I'm back in the US? I can try and help you." Harvey asked, hoping that Hayley would accept his help.

"If you could that would be great Harv. I'm really freaking out! I'll tell you everything he's done when you get here. Not a word to anyone else though please? I don't want to worry anyone." Hayley insisted.

Harvey felt happy that she was confiding in him, in a selfish kind of way. At the same time he was disturbed that she had become so scared of the man she loved and couldn't wait to get back to Texas to be by her side.

Hayley thanked Harvey, said goodbye, then took a picture of her neck; after adding Harvey's number back into her mobile she sent him the photograph.

Harvey's phone buzzed, he was shocked the image Hayley had forwarded to his phone. He messaged straight back. *"I'll be there as soon as I can. Delete this message and the photo, I've got it now."*

Hayley knew Harvey was right and deleted everything from her phone, then sat in the kitchen and had a cry.

Mitch and Jane arrived a couple of hours later looking happy and relaxed. They'd had a lovely break away from everything; it had been a long time overdue.

They hugged Hayley and sat in the kitchen chatting about their trip to Mexico. Basically they had just chilled in a posh hotel, doing nothing much except wining and dining and lounging around. Something they hadn't had the opportunity to do for a while.

"So how was your time with Wayne?" Jane asked with a big beaming smile, "Did you see the wedding coordinator? Ooh I'm so excited! I was dying to phone you to find out how the meeting went but your father wouldn't let me. What colors did you choose? Anything but red and white I hope. Red and white symbolizes blood and bandages… Oh honey! When did you want to go shopping for your dress?"

Hayley smiled a little smile, almost in tears at the thought of what her mother said about red and white. How poignant, blood and bandages and she wasn't even married yet!

"Are you alright my love?" Mitch asked, looking at the tears welling up in his daughter's eyes.

She bluffed a smile. "Hey Pa, it's been crazy! Of course I'm all right! I'm just a bit emotional at the moment."

He hugged his daughter and kissed her forehead. "As long as you're happy my darlin'."

Jane hugged her too. "Ooh group hug, we've missed our gal."

Hayley held her forehead. "Mama, I've got a bit of a headache, I think I might be coming down with something. Do you mind if I tell you about our plans later? I need a lie down."

"Oh honey, bless your heart, of course. You go ahead."

Hayley slipped under the soft thin summer comforter as she did she felt something touch her leg. She lifted the cover to see the bear that Wayne had bought. He had slipped it into her bed before he'd left. She remembered him saying. "When I'm in Nashville, hug the bear and think of me." Hayley threw the bear across the room, it hit the wall and landed face down. "Oh I sure am thinkin' of you, you've made darn sure of that!" Then she pulled the comforter over her head and cried herself to sleep.

A couple of hours passed, Jane opened the bedroom door with a cup of coffee. "Hey sweetheart, are you awake hun?

How are you feelin'?" She picked the bear up from the floor. "He's cute!"

She placed the bear on the dressing table and sat on the bed, handing Hayley her coffee. "You look a little peaky honey." Jane brushed the hair from her daughter's face, as she sipped her coffee.

"Mama I'm fine, honest I am." Hayley quickly pulled her hair over her neck to hide the bruise.

She didn't know how to begin to tell her parents what Wayne was like and didn't intend to tell them yet.

Jane and Mitch lit the grill and invited the ranch hands and their partners. Jeff and Kelvin, the two head hands, had two separate bungalows in the grounds of the ranch with their wives and children and were often invited to join Mitch and the family. The younger ranch hands lived off-site and had already headed home for the night. Hayley felt anxious about spending the evening with Jeff and Kelvin. She suspected that they didn't believe her when she made excuses about the bruising on her neck.

Mitch sipped on a beer whilst he flipped the burgers and steaks. The adults were seated around the table; the three children played with a ball on the grass in front of the house.

The evening started with lots of laughter as Mitch and Jane talked about the very funny head waiter at their hotel. He did impressions, told jokes and did magic tricks and entertained the hotel guests every evening.

Mitch laughed, "How about this one?" They all chuckled as Mitch reeled off all his corny jokes trying to keep them clean in front of the ladies.

Jeff brought up the subject of the accident which happened whilst they were away. Mitch was full of questions and turned to Hayley. "You didn't mention this to us! Why didn't you tell us, you could have let us know! There we were enjoying our vacation with no idea! Honey, you should always tell us if there's a problem."

Hayley fiddled with the scarf around her neck.

Jeff went into detail about what happened with the horses and the storm and mentioned that Hayley took a bad fall, causing some nasty bruises.

Hayley was quick to pull her shirt sleeve up and show Jane the large blue and yellow bruise. "It's not as bad now Mama, Wayne drove me to the hospital and they told me to rest up for a couple of days. The storm was really frightening for the horses, I was scared stiff."

Jane had to smile to herself. She knew what a drama queen her daughter was when it came to injuries and a coward when it came to thunderstorms. Not without reason, she understood that her childhood experience of the tornado had left a fear that would never go away.

After they'd eaten, the guitars came out and the sing-along started. Everyone joined in, singing and dancing on the porch. Kelvin pulled Hayley up for a dance and whispered in her ear. "I don't like the look of the bruises on your neck Missy. If you've any problems with that man of yours, just let me know. I'll soon whip his ass."

Hayley held Kelvin away and looked him straight in the eye. "It's fine Kelv. It's fixed… Really it's OK. Harvey is going to help me. Not a word to my mama and pa. Please, promise me?"

Kelvin looked worried. "Your father would kill him if he knew that he'd hurt you."

Hayley held Kelvin's hand and did a twirl. "That's why I don't want him to find out. Together Harvey and I will sort things, I don't want my pa to do anything stupid."

Jeff took Hayley's hand from Kelvin's and took over the dance. "I detect that Kelvin has been talking to you about the man in your life. I've known you almost all your life, if I find out that he is hurting you, I'll sort him out. He's not worth it Hayley. Far be it from me to tell you what to do. I can only give my advice. He's not worth it; there are better guys out there. You need someone you can trust. I might be talking out of turn but I think I'm right."

Hayley hugged him. "I'll say the same to you as I did to Kelvin. It's fixed, but I don't want my folks to know anything yet. Please don't mention anything to them."

Jeff nodded his head as Kelvin was watching him and his reactions. Mitch was oblivious to their conversation and was having a good time singing songs and playing his guitar.

"Let's step it up a bit!" Mitch said reaching for his banjo, which he vigorously played. Kelvin and Jeff started a hoe down. "Yeeha!" They were all having a great time.

Hayley's phone was on the table and she noticed it had lit up, meaning that someone was trying to call her. It was Wayne's number, so she slipped into the house to answer. Wayne spoke. "Hey honey! How are you doin'? Are you missin' me as much as I'm missin' you? Don't answer that because I know you're not!" Wayne said sarcastically.

Hayley had to play it cool, although she was shaking. "Honey! Did you get back safely? Of course I'm missing you! Why did you say it like that?

Wayne was smug in his reply. "I expect that you're sitting on your porch with the guys from the ranch and you've been singin' and dancin' with them."

Hayley felt really uneasy, as if Wayne could actually see what she was doing. "Oh my God! Maybe he can! Maybe he has a web cam set up somewhere!" She thought. "Ma and Pa are back from their vacation so before we start work tomorrow we thought we'd chill out. We often have a get together with Jeff and Kelvin."

Wayne listened to her defending words and tried to cool it with her. "Honey, I love you and I trust you. I know that you wouldn't go with anyone else. You have too much at stake."

Hayley mulled over his words. Feeling confused she asked "What do you mean, I have too much at stake?"

The phone line went dead. "Hello? Hello?" Hayley repeated. Then she tried to call him back but the line was engaged.

Feeling spooked, she went back outside. She sat down and looked around to see if there was any evidence of hidden cameras. How did he know what she was doing? Was he just guessing, perhaps?

Jeff glanced her way and mouthed silently, "You OK?" Hayley nodded and smiled but Jeff could tell that something was wrong as she seemed very jittery.

CHAPTER TWELVE

Harvey boarded the plane at Heathrow, feeling a little excited that Hayley had asked for his help. He'd had several missed calls from Dorothy, which he'd deliberately ignored.

When he was seated, the flight attendant handed him a newspaper. He thought he would save it to read later and placed it underneath the seat in front of him. He looked upon his journey to Austin as a chance to spend some time in solitude and put his life in some sort of order.

He sat in his first class seat and looked up and down the aisle. People from all walks of life were buzzing around, organizing their hand luggage and duty-free bags, fussing over children and babies. He noticed a man of a similar age to himself, who had a cute little baby daughter, and suddenly he felt more alone than he ever had before. If he could help Hayley eliminate her problem, he might be able to win her love and in a few years' time, they might have a small daughter too, a family even. He imagined life as a father and pictured what his children would look like, a boy much like himself as a youngster and a cute girl with pigtails, just as he remembered Hayley when he used to chase her and pull them.

An hour and a half into the flight Harvey fell into a deep sleep and dreamed of Hayley. In his dream, he was in her bed, it was their first time and the sex was hot and passionate. The bedroom door opened and there stood a figure, dressed all in black with a bandanna around his face, which showed only his eyes, which were glowing red. He was holding a shotgun in his hand which he aimed at Hayley. Harvey shouted at Wayne, demanding he put the gun down. Hayley sat in silence, in disbelief and scared stiff as Wayne pulled the trigger and shot her in the head, showering Harvey with blood and bits of her brain.

Harvey woke up feeling frantic, slapping and wiping his face with his hands; he was clearly distressed and for a moment he couldn't fathom where he was. The dream had seemed so real. He composed himself and looked upon it as a sign that he must help Hayley to get rid of this man from her life. A flight attendant walked passed and noticed Harvey was looking a bit hot, sweaty and disoriented. "Is everything alright sir?"

"Yes thank you Ma'am, bad, bad dream. Could I have a Jack and Coke please?"

Harvey drank his drink and settled back down for a sleep, hoping that he wouldn't have the same nightmare. After half an hour it was clear that his dream had disturbed him so much that sleep was out of the question, so he reached down for the newspaper. The front-page headline was, "The New Face of Silent Senses quits!" Accompanying the headline was a photograph of his half-sister Florence, taken leaving Claridge's, with Dorothy hot on her heels, both looking very anxious.

"Jeez, not only have I gotta get Hayley away from Mr Psycho but I've got a sister to deal with!" thought Harvey, throwing the newspaper on the floor and closing his eyes tight with frustration.

Having managed a few hours' sleep Harvey woke in time for a soda water before the cabin crew checked passengers' seat belts for landing. He got a cab straight from the airport to Mitch's ranch, texting Hayley on the way so that she was ready to explain his arrival imminent to her parents.

Hayley felt relief when she received Harvey's text and went

to tell Mitch and Jane that he would be arriving to help her sort out a problem.

"What problem honey? Couldn't we help you, save Harvey coming all the way from Dallas?" Mitch asked curiously.

Little did he know that Harvey had come all the way from London.

"It's just a little problem of mine and Harvey knows how to deal with it Pa. Nothing for you to worry about." Hayley said giving both her parents a kiss on their cheeks.

They knew that if she didn't want them to know what was going on they'd better leave well alone. She would tell them in her own time what was going on. They trusted Harvey and were happy, for now, to leave it at that.

Hayley eagerly waited for Harvey to arrive, pacing back and forth in the kitchen. When she saw the cab pull up outside the ranch house she ran down the front steps to meet him and stood waiting whilst he paid the driver, before helping him carry his bags into the house.

Mitch and Jane welcomed him, whilst Hayley poured a coffee. "Black with sugar still Harv?"

"You remembered!"

"Right Harv, I don't know what is so important that you have to come from Dallas to help Hayley with?" Mitch declared. Hayley put her finger to her lips, hoping Harvey would understand that not only did she not want her parents to know about her problem but also she didn't want them to know that Harvey had just travelled from London and not Dallas.

"I suppose we had better make ourselves scarce so you guys can talk." Mitch said, hooking his arm in Jane's before edging out of the door. "See you guys in a couple of hours."

Hayley sat at the kitchen table with her mug of coffee cradled in both hands. She stared at Harvey, not really knowing how to start. Then the words just poured along with some tears.

"I have made a huge mistake. I thought I was a good judge of character but Wayne is so not the man I thought he was. He is some sort of control freak. He doesn't want me to carry on as a personal trainer. He seems to know, or guess what I'm doing. He texts me in the middle of the night, he Skypes me at various times throughout the day or night... I feel as though he's spying on me. At first I was flattered by all the attention but I know that he has hacked my Facebook and Twitter accounts. He's even been bad tempered and violent, he tried to strangle me! He swore that it would never happen again and wept like a child. I felt sorry for him, he seemed so genuine. Then I got back from dropping him at the airport to find he had been in my gym and wiped the names and contact numbers of all my male friends and clients, even you!"

Harvey looked worried. "He tried to strangle you! Hayley, why haven't you told the cops?"

She gingerly pulled open the collar of her blouse to reveal the bruise hidden beneath.

"I felt sure that he was sorry, he was so upset! I didn't want the police involved. He's my fiancé, he isn't supposed to do things like that but I don't trust him anymore. He really scares me! Do you think I *should* tell the cops?"

Harvey took hold of her hand, "Take me to your gym and let me have a look around."

They opened the door to the studio and the heat from the room enhanced the gorgeous aroma of the dozens of roses left by Wayne.

"Good Lord! He sure is very sorry!" Harvey said sarcastically before he started looking around the room.

"What are you looking for?"

"Not sure… Hmm, where could he hide a camera?… Hey Wayne! Are you watching us?" Harvey shouted.

"Oh Jeez, do you really think he is?" Hayley screeched, looking petrified. "He will go mad if he sees you here Harvey!"

They both searched but found nothing.

Harvey felt quite satisfied that Wayne hadn't bugged Hayley's workplace. "Right, now then, you say he knows what you are doing. In what context?"

"The other night he knew that I had been singing and dancing with Jeff and Kelvin. It was as if he had been watching me. Oh God! You don't think he's here somewhere on the ranch? I took him to the airport but he could have come back here if he didn't catch the plane, couldn't he?"

Harvey suggested Hayley find the telephone number to Wayne's recording studio, so she hurried back to the house to get her phone, which she had left on the kitchen table.

It wasn't there! She was panic-stricken. "I know I left it on the table!" She said aloud.

The kitchen door slammed, Hayley looked up. There was Wayne. He was standing in front of the door holding Hayley's phone.

His face looked sinister and distorted. "Looking for this my darling?"

"Yes, Wayne, y-y- you made me jump! Honey, darling, w-w-what are you doing here? I thought you were in Nashville!"

"Well as you can see, I'm not in Nashville, I'm here with you!" He said, turning around to lock the kitchen door. "It seems that you can't be trusted honey, my suspicions were right about you and other men."

"What are you doing? Don't lock the door, please don't lock the door. Let's sit down and talk honey. It's such a nice surprise to see you back again. Won't they be expecting you in Nashville?" Hayley asked, beckoning to Wayne to come and sit at the table.

Wayne ignored her and locked the door, then sat down at the table opposite Hayley. She wished that she had changed the password on her phone. Luckily she had erased the messages and calls from Harvey but it was obvious that Wayne knew Harvey was around.

"So!" Wayne shouted, slamming her phone down hard on the table, which made Hayley jump off her seat! "You don't need me anymore then?!"

Hayley was scared. "What do you mean, I don't need you

Wayne? Of course I need you. I am going to marry you aren't I? The wedding is still on isn't it?" She asked shakily, trying to keep him sweet.

"Why would you still want to marry me when you have Harvey?"

"I don't have Harvey, I have you!" Hayley said, in a quiet voice. She felt sick.

"Why is he here then?" Wayne shouted.

"He's here on business."

"I don't believe you, he said he missed you. I can't get past that!" Wayne shouted and kept looking around at the back door, expecting Harvey to peer through the window at any minute.

Meanwhile, Harvey was wondering why Hayley was taking so long and sensed that something wasn't right. He crept up to the house and along to look in a side window. He saw Wayne sitting opposite Hayley. He wasn't sure what to do next but saw Kelvin and Jeff in the distance; he made his way over to them, running as fast as he could. When he reached them he was out of breath and panicking but managed to briefly explain what was happening.

"He's a son of a bitch. We should have said something to Mitch but Hayley made us swear not to." Jeff said, gritting his teeth with anger.

Harvey beckoned them to follow. As all three ran back to the house, Jeff reached into his pocket for the front door keys. "It's rare that anyone uses the front door. I hope it's not bolted from the inside."

They quietly crept up the steps to the front door. Jeff tried the lock. "Dang, it is. Now what?" He had panic in his voice.

"I think I should call the police and fill Mitch in, he might come back with Miss Jane and who knows what will happen." Kelvin said, while dialling Mitch's number, walking away so that he could talk. Meanwhile the other two waited for instructions.

"Right the cops are on their way. They will use a silent approach. Mitch is havin' a conniption fit but I told him to try and keep calm. He's on his way back from town. It's best that we just try and keep an eye on Wayne and Hayley but don't let them see us. We don't want Wayne to hurt her before the police get here." Kelvin advised, whilst creeping along the side of the house, with the others closely following.

Harvey peered in through the kitchen window. It looked pretty calm. "They are still sitting at the table and look like they are just talking." He ducked down quickly, as Wayne turned to look over his shoulder. "Dang it, I think he saw me!"

Wayne stood up! "Well I'll be! So lover boy is out there! Let me tell you bitch, if I can't have you, no one will!" He said with pure evil and jealousy in his voice. He grabbed hold of Hayley by her hair and dragged her to the window. He banged on the window with his fist, Harvey stood up whilst the other two men stayed out of sight. "See this?" he said, pointing to Hayley, "She's not yours, she's mine, and that means I can do whatever I want to her, right?" He grabbed her face and licked her cheek with his long tongue. Then he spat in her face. Hayley was crying uncontrollably. Her whole body was shaking.

Harvey shook with anger. The other two men stood up and started cursing and shouting at Wayne to let her go.

"Oh yes! Another two of your admirers! Shall we let them in and we can all have a go on you?!" Wayne asked, laughing at the three men outside. They started kicking the kitchen door. Wayne went from angry to furious; he grabbed a large kitchen knife and held it to her throat.

"Please Wayne, don't hurt me, please." Hayley begged. She screamed, "Don't kick the door down, he's got a knife!"

Wayne held her tighter. She could smell his sweaty body and feel his anger.

The men peered through the window. Wayne looked deranged, his eyes were bulging, his face bright red, he was gritting his teeth and shaking.

"Is there any other way in? Check for open windows." Harvey whispered.

There was a small bedroom window open. Kelvin lifted Harvey up so that he could reach in and try to unlock the larger side window. "Yes!" Harvey whispered with relief as he managed to open it and climbed in as quietly as he could. He crept along the hallway and stood outside the partially closed kitchen door. He could see Hayley and part of Wayne, who was still holding the knife to Hayley's throat. He felt Kelvin breathing down his neck; both he and Jeff were right behind him.
Harvey whispered to Jeff to unbolt the front door, which he did. Then he came back and stood behind Kelvin.

Harvey knew he couldn't let this psychopath hurt his oldest

friend and was determined to save her.

Hayley stopped crying, intrigued as to why everything had gone so quiet. She knew that she had to keep her cool, no matter how difficult it was with the madman holding a knife at her throat.

"Wayne, why are you trying to hurt me? I'm going to be your wife. I thought that you loved me! Come on honey, put the knife down please. You promised me that you would never hurt me again, didn't you?" She pleaded with him and for a moment she thought he was going to put the knife down but then he caught a glimpse of a police officer outside. He turned her to face the kitchen window and he stood behind her, still holding the knife. He opened the window and shouted at the officer. "Don't try and get in, or I will slit her throat! I mean it! I will kill the little slut!"

Hayley's heart was pounding so hard that it felt as though it would burst from her chest. She felt like her face was on fire, she was so hot that beads of sweat started to trickle from her brow. Wayne was enjoying the fact that he had such control and he'd managed to frighten her so much.

Harvey could see everything through the gap in the doorway and took the opportunity to silently crawl along the floor, whilst Wayne had his back to him. His heart was beating so loudly, he felt sure Wayne would hear it. He crawled along unseen until he was directly behind Wayne. He took his chance and stood quickly, grabbing hold of his arm tightly, he skilfully pointed the knife away from Hayley's neck. Hayley managed to run to the back of the kitchen, collapsing in a heap on the floor. Wayne struggled to free himself from Harvey's tight grip. Harvey squeezed Wayne's hand so tightly that he dropped the knife.

Wayne turned and threw a punch, hitting Harvey straight in his left eye. Harvey fell to the floor on his knees in pain, for a moment he couldn't do anything. Wayne held Harvey's head in a tight grip and bent down to bite him. The other men were close behind and wrestled Wayne to the ground, Jeff sat on his chest whilst Kelvin undid the back door, letting two armed police officers in.

Hayley was so grateful to Harvey, she threw her arms around his neck and sobbed, then hugged Kelvin and Jeff.

The police cuffed and searched Wayne before taking him away. The police were still taking statements as Mitch and Jane arrived and both sat and wept as they heard Hayley's account of everything that had happened. Jane hugged her daughter and opened her daughter's collar to see the bruises Hayley had vividly described. She couldn't take it all in and thanked God for a lucky escape.

The officer ran a background check on Wayne and told them all that he wasn't destined to be a famous country singer. He had fabricated the whole thing. He was an ex-convict who had previously been jailed for stalking woman.

Hayley felt exhausted, yet so thankful to be surrounded by so many caring people. She noticed Harvey who was standing at the door talking to her father. He had been so brave, how much he'd changed since their childhood days.

The police searched the ranch and found that Wayne had been camping in the large disused shed on the property. There was evidence that he'd been there often, including clothes, bedding, old drink cans and food packaging. He had a couple of cameras, some binoculars and his phone, along with a large knife and a gun. When they looked through the photographs on the camera and phone, they were nearly all of Hayley. He'd photographed her dancing with Jeff and Kelvin on the porch. He had photographs of her talking to Harvey. He also had a few photographs of Hayley in the shower and her getting undressed.

"Creepy bastard!" Jeff exclaimed.

Hayley shook her head in disbelief. How could she have fallen for such a monster?

CHAPTER THIRTEEN

Expecting her friend to arrive home late after her exciting evening at Claridge's, Lucy prepared dinner for one - jacket potato, bacon, egg and beans. She hadn't had that for ages; it was an easy meal and one of her favourites. Having worked late into the evening on a canvas, the time had slipped away quickly and hunger had forced her to take a break.

Just as she was sitting down in front of the TV and was lifting the first fork of potato to her mouth there was a loud crash in the hallway as the front door burst open and Florence made her appearance.

"Ooh Flo! You made me jump out of my skin. What on earth are you doing home so early?" Lucy exclaimed, jumping to her feet.

Florence, who was in floods of tears, threw down her bag, kicked off her shoes and pulled the bow from her hair, shaking her head so that her curls flopped into her face. She looked a real state, with black mascara down both cheeks and a false eyelash stuck on her nose. It was all Lucy could do to stop herself from laughing, but she could see that her friend was genuinely upset.

"What's happened?"

Florence wiped her cheeks with her hand and sniffed, "I have been conned Lucy."

"What?" Lucy pulled a tissue from the box on the side and handed it to Flo.

Flo blew hard. "It was all a ploy to get me face-to-face with a long-lost aunt and a half-brother that I knew nothing of until today!"

Lucy was dying to find out all the details. "I'll put the kettle on." she said, grabbing hold of Flo and sitting her down on the kitchen chair.

Florence blew her nose again, sounding as loud as an elephant blowing its trunk. "Oh God! My life was so simple, now it's so complicated I do not know what to do!"

Lucy put a large mug of tea in front of Florence. "Tell me more! Who is this aunt? And more to the point, who is your brother?"

"Oh Lucy, you will not believe it! Dorothy Hamilton-Smythe is my great-aunt and Harvey Dove is my brother!"

"What? How?" Lucy was shocked!

Florence buried her face in her hands and sighed. "I had no idea that my beautiful mother just up and left America and her family to start a new life in France with my father. What sort of person does that? My father has never mentioned any of this to me! My life has been turned upside down. Everything is such a mess! She changed her Christian name, and married my papa, even though she was already married to Harvey's father. How on earth am I going to bring up the subject to my papa? He obviously didn't ever want me to find out! I feel as though my life is a lie!"

Florence looked up; one false eyelash had dropped into her tea and was floating around like a drowning spider. The other was hanging off, partially covering one eye. In frustration she ripped it off, causing her to wince.

Lucy put her arm around her. "Hey hun, come on! It's not all that bad. You loved your mum and missed her when she died. I admit it must be a shock but you have family now! This could be good for you."

Florence shook her head. "Papa is getting married to the lovely Eloise. What will she think? This could ruin them!"

Lucy brushed the curls from Flo's hair and looked at her face. "It's a shock for you but once you can get your head around it you will see things in a different light. You look done in, my lovely girl. Drink your tea; make sure you don't drink the eyelash that's floating in it!"

Both girls laughed.

"You are such a good friend Lucy, I can talk to you about anything!" Florence said, as she fished out the eyelash.

"Of course my lovely! What are friends for? I can tell you anything as well. So I'm telling you now, drink up and off to bed!" Lucy said, digging her fork into her cold dinner and pushing the plate away.

"Ugh, I don't fancy that now!"

"I'm so sorry. I have put you off your dinner now!" Flo looked over her cup with sad eyes.

Lucy patted Flo's hand. "Don't be silly, I'm not hungry now and it's too late to eat anyway! Bed I think, don't you? Come on, let's get your makeup cleaned off and get you a couple of headache pills."

Flo did as she was told and stood still whilst Lucy gently removed her makeup with a wipe. "I vaguely remember my mother wiping my face. I can still smell her perfume and see her beautiful smile. She would spit on a tissue and use it as a wipe."

Lucy laughed. "I think all mothers have done that to their children!"

Flo mocked. "Yes Mum! Do I really remember those things Lucy, or am I just wishful thinking? I was only five when she died, would I really remember?"

Lucy looked sympathetic, "Even if those things are in your imagination, keep hold of them in that lovely head of yours. I'm sure your mother was a wonderful woman and there was a perfectly good explanation for her leaving your brother and his father."

The girls hugged and made their way to their bedrooms.

"Sweet dreams." Lucy called out.

Florence couldn't imagine for one minute that she was going to have sweet dreams ever again, just big scary nightmares! She lay awake for what seemed like hours, looking at the clock every ten to fifteen minutes, wondering how to bring up the subject to her beloved father Jack.

Finally, at precisely 3.24am, Flo drifted off to sleep.

"Morning! Rise and shine!" Lucy called on her way passed Flo's bedroom door. She stopped, stepped back and popped her head around the door to see Flo pull the duvet over her head. "Hey, it's ten o'clock! Wake up lazybones! I'll make you some tea in a sec. What are you doing today?" Flo's immediate thought was her father. She sat up. "Oh mon Dieu! I was hoping that last night was just a dream. I thought long and hard about everything last night. What's done is done. I think I will arrange to meet my aunt Dorothy, I need to find out more about my mother. I can't understand how a woman can just leave a husband and son behind like that! Harvey, poor Harvey, he must hate my father, and he is my brother! I have a brother! What will his father think of that?"

"Think about it Flo, your father must know about Harvey, mustn't he?"

"Yes, you are right of course. Unless my mother kept Harvey a secret, but I cannot imagine any mother being able to do that!"

Florence and Lucy sat at the breakfast table eating croissants and drinking tea and fruit juice. In the background the radio was playing but neither of them were listening to the music, instead they were listening to their inner thoughts. Flo's head was in conflict. Should she ring her father with her news, or should she wait until she was face-to-face with him? Lucy was reflecting on the past. Her parents cropped up in her mind and she wondered when she'd last spoken to them and made a mental note to call them sometime, maybe next week.

CHAPTER FOURTEEN

Ella was a very quiet young woman, deep and introverted. She didn't have many friends, was happy with her own company and didn't feel the need to fit in with the crowd. Her belief was that everything happens for a reason, so when she met Ed at the young age of eighteen, she truly believed in love at first sight.

Edward was a very handsome young man and a hard worker. People said he would be a millionaire some day with his entrepreneurial skills. Never too busy to help others, a kind heart and a generous nature were amongst his many good qualities.

Their eyes first met when they both looked up at exactly the same time, whilst drinking milkshakes in the diner in town. Both had chocolate shakes which left them chocolate froth on their top lips, resembling a moustache, which made them both smile at each other. They shared several glances across the half empty burger bar until they both made their way to the jukebox at the same time where they stood next to each other scanning the hundreds of tracks.

"Hi, I'm Ed, here's a dime you choose." he said, handing Ella a coin.

"Oh, it's fine, I have a coin let's both put some money in and both choose." Ella suggested, blushing slightly.

Ed was much taller than the young woman standing next to him. He could smell her sweet perfume and looked down on her, admiring her shapely figure.

"My name is Ella and I like country music. How about you?" she asked, placing her money in the slot and selecting a few of her favourite country singers.

"I sure do." Ed was impressed with Ella's selection and went on to choose some country music and rock and roll tracks.

Music broke the ice as it so often does. They sat together and ordered more milkshakes. Ella had heard of Ed from gossip at school but never imagined he was really that nice. They chatted for over two hours; never had words flown so freely for Ella. They left the diner hand in hand, as if they had known each other all their lives. He gallantly drove Ella home, giving her a gentle peck on the cheek before thanking her for her company. He opened the glove compartment and rummaged around for a pen and paper. "Can I have your phone number? I'd like to take you to the movies. If you'd like to, that is?"

Ella's heart was racing, she had never been on a date before, so with a shaky hand she nervously wrote down her number, drawing a little smiley face next to it.

Ed was smiling all the way home. He turned up the music on the radio and sang loudly, causing a few raised eyebrows from passersby.

That night, whilst tucked up in bed, after lending a hand on his parents' ranch, he drifted off to sleep, thinking about the beautiful young woman he had met that afternoon. The smell of her delicate perfume, her pretty face, and long wavy fair hair, the way she was dressed in a pale blue top and a red checked skirt. He couldn't wait to see her again.

Edward's mum was impressed with her handsome son, admiring his good looks as she handed him a freshly laundered pure white shirt. "Thanks Momma." he said, standing in front of the kitchen mirror, greasing and combing his dark hair into a large quiff.

His mother was so proud of her boy. He had grown into a lovely young man, everyone thought so and quite often told her, making her feel that she had done a good job at raising him.

"Behave yourself with that young lady." Rose called out as her son pulled the front door shut behind him.

Ed grinned to himself. He knew what she meant. They'd had the chat about the birds and the bees a long time before. He cringed; remembering the day Rose had sat him down and tried to explain the facts of life. He must have been eleven and thought the whole thing sounded disgusting.

The first date went well. Ella was eagerly waiting outside her parents' house and smiled when Ed pulled up and tooted the horn in his father's car. She looked stunning, standing in front of the white picket fence, in a pink gingham blouse and white skirt. Ed got out and opened the passenger door wide for Ella to get in. He skipped around the front and hopped into the driver's seat, smoothly accelerating down the dusty road towards the drive-in.

They settled down in the cool leather seats in the spacious Cadillac to watch the movie at the open air cinema, along with dozens of other courting couples. After a while, Ed nervously put his arm around Ella's shoulder, which made her shudder with delight. Ed was intoxicated by the familiar soft aroma of her perfume and before long they were hugging and kissing, not taking any notice of the movie on the large screen in front of all the rows of parked cars. His father's words kept ringing in his ears "Treat her like a lady." It was a first date and Ed didn't want to push his luck so he kept to his word and treated Ella with respect; he was a red-blooded cowboy and really wanted to go further but he didn't want to put his date off by being too forward and kept his hands to himself, trying hard to hide the bulge in his tight jeans.

Four months passed. Ed and Ella were seeing each other every day. It was Ella's nineteenth birthday and they had planned a romantic evening out. "Could this be the night he takes things just that bit further?" Ella thought, painting her lips with powder pink lipstick before straightening her black skirt and putting on her patent shoes.

The familiar toot sounded outside. It was dark and the evening air was chilly under the large Texas moon which shone down upon her handsome date, patiently waiting with the passenger door open for her.

She skipped down the pathway to the car, leaving behind the aroma of the rambling rose and evening jasmine.

"Hi honey, where are we going?" she asked wide-eyed with wonder, slipping her bare arms into the cardigan which was draped around her shoulders.

Ed kissed her lips, long and hard. "Happy nineteenth birthday! We are going on a picnic!"

"Ooh isn't it a bit cold for a picnic?" she asked, imagining sitting in the middle of an open field on a rug, sipping ice-cold Cokes and eating crusty bread and cheese.

"No, our picnic will be in here. I have supplies in the trunk, along with your favorite munchies, not to mention, your birthday present!" Ed proudly announced, feeling he'd thought of everything needed to suitably impress his girl.

Ella leaned over and kissed him, her eyes closed as she teased her tongue around his lips, hoping that Ed was thinking the same thoughts as her.

Ed put the car in drive and headed down the moonlit road towards a quiet lane a few miles away.

He pulled into a rest stop. Ella had rested her hand on his leg the whole drive. She'd been gently stroking his jeans, making Ed wonder if Ella was teasing him or if this was the night he would be able take things a step further.

He cut the engine and dimmed the headlights; the moon was all the light they needed. Ed jumped out of the car and opened the trunk. Ella could hear him fumbling around and felt excited to find out what her birthday present was.

"Here you are, birthday girl," Ed said, kissing her on the cheek and presenting her with a large envelope and a small elegantly wrapped box, tied with a lavender ribbon.

Ella excitedly opened the envelope and read the words inside the card. Then she untied the bow and pulled the paper from the box, opening it to reveal a silver heart shaped locket on a delicate chain.

"I love it! Thank you honey! It's beautiful."

Ed took it from her, "Here, let me do it up for you." He said, pulling Ella close so he could fasten the clasp for her. "Perfect! You are just so perfect!" He said before kissing her with a passion she had never known before.

"Oh my, I love you my Edward Dove." Ella said between

heavy breaths and passionate kisses.

Ed slowly undid the buttons to Ella's blouse, revealing a white lace bra which cupped her small breasts. She pulled her blouse off and let it slip to the floor, then undid her bra and let that also slip to the floor, allowing Ed to gently kiss her breasts.

Ella sighed with pleasure at every touch and every kiss. "I want you to make love to me."

Ed knew that tonight was the night and was overcome with passion. It was a first for both of them and neither had anticipated the overwhelming feeling of complete love for each other. Ella didn't feel shy like she'd always imagined she would for her first time. She wanted to take control and began to lift her skirt and pull down her white lace panties.

Ed pushed the seat back as far as it would go and climbed over on top of Ella, kissing her all over. It wasn't long before all the windows steamed up, both climaxing at the same time, proving to Ella that they were made for each other.

Four months passed. Ella had been feeling unwell and twice had to cancel going into work at the drugstore.

"I'm not feeling so good again today Mama." Ella's mother heard as she called down from the bathroom. She listened at the bottom of the stairs and could hear Ella retching. She'd noticed her daughter had gained a little weight and had been eating odd combinations such as pickles and cabbage on rye bread.

As Ella appeared looking peaky and tired, Rose sat her down with a glass of ice-cold water and said. "I think you need to see Dr Jones, because I think you are expecting my first grandchild."

Ella burst into tears, knowing her mother was right. She'd missed three periods and believed that their first night of passion was when she had conceived.

Ella and Ed quickly married at the local courthouse, with both sets of parents and two passing strangers for witnesses, then five months later, Ed was pacing up and down the landing, listening to encouraging words from Rose and the midwife from inside Ella's bedroom. He felt Ella's pain as she cried out in agony. Ella's father Grant and her older sister May ran up and down the stairs with drinks for Ed who couldn't stand still. Eventually they heard a baby's cry and Rose stuck her head around the door. "It's a boy! Ed you are a Daddy, Grant you are a grandpa and May, you are an aunt!" Rose was so excited. They all hugged and waited for the midwife to leave before showing Ed into the bedroom to meet his baby son for the first time.

Ella was exhausted but sat proudly holding a little six pound bundle with a mop of dark hair.

"Hi, this is your daddy." she said, proudly handing Ed the baby boy who was tightly wrapped in a hand knitted white shawl.

"I think Harvey suits him, what do you think honey?"

It was settled, Harvey Grant Dove was christened two weeks later in the small local church while his very young but happy and proud parents looked on.

CHAPTER FIFTEEN

Ed and Ella lived on a small ranch in Texas with their young son Harvey. He was a perfect and happy baby, making motherhood easy for Ella, which was good because she spent most of the time alone with her son whilst Ed worked all hours on the ranch.

Ed strived to make his ranch bigger and better. He had good business sense and wasn't shy of hard work. He knew what he wanted to achieve and was prepared to do anything to reach his goal in life, which was to become a millionaire.

When Harvey was three, Ella had the same sickly symptoms she'd had with him and suspected that she may be pregnant again.

The doctor confirmed it and they all looked forward to this time perhaps a little sister for Harvey to play with.

One night Ella woke in alarming pains.
"Ed… Ed, are you awake?"

Ella felt an empty pillow next to her and crawled out of bed and down the stairs to fetch a glass of water. Ed was nowhere to be seen, the house was quiet and the truck was gone. Moaning in agony and losing blood, Ella feared the worse and telephoned Rose.

"Mama, I'm sorry," Ella said sobbing, "I know it's the middle of the night but I've just called the hospital and they want me to go in. Could Pa bring you over to look after Harvey? I'm bleeding. I think I'm losing the baby. I'm not sure where Ed is."

The ambulance came and took Ella to the hospital, whilst

Rose and Grant waited for Ed to return home.

At ten minutes past four in the morning, Ed came in looking fraught.

"What are you guys doing here? Where's Ella? I've been trying to save one of my horses, she has colic."

Rose was angry, even though she thought he was a kind young man, he should have been home with his wife, instead of looking after a horse.

"Well, whilst you were tending to a sick horse, your sick wife has been rushed to hospital! I fear that she has lost the baby!"

Ed found the information hard to hear and grabbed the truck keys that he'd just thrown on the kitchen side.

"I'm on my way. Are you alright to stay with Harvey? I'll call you when I know what's going on. Try and get some sleep, there's nothing you can do. Go to bed the pair of you. I won't call until the morning. Thank you so much for coming."

Ed had tears in his eyes as he left the house. He knew how much Ella was looking forward to having another baby and he felt very guilty at not being there with her.

When Ed arrived at the hospital a very strict nurse guided him to a room where Ella was sleeping. She wasn't going to let him in but could see how upset he was. "The baby?" He asked with hope in his voice.

The head nurse shook her head. "I'm sorry."

Ed's tired eyes filled with tears as he stood looking at his beautiful wife. "Was it a boy or girl?"

"A girl."

He sat with Ella until dawn, when she started to stir from her sleep.

"Hey." She said quietly, just managing a smile.

"Hey." Ed said, unable to control the tears.

"She was a little girl Ed."

"Yes, the nurse told me. I'm so sorry I wasn't with you honey. I was with Tilly. I sat with her all night, I was frightened she would die." Ed pulled a white handkerchief from his pocket and wiped his eyes. "I should have been with you. You shouldn't have gone through that on your own."

"The hospital doesn't let fathers in when their wives are having babies, there was nothing you could have done. Tilly needed you. Is she OK?" Ella asked, hoping that she was. Tilly was an expensive horse and Ed's favourite.

"Yes, I think she's going to be fine."

Ella wept uncontrollably. "I had to give birth to our baby girl. She was so tiny and yet so perfect. I was allowed to hold her. Why? Why do things like this happen? What have I done to deserve this misery?"

They both hugged and sat weeping until the nurse came in and told Ed he had to leave.

"I'm sorry Mr Dove, I can't allow you to stay any longer. Visiting hours are from two p.m. tomorrow, your wife needs her rest."

Ed kissed Ella and made his way back home. Harvey was sitting in his wooden chair and Rose was feeding him a soft boiled egg.

"Daddy!" Harvey shouted, pleased to see his father. He didn't get to see him very often, in fact he was more familiar with his grandfather, Grant.

Rose could tell it wasn't good news and tried hard to hold back the tears. Grant took over feeding Harvey and listened in silence as Ed explained what had happened.
Rose hugged her son-in-law. "You look wrecked boy. Go sleep for a couple of hours. We'll watch Harvey."

Rose knew what Ella was going through; all the emotions, the heartache and sadness, along with the feeling that she had done something to cause her miscarriage because Rose had been through it twice herself. She'd lost two babies between May and Ella.

Ed started to doze, promising himself to take more time with his lovely wife and son and not to carry on working so much. In reality he knew that at the moment it was out of the question, he needed all his spare time to build up the business and work on the ranch. His brain was on overload, with conflicting thoughts and emotions running around in his head, until eventually sleep took over.

Ed woke four hours later, wondering how Ella was and worried about Tilly. He could hear his son happily playing downstairs with his grandparents. He flew out of bed, washed and dressed and rushed downstairs.

"Hey, little guy! How are you doin'? Has he been OK?" Ed asked Rose, kissing Harvey on the top of his head.

"He's been fine. Did you sleep?" Rose asked, feeling concern for her son-in-law.

"Yes, I did. Thanks Rose. I must phone the hospital."

Ed reached for the phone but Rose quickly placed her hand on his.

"Grant phoned half an hour ago. Ella is fine. They will keep her in for a few days, so if it's OK with you, we shall stick around to take care of the little man."

Ed smiled with relief. "Thank you Rose. That would be awesome. I really don't know how I would manage without you now that Ma and Pa have moved so far away. Oh! I must check on Tilly!"

Rose pointed to her husband, who was crawling on the rug on all fours, pretending to be a wolf and chasing Harvey, who was screaming with delight! "Grant has already been down to the stable and checked on her. She is fine, she's better."

"Thank God and thank you!"

A few weeks later and life was back to normal, although Ella was still mourning her baby girl. She suggested to Ed that they try again soon. Ed was keen, he was working on the ranch even more and wanted to make his young wife feel happy again.

Ed sat down to supper, sighed and yawned. "I'm gonna

have to hire a couple of hands soon, I can't do all the work by myself hun."

"You look so tired, the sooner the better honey, you need a break!" Ella poured a couple of beers and sat down to eat the beef stew she had prepared.

She looked around her kitchen. Everything was in place and sparkling clean. Harvey's toys were neatly piled in a wicker basket in the corner, Ed's boots were polished and sitting on the mat. The fruit bowl was piled high with produce from the garden and so was the vegetable rack. Life seemed perfect but Ella was lonely. She hoped that if her husband hired a couple of hands she might see a little more of him.

They soon settled down for the evening, falling asleep in each other's arms, upon the couch. Ella loved her wonderful husband so much and it was so nice to spend quality time with her man.

Ed woke and gently roused Ella from her sleep. "Hey hun, it's two a.m.!" He picked her up and carried her up the stairs, then gently lowered her upon the bed. He kissed her eyelids gently, then nibbled her earlobes, before undoing the buttons of her dress. "I think we'll have another go at trying for our baby." Ella stretched her arms up and let Ed pull the dress over her head. She thought of the first time they'd made love in Ed's father's car and was overcome with passion. She kissed his handsome face all over, teasing his mouth with her lips. Then pushing him down on the bed, she straddled him, undoing his shirt and kissing him down to his belt buckle. He undid her bra and admired her beauty, then kissed her breasts, making her tingle all over. They made love twice, then fell asleep on top of the bed, entwined in each other.

Harvey woke them by calling out to them instead of the alarm which hadn't gone off. Ed leapt out of bed! "It's seven thirty! I've got a busy day!" He rushed into Harvey's room, lifted him from his bed and took him into Ella, who was getting dressed. Ed kissed them both, washed, brushed his teeth, called out "Goodbye!" from the bottom of the stairs, and was gone.

Two months later, Ella was over the moon to be told by the doctor that she was pregnant again. Everything was going to be fine this time. They even redecorated Harvey's little room in neutral colours and gave him the larger one, which they painted in blue. Ella made sure that she did everything right and didn't over do things; at fourteen weeks the same thing happened again, ending in more heartache.

Ella suffered deep depression. Why couldn't she have the baby girl she longed for? What was she doing wrong? Her days were black. Some days she didn't even bother getting dressed, and slouched around in her housecoat and slippers, not even bothering to brush her hair. She resented Ed for being able to carry on as normal, hating him for being able to whistle a tune or laugh at someone's jokes. She couldn't bear to have the wireless on because music always used to make her happy and she didn't want to feel happiness.

In time Ella accepted that she wouldn't have any more children and by the time Harvey was ten, he was still an only child. His parents made sure that he had the company of other children, allowing him to stay over at Mitch and Jane's some weekends where he enjoyed spending time with their daughter Hayley and his best friend Joe. Ed never seemed to be around much but Harvey occasionally enjoyed time with his father when he took him to the rodeos. Harvey was very good at riding sheep when he was small but had progressed to riding the horses, his mother forbidding him to ride the steers. Ella was proud to go and watch her son and shyly joined the other parents at the barbecue cook-offs held at the rodeos.

One evening at the Stockyards Championship Rodeo, Ella as usual was seated on her own, eagerly waiting for everything to start, when a man came up and asked if she would mind him taking the seat next to her. He had a gorgeous French accent and had the most amazing blue eyes she had ever seen. Immediately attracted to the foreign accent, Ella agreed that he could sit next to her.

"My name is Jack. I'm here for six months, this is the first rodeo I've ever been to. I do not know what to expect. I only hope that it does not get too dangerous!" He laughed.

"Don't worry, it never gets too dangerous, it's pretty controlled. My boy is in it. I would never let him do anything too bad!" Ella said, studying the handsome Frenchman's striking features. "Why are you here? You sound French and France is such a long way!"

"Yes I am French, I'm from Auxerre. My father died, he left me a bit of money and I've always wanted to do Route 66. I'm a modest builder and before I get settled down, I thought I'd fulfil my dream and visit America."

Ella was fascinated and charmed by Jack and sat talking to him for the whole afternoon and evening. Ed was around but hadn't even found the time to make sure that she had a drink.

At the end of the evening, Ella handed Jack a piece of paper with her telephone number and said if he was stuck for somewhere to stay, to give her a call and he could stay with them.

Jack thanked her and said he was staying at the Homestead Ranch, which surprised Ella, because by coincidence it was the ranch next to hers.

Ella lay in bed alone, whilst Ed was outside working with his ranch hands, mending fences in the top paddock. All she could think about was Jack's sexy French accent and his attentiveness at the rodeo the day before.

"I have to think of an excuse to see him again." She thought, pulling the bed sheets up under her chin.

Jack was lying in a bed, in the ranch along the way, thinking exactly the same thing. How could he make an excuse to see her? Jack made his mind up that he would telephone Ella in the morning.

Ella took Harvey to school, stopped at the store for some milk and headed back home to feed the hens and water the vegetables. Just as she was hanging out the laundry, she heard the telephone. She ran inside and answered, out of breath. "Hi, Ella Dove speaking."

The phone was silent for a few seconds and then she heard the sexy French accent. "Bonjour, it is Jack speaking. I hope that you do not mind me calling you? I just wondered if you would mind accompanying me for lunch somewhere? Euh, just as friends. I haven't anyone to spend time with while I stay in Texas. I do hope that I am not sounding too forward! I don't even know where to eat! If your husband would prefer you not to, then I understand."

Ella felt excited and alive and answered "Yes!" immediately. "Yes, that would be nice, thank you. My husband won't even notice that I've gone, so don't worry about that. I'll pick you up. I don't know the people that you are staying with. My husband probably does but I don't know any of our neighbors and because the ranches are so far apart, I'm never likely to! Ed has never invited them around for a drink or a cookout, he's always working and never has the time… Anyway, I'll be there at noon. Is that OK with you Jack? I shall need to be back to pick up Harvey from school."

"Oui, I mean yes. Thank you, I am looking forward to seeing you again." Jack put the phone down, feeling a strong connection with Ella and hoping that she felt the same. He sensed that her marriage was not a happy one; he'd observed that she was a bit of a loner and that her husband worked hard and didn't pay much attention to her. There was definitely a strong attraction between them both.

It was noon and Ella pulled into the driveway of the Homestead Ranch to see Jack waiting with his jacket thrown over one shoulder.

Her heart was pounding, like a school girl on a first date, just as her heart used to pound whenever she saw Ed.

Jack opened the passenger door and sat next to Ella. "Bonjour."

Just then Ella panicked. What was she doing?! He could be a murderer, escaped from France and trying to make a life in the US. Then he spoke again in his gentle French voice, and Ella just knew that he was a good guy.

"I do not want to cause you any problems Ella. Are you sure this is all right with your husband?"

Ella sniggered and said bitterly, "He doesn't even know!"

They drove for a while, came across a small café and sat for two hours, talking about life, love and their expectations. Ella didn't notice the time, she was simply enjoying Jack's company, until he looked at his watch and said, "I think it's time we left, your son will be needing a lift from school."

After leaving the café and arranged to meet again the next day, which they did for the next two weeks, Ed never knowing that his wife was with another man. After meeting on the fourteenth day, the owners of the café, had got to know them and commented that they made a lovely couple. They giggled feeling like they were actors in a play, but this was real life. How was this going to end up? They were both asking themselves the same question.

"So at what point are you going to do your Route 66 trip?" Ella asked inquisitively. Jack shook his head. "I do not want to do it alone. I would like company." He held Ella's hand. "How about it? Do you fancy an adventure?"

Harvey's face flashed in Ella's mind. Her handsome boy, what would he think of his momma if he knew what she was doing?

"I have my son, Jack. I can't just up and leave! Are you also forgetting that I'm a married woman?"

Jack was full of apologies; he had obviously read the wrong signals and made incorrect assumptions.

He stood up, embarrassed by his suggestion; he hurriedly paid the check and beckoned Ella to leave with him.

In the car on the way back to the ranch, Jack sounded so sincere with his apologies. "I didn't want to offend you Ella.

Of course you have to think of your son. Maybe we should stop meeting like this. I will start my road trip and you can forget all about me. I will leave you alone to get on with your life with your husband and son, then I will return to France and you will never hear from me again."

Ella stopped the car. "I think I'm in love with you Jack but I don't know what to do about it! I'm torn, my son needs me. I know that Ed would never let me take him with me should I leave and I wouldn't want to break Ed's heart by doing so. I am trapped, trapped in a lonely marriage and a lonely life. I have no friends, I lost the ones I had when I married Ed, I was so engrossed in my life with him. I wanted to be the perfect wife because everyone said that we were too young to marry. My friends all thought I was crazy, but I was pregnant! I've never had the fun part of life! I raised Harvey virtually alone."

Jack put his arm around Ella; it was the first actual close contact that they had shared in their two weeks of friendship. Ella buried her face in his shoulder; he lifted her chin with his hand and looked into her tired, tear filled eyes.

"I do not want to break up a marriage but I can see that you are not happy, I know that I could make you happy. I want to make you happy, I cannot bear to see a beautiful woman like you living a life of loneliness, and should you decide to stay with Ed, I can only hope that you would try to change your life, and live a little."

Ella sighed, "I have tried Jack, I'm tired of trying to make Ed notice me! We haven't made love for over a year, he is just too tired. He says he loves me, and it is work that's preventing him, he's just too tired at the end of the day! I am so tempted to come with you, but it will break my heart to leave my son. What am I going to do?"

Jack shook his head. "I do not know what else to say ma chérie. I know everything about you and you know everything about me. I am an honest and truthful man, I can offer you a modest home in France and all of my heart. If it means that Route 66 has to be put on hold so that you can make a clean break from the US, so be it. You can bring Harvey too, I will welcome your son with open arms, if that is what you would like."

Ella looked anxious, "I couldn't take him away from Ed but I can't leave him either. I'm so confused! I've only known you for two weeks and yet we have such a connection. I can tell that you are a good man Jack. I need to be loved. Ed has just forgotten what love is. It would take all my inner strength to kiss my son goodbye and never see him again."

Jack stroked her hair and kissed her cheek with such tenderness. "It wouldn't have to be forever mon amour. He can visit when you are settled. He can come for the holidays, if Ed is too busy for you, how could he refuse his son having holidays in France?"

Ella held Jack's hands in hers. "Thank you but I wouldn't want you to give up your dream of travelling America."

"That does not matter, it can wait. You are more important. Take time to think about it. I know it's a huge decision. Try and save your marriage and if it's beyond saving, you know that there will be happiness if you want it." Jack gently kissed the top of her head and squeezed her hands.

Ella's heart was pounding, what should she decide? "I owe it to my marriage to try and save it one last time. I feel such a special kind of love for you Jack. You are the nicest man I've ever met but I once had feelings like that for Ed. Can you give me a week to decide? I won't play games, it'll be a yes or no."

Jack hugged her tightly, "Of course, I hope that you make the right decision."

Ella drove Jack back to the ranch, then collected Harvey from school. She kissed her son on the cheek as he jumped into the car.

"Hi Momma, what's for dinner tonight? Will Pa be home for dinner, it's ages since he sat with us! The last time was when Mitch, Jane and Hayley came over and that was months ago! She's such a funny little girl, I sometimes wonder what it would be like to have a little sister like her, she's so cute. She wanted to ride Samson but she's way too small."

Ella felt a single tear trickle down her cheek, as she thought of her four miscarriages. "Honey, I don't think your father will be able to have dinner with us tonight. He has gone to see Mitch and won't be back for a couple of days. We could ask one of your friends over if you like?"

Harvey stared out of the window at the vast open landscape.

"It's OK, I have stacks of homework to do. I should sit in my room and get it done Momma."

Ella knew she was going to spend another evening on her own and longed for Thursday, when Ed would be back and she could try and change things.
The next day Ella met Jack, and drove him to the park, where they walked hand in hand, then sat on the bench putting the world to rights. They had so much in common

and yet they were worlds apart. Jack put his arm around her shoulder and Ella comfortably snuggled into him. She really wanted him to kiss her and looked up into his eyes. She felt a shiver run up her spine as his lips covered hers with the most tender and loving kiss.

"Come on, let's go and eat some lunch." Jack suggested.

Back in the café again, they sat at their usual table, drinking coffee and eating lunch. Ella had butterflies in her stomach; she admired Jack's flawless face and beautiful blue eyes. His smile was captivating, she had definitely fallen in love with him but how could she when she still loved Ed?

"I'm going to give it one last go at saving my marriage tonight Jack. I'm so sorry but I have to try. I'm drawn to you and it feels so right but oh so wrong."

The juke box was playing Connie Francis's "Everybody's Somebody's Fool." Ella listened to the lyrics, which rang so true. "Listen Jack…"

The tears I cried for you could fill an ocean
But you don't care how many tears I cry
And though you only lead me on and hurt me
I couldn't bring myself to say goodbye

'Cause everybody's somebody's fool
Everybody's somebody's plaything
And there are no exceptions to the rule
Yes, everybody's somebody's fool

I told myself it's best that I forget you
Though I'm a fool at least I know the score
Yet darlin' I'd be twice as blue without you
It hurts but I come runnin' back for more

'Cause everybody's somebody's fool
Everybody's somebody's plaything
And there are no exceptions to the rule
Yes, everybody's somebody's fool

Someday you'll find someone you really care for
And if her love should prove to be untrue
You'll know how much this heart of mine is breakin'
You'll cry for her the way I've cried for you"

Jack took her hands and kissed them. "The only fool is Ed."

Thursday came; it was late afternoon when Ed returned. He rushed into the kitchen and kissed his wife on the lips.

"I managed some good deals whilst I was at Mitch's."

Ella had her best dress on and had done her hair and makeup. She looked stunning but Ed didn't even give her a second glance. "Where's the boy?" Ed asked, whilst washing his hands in the sink.

"He's staying over at a pal's. I thought maybe we could spend a nice evening together? I've cooked your favorite, chicken pot pie. We need to talk Ed, what do you say?" Ella walked over and put her arms around him.

Ed dried his hands and turned to look at his wife. "You smell nice, is that a new perfume?"

Ella shook her head, "It's my usual Ed, the one I always wear."

Ed took a beer from the fridge and talked about the work

he and Mitch had been doing. He wiped his brow and yawned. "I'll take a shower and then we can talk hun."

Ella served the meal while Ed showered. Ten minutes passed and Ella called out, "Supper's on the table."

She had laid the best white linen tablecloth, lit a small candle and poured two glasses of red wine.

Five minutes later, he still hadn't appeared, so she made her way up the stairs, only to hear loud snoring coming from the bedroom. Ella peered around the half-open door, there he was, sprawled on top of the bed, fast asleep.

CHAPTER SIXTEEN

Ella phoned Jack. "I'm coming with you. How soon can we leave?"

The next day Ella and Jack drove to the café, where they sat and made plans. Ella had to send for a passport, as she'd never owned one. This was going to take a few weeks, so they had plenty of time to plan everything. It was decided that she would just disappear and not contact Ed again, until she felt she could face Harvey. It would be hard, but this was the best way.

Three weeks later, her passport arrived. Her stomach churned, she ran to the toilet and threw up. This was it! She couldn't go back now. This was her chance at happiness.

They booked flights for the end of the week. Ella arranged for Harvey to stay at his friend's house straight from school, so that she knew someone was there to pick him up, and he would be away from home when Ed found her letter. She couldn't bear the pain she was causing, her heart was aching.

As they sat on the plane, holding hands, Ella sobbed at the thought of not seeing her baby boy again, at least not for a while. The note left on the kitchen table explained why she would not be returning home.

When they arrived in France, Ella would change her name to Annette Dubois, taking the same last name as Jack. He would buy her a wedding ring and everyone would think that they were married.

Back at the ranch, Ed walked through the door, expecting to find either Ella cooking his supper, or a dried up meal in the oven, often the case if he hadn't returned home at the expected time.

"Honey!" he called up the stairs. No answer. He checked the oven, no supper. He remembered that Ella had told him that Harvey was staying with a friend. The house was really quiet.

As he headed to the fridge for a beer, he noticed an envelope with his name on it on the table. He opened it and took out the letter, it said simply:

"Ed, my darling man, I have tried to make you notice me. I know you are an honest, kind man, but my needs have gone by the wayside, replaced by your love for your work and the ranch. Your son still needs you. He often asks where you are. If you don't want to ruin your relationship with him as well please make an effort not to ignore him."

Ed couldn't believe the words before him, his wife's elegant handwriting, expressing painful truths. He knew he had pushed things too far. The letter went on…

"I won't get in touch just yet, maybe when the dust has settled. I loved the man you used to be. I'm leaving for a foreign country. Please don't try and find me. My life is taking a different turn. I'm so sorry to do this to you both. Ella."

Inside the envelope was another note to Harvey and her wedding ring.

Ed walked into the living room and stood in front of Ella's portrait. "What have I done? He hung his head in shame and cried, flashbacks of all the happy times as well as the traumas of their eleven-year marriage racing through his mind. He knew he must make it up to Harvey or his son would want to go and live with Ella, and he would be left alone.

The following day, Harvey was surprised to see his father sitting in his mother's car. He couldn't remember the last time his Pa had picked him up from a friend's house.

"Hey Pa, where's Mom?"

What Ed had told him through his tears was to remain in Harvey's memory for ever.

Ella wrote to her parents Rose and Grant and to her older sister May, mailing the letters on the way to the airport. They were all fraught at the news, none had any idea that anything had been wrong with what had always seemed to be Ella's perfect life, aside from losing her babies, Ella had everything she wanted; Ed was a good provider and seemed to be a loving and loyal husband.

May was now living in Canada. She'd never been that close to her sister. It seemed that whatever Ella did she was never in the wrong so it was a shock to find out that Rose and Grant thoroughly disapproved of Ella leaving Ed and Harvey. She had half-expected them to stick up for their daughter.

The letters explained that she had been in an unhappy marriage for a long while, that she had met someone else, not to try and find her, and she would contact them after she was settled.

CHAPTER SEVENTEEN

Dorothy Hamilton-Smythe telephoned Florence to arrange a meeting. She desperately wanted to get to know her great niece as time was running short and there was a lot of making up for lost time.

Florence ignored her calls, every one of them, and there had been a couple of dozen! Back in France, Jack and Eloise woke to hear someone fumbling with a front door key. They lay in silence, listening, as the front door chain prevented whoever it was from entering.

Jack flew out of bed and rushed down the stairs in just a pair of boxer shorts.

"Qui est là?" He asked grabbing hold of an umbrella from the brass stand in the corner of the hallway.

"C'est moi Papa." Flo answered, still trying hard to enter.

Jack opened the door with a relieved look upon his face.

"Why did you not say that you were coming ma chérie?" He hugged his daughter tightly, then called up to Eloise that Flo had arrived. Florence smiled at her father, who looked fit and well, and noticed that since Eloise had been caring for him, he'd put on a few pounds.

They all sat down to breakfast. Eloise hurriedly ate hers so that she could rush down the road and open the shop.

"Enjoy, mes amours, take your time, I will see you both in a while."

And off she went, leaving Flo feeling relieved now that she

could talk to Jack alone. She didn't want to ruin his chance of happiness by discussing revelations in front of Eloise.

"Papa." she said with a mouthful of croissant, "Papa, I have something to tell you. I do not want to give you another heart attack, so please stay calm. The woman that wanted me to work for her as a model for Silent Senses is actually related! She is my great-aunt Dorothy."

She looked at Jack who sat there expressionless. She was hoping to see some sort of recognition but he had obviously never heard of her.

"She also told me that I have a half-brother."

Her father went white.

"His name is Harvey. I've met him a few times and didn't even know who he really was until the ball. Then Dorothy revealed the truth and he wasn't pleased. He blamed me for growing up without his mother… Ma maman!"

Jack swallowed his mouthful of tea and choked on it. His mind went racing back to the day he met Ella.

"Papa, if what Dorothy says is true, my mother was married to two men at the same time."

Jack banged his cup on the table. "How dare anyone assume that your mother was a bigamist! The truth is, we never married! I wanted to marry her but she wouldn't get in touch with Ed for a divorce. The longer time went on, the harder it became for her to see Harvey again, she thought that her son hated her. She sent him cards but never revealed our address, so we never found out if he received them."

Flo took her father's hand. "Then why was my mother's last name the same as yours? And why did she change her name to Annette?"

"She changed her name so that everyone would think that we were married and Annette was to cover her tracks so that no one could trace her."

Flo looked sad. "How could she leave her son?"

Jack looked sad. "It was the hardest thing she ever had to do; she regretted every day that they were apart. She only really found happiness again the day you were born. She had always wanted a daughter; she'd had several miscarriages with Ed's babies, all girls. I tried so desperately to make her happy and I'm convinced we were, at least, happier here than her life was with Ed back in Texas. Then came the tragic day that my beautiful Annette drove home in fog and hit a car head-on. Thank God she didn't suffer, she was killed instantly!

"I wrote to Ed and Annette's family, I gave them my address and telephone number but I did not hear a damn thing! They had wiped her from their lives! It is unbelievable, I know that it was wrong of her to leave a husband and son but not even to acknowledge that she was dead is inconceivable to me!"

Flo looked at the small photograph in the gold frame which had lived on the oak dresser ever since she could remember. She held the silver locket around her neck. As a child she would kiss it every day, and daydream about what life would be like to have Annette by her side to wipe away her tears and patch up her grazed knees. Her wonderful father had taken great care of her but she had still missed out on what life would have been like to have her beautiful mother.

"Oh Papa, does Eloise know all about how Annette came into your life?"

"Yes, she does. Florence, you know that I am an honest man. I wanted Eloise to know the truth. I am not proud of the fact that I took your mother away from her son, but under the circumstances, at the time, it was the right decision. Who knows, you may one day become close to your brother?"

"Hmm, I doubt it; he did not want to know me!"

"It was a shock Flo, to you and to him!" Jack made another pot of tea. "How long are you staying?"

"I'm flying back tomorrow, just the one night Papa. I'm going to get in touch with Dorothy when I get back to London. I've been ignoring her calls. I shall also try and reach Harvey. He was so desperate to own the painting that Lucy did of me; I should think that all he will want to do now is throw it away!"

Flo explained how Dorothy found them both. It was a long story and they sat for a couple of hours chatting. Jack was glad that it was all out in the open now. He had never liked keeping things from his precious daughter.

Flo cleared the table, in doing so she accidentally knocked the teapot on the butler sink, causing the spout to break off.

Jack laughed, and laughed.
"You still haven't lost your touch Flo!"

"I am sorry Papa, I will buy you a new one."

He laughed again. "I have a spare, do not worry about it ma chérie."

CHAPTER EIGHTEEN

Harvey waited until the police had gone, happy to see the back of Wayne, once and for all. Now was his chance to win Hayley over. Mitch and Jane were so grateful to Harvey, Jeff and Kelvin for being so brave and saving their girl from God knows what, perhaps even her murder if Wayne had done what he'd threatened.

"Stay the night Harvey, it's been a heavy day, you must be worn out." Jane patted him gently on the back and handed him an ice-cold beer.

"That would be great Jane, I'm tuckered out! I've got jet lag." Harvey admitted, rubbing his eyes.

Mitch looked a little puzzled.

"Jet lag? From Dallas?"

Harvey shook his head and smiled, "From London."

They all sat down to eat pizza and salad which Jane had quickly thrown together and went over the events of the past twenty-four hours, Hayley shuddered at the thought of how terribly things could have turned out had the guys not been so brave.

Harvey was falling asleep at the table so Jane quickly made up the bed in the guest room and put clean towels out for him.

As soon as Harvey had showered, he slipped under the clean sheets and drifted into a deep sleep.

A little while later as the others decided to turn in for the night; Hayley popped her head around the door and in the dim light, silently watched Harvey, who was sleeping like a baby.

Jane was passing and doubled back to stand next to Hayley. She whispered "He's a good guy, ya know, and he's sweet on you."

"I know Mama, he's awesome but there's just nothing there for me, he's more like a big brother."

Jane hugged Hayley. "The right man will come along. Ya know that don't you?"

"I hope so mama, I hope so."

The next morning, Hayley was up bright and early and headed to her gym with trash bags to throw away all the roses. Her temper got the better of her as she angrily threw them all away, cursing as she did so.

"Wayne, you bastard! You bastard! I hate you! I hate you so much!"

As the last lot of roses went into a bag, Hayley burst into uncontrollable sobs. One of her clients had arrived and stood back looking confused, not knowing how to deal with the situation.

Harvey ran in, grabbed the bag and threw it across the room, then held Hayley tightly, letting her sob.

"I'm sorry man, Hayley isn't working today." Harvey said to the client.

She sobbed and sobbed. Harvey was extremely concerned

about her, but just held her, saying nothing, just hugging her tightly and stroking her hair.

Meanwhile back inside the house, Mitch was on the phone to his old pal Ed, explaining everything and telling him how grateful he was that Harvey had been so brave.

Ed was horrified and once the conversation had ended he packed a bag and was straight on the road to Austin.

Once Hayley had calmed down, Harvey planted her on a bench with his arm around her and spoke gently about sorting out the business.

"You need a break now, why don't you let me help you cancel your appointments and maybe take you away for a few days? I need a break and would appreciate the company."

Hayley drew away from him. "No, thank you Mr Dove! I most certainly do not need a break! Work will be my focus now! It will help me to forget that scumbag! I need to try and get my appointments rescheduled, and try and find my missing contacts, who will hopefully start to turn up for their training sessions. If I'm not here and they turn up, then what?"

Harvey shook his head. "Fair enough. I'm still going to take a break though, so if you change your mind hun, you just call me. Meanwhile, at least let me take you out for supper tonight?"

Hayley stood up as another client entered the gym. "I'll be five minutes Sam." Hayley called as she disappeared into the back room to splash her face with water, and re-apply her mascara, leaving Harvey without an answer.

Harvey and Mitch saddled up and took a ride out on a couple of the horses. They needed the wind in their hair and the sun on their faces. After about half an hour they stopped and looked at the creek. The sun was glistening on the dancing ripples in the vast stretch of water, the tall pine trees shading them as they admired the view.

"Takes me back to when you were a boy Harv. Your pa and I used to ride up here and we'd all skinny-dip in that there creek."

Harvey chuckled. "I remember it as though it were yesterday Mitch. It was kinda our own guy thing. No women allowed. Made me feel like a man. It was when Momma left us, and Pa realized that he had to take care of me. I used to love coming to stay here with you guys. Your life seemed so normal, compared to ours."

Mitch lifted his Stetson and scratched his head, in deep thought.

"Your pa worked too hard, still does! I keep telling him to slow down. That was partly to do with why your folks broke up."

"How do you mean?"

Mitch was scared to say too much. It was up to Ed to tell Harvey why his mother had left and why he hadn't given Harvey the cards and presents she'd sent and that his mother was killed in a car crash.

"It's not for me to say, it's really time your pa told you everything. You are so much like him Harv, look at you, always working, always jetting off here and there. You've made your millions, take it from me, money isn't everything. My Hayley's the same, it's as though it's her mission to earn as much money as she can, but she doesn't have to!"

Harvey knew Mitch was right. He didn't need to work. His father didn't need to work either. They both had ranch hands and he could give up dealing in art just like that, but art was his passion, he enjoyed nothing more than discovering new talented artists and purchasing exquisite paintings and drawings to sell on or keep for his own collection.

"I asked Hayley to take a break with me but she said no. She needs to work, I think it's so she can forget that psycho. I asked her out for supper tonight but she didn't answer. I'm gonna ask her again when we get back, I won't take no for an answer."

"Hell boy! Good for you. It's just what she needs, a nice relaxing evening with someone who cares for her."

Harvey stared at the creek. "I care for her more than she will ever know."

Mitch nodded. "I can see that you do Harv but I don't think she wants a relationship with anyone else just yet. Give her time to get over the shock of Wayne."

He looked at his watch. "Your pa will be here soon, we should head back to the ranch."

As they galloped back to the ranch so many happy childhood memories came flooding back. Long hot sunny days, filled with fun and laughter. The smell of a short, sharp rain shower on parched sunburnt land. Fishing in the creek with Mitch, Hayley and his best friend Joe. Swinging on the rope from the large tree branch, until they could hold on no more, then letting go and splashing in the water in fits of laughter. Delicious picnics of cold fried chicken and potato salad with Jane's special cheese coleslaw and home grown strawberries, cold lemonade and home brewed beer for Mitch, all packed neatly in a basket with a red gingham cloth to lay it all out on. Hayley being stung on the butt when she sat on a bee, and Mitch having to try and remove the sting, while Hayley screamed and hid behind a bush from the boys' curious eyes. Harvey rode alongside Mitch and admired the vast surroundings, making up his mind that he didn't want to get much older before he had a son of his own to make similar memories.

Back at the house, Jeff and Kelvin unsaddled the horses and let them loose in the paddock with the others. Mitch and Harvey opened the door to Michael Jackson blasting from the twin speakers and Hayley happily teaching the ladies aerobics in the afternoon session. Totally engrossed, she didn't even notice her father waving at her, trying to attract her attention.

"She seems fine." Mitch said, giving up and pulling the door closed, instantly muffling the sound of "Beat It."

"She looks fine, she seems fine, but that's because she has her work." Harvey was quick to point out, concerned that deep down she really wasn't.

Ed arrived late in the day, pulling up outside the steps to the ranch house.

"Howdy all y'all. Thank the Lord you're all OK! So... Tell me all about it! Who'd a' thought that nice young fella would turn out to be as mean as a mama wasp!"

Jane kissed Ed affectionately on the cheek and pulled a chair out for him.

Harvey shook his father's hand. "Howdy Pa, uh huh, thank the Lord! Hayley could've married the sadistic asshole!"

They all sat around the table mulling over the ins-and-outs, when Hayley came around the corner and ran up the steps.

"Don't let me stop you guys! I know y'all are talkin' 'bout what a fool I've been, just carry on, don't mind me!"

Ed stood up and stopped Hayley in her tracks. "Whoa! Wait just a doggone minute! We were all taken in by his charms!"

Mitch firmly took hold of her shoulders and sat her in the spare seat.

"Right! I understand how angry you must be feeling hun, but there is no need to take it out on us! You've worked way too hard today! Now sit!"

Hayley looked totally washed out. "I'm sorry guys, I'm just tired."

Harvey frowned. "There's no chance that you will let me take you out for a quiet meal tonight then?"

Hayley looked at him and felt sorry for the way she had treated him. She must have seemed ungrateful; after all he'd saved her life.

"Ya know what? Why not, though not tonight Harv, I need to get some sleep. If you still want to then stay another night, tomorrow would be better for me."

Mitch winked and nodded approvingly, while Hayley went inside.

"Could you excuse us please?" Harvey nodded to Ed and beckoned him to follow down the steps.

They walked along the dusty road, Ed was a little uneasy and wondered what was going to crop up in the conversation.

"What's wrong son?"

"I don't know how, or where to start Pa."

Ed chuckled. "Oh hell… was she an Ugly Betty?"

Harvey turned to Ed, thinking back to the Ball and Wren. "Uh? Oh, no she was a looker, but that's not what I want to talk about."

"This is so hard, I'm sorry for what I am going to tell you. It's bad news. The portrait I wanted to buy? The one I was allowed to buy, for being chaperone? It's so complicated, I'm just gonna blurt it out! Dorothy Hamilton-Smythe is Momma's long-lost aunt, my great aunt! And the girl in the painting is my half-sister Florence! Momma had a baby girl! She is my sister Pa, and I was awful to her! I blamed her for me not having a mom, then she told me neither did she cause Momma was killed in a car crash."

Harvey had tears in his eyes. "My momma is dead!"

He looked at Ed waiting for a reaction. Ed kept his head down.

"Pa? You knew didn't you! You knew that Momma was dead! Why didn't you tell me?"

Harvey was angry!
Ed couldn't look at his son.

"I knew but couldn't tell you Harv. You were heartbroken when ya momma left. How could I hurt you anymore? How could I add to your pain?"

"So, she lived in France, had a daughter, and then was killed in a car crash. You told me that you thought she'd emigrated to Australia. Was that to put me off searching for her and finding out the truth? I did search for her but it was like hitting my head against a brick wall! Why have my grandparents Rose and Grant never tried to contact me?"

"They were ashamed of Ella just up and leaving you and thought it best to wipe their hands of anything to do with any of us!"

"Oh come on Pa, would they really have abandoned me? I don't believe you! You aren't telling me everything! Tell me the real reason Momma left, because I blamed myself. I thought it was because I'd done something to upset her. Was the real reason because you were always working and because you didn't take any time out to spend with us? "

Ed looked a bit shocked. "Look Harv, things just went wrong. We were too young to get married, everyone said so. Yes, I worked hard and I do sometimes regret not paying as much attention to Ella as I should have but it was because I wanted you both to have everything. I gave her everything she wanted, except the one true thing, and that was another baby."

"Pa that still doesn't ring true! Grant and Rose, I meant the world to them and all of a sudden they stopped sending

cards and gifts, Momma never sent any either! Not to mention Aunt May."
The penny dropped.

"They did, didn't they? They sent me stuff, so did Momma, and you didn't let me have any of them! You punished them for Momma leaving!"

Ed could see Harvey was getting really angry and frustrated.

"Tell me Pa, don't lie to me!"

Harvey stopped and started to walk back to the ranch, kicking stones along the way. Ed followed, grabbing hold of Harvey's left shoulder.

Harvey was so angry he turned around and threw a punch, knocking Ed off his feet, leaving him on his back in a cloud of dust from the dirt track.

Harvey marched on, not looking back to see whether his father had got to his feet. Further down the track, Harvey felt a hand on his shoulder again. Before he could throw another punch, Ed tried to explain.

"I kept them all. I wanted you to have them eventually. They're in the attic, you can have them Harv. I'm so sorry son."

Harvey ignored him and marched back to the ranch, he had a face like a raging bull when he walked back inside.

Mitch guessed what had happened between father and son and felt as though he was somehow to blame as well because he knew all the family secrets.

Ed followed Harvey into the kitchen, his mouth was bleeding and his cheek bruised.

Jane jumped to her feet. "Here, let me fix that for ya Ed. What in heaven's name has happened?"

"I deserve a good punch! Harvey knows everything now Jane. I've admitted that I kept the letters, cards and presents from his family and I've admitted that I knew that Ella was dead and that I didn't have the guts to tell my only son all those years ago. One of the biggest regrets of my life!"

He looked at Harvey, who was standing with his arms folded and looking out of the window.

"But hey! Hang on! I regret everything in my life, except my only son! I loved Ella, Jane; you know how much I loved her. I would have given her the moon! Why oh why didn't I listen to your advice Jane? You told me to slow down and pay my family more attention, you've been through it, you and Mitch, same as us. You slowed down Mitch, why didn't I? I lost everything the day she left me, everything except Harvey, now I think I've lost him as well."

His son was still standing with his back to everyone, listening to the conversation, and was seething inside.

Jane dabbed some cotton wool in antiseptic and bathed Ed's lip.

"Now Ed, you know how closed off Ella was. She hardly spoke to anyone, except you! She didn't make friends easily, Lord knows I tried plenty of times, inviting her on shopping trips, or barn dances, or just coming here for the weekend while you boys went off fishin' She was a hard one to get through to. It seemed that the only people she wanted were you, Harv and her ma and pa. She didn't even like her sister that much did she?"

Harvey listened to Jane's words with curiosity. He hadn't imagined his mother to be like that, but thinking back, she didn't mix with any of his friends' parents when they invited her around to their houses to socialise.

Ed winced as she dabbed his lip again with the antiseptic.

"Yes she was intense, but I thought I knew her well enough not to go off with another guy! I thought I could trust her. I've blamed myself but I guess it takes two to make or break a marriage. It's not all clear-cut."

Mitch patted Harvey on the back. "Come on Harv, don't be too hard on your dad. Listen to his regrets, my regrets too! I knew everything. It's hard Harv, it's so hard!"

Harvey turned around and saw what he'd done to his father. It was the first time they'd fallen out and he'd hit him.

"I'm going to bed. When we get back to Dallas, I wanna see all those cards, letters and presents!"

He went to bed, leaving the other three sitting around the table, talking about life, their kids and Ella.

CHAPTER NINETEEN

Dorothy, a stunning dark-haired beauty, lived in Dallas until the age of twenty-one, she was orphaned at ten and lived in a children's home until fifteen, when she got a job working in the mailroom at a local newspaper.

Her life was her work. Dorothy was determined to work up from mailroom assistant to better herself. Six months later, she was working the switchboard, two years later she was secretary to the editor and finally his personal assistant.

Mr Hamilton-Smythe, Dorothy's boss, was very impressed by her hard work and enthusiasm and when he was offered a job as editor for a top London newspaper he asked Dorothy to go with him.

Dorothy ended up marrying her boss, who was twenty years older. Life was great for them both. Dorothy went on to own a fashion magazine and had her own brand of lingerie and eventually her own brand of perfume.

John idolised his wife. There was nothing he wouldn't do for her. He encouraged her to start her own business, whilst he carried on as a newspaper editor. They owned a six bedroom house in Buckinghamshire, with a swimming pool and tennis court, and a large town house in London; they often entertained many rich and famous people. Life could not have been better. They had a very happy marriage, never argued, and had plenty of close friends.

John became ill and very frail, needing constant care. Dorothy sat at John's bedside and held his hand tightly.

"I love you, my darling man." she whispered quietly in his ear, as he managed to gently squeeze his wife's hand before peacefully slipping away.

Dorothy kissed his cheek and said "Thank you my darling man, for being the kindest most supportive boss, my lover, my husband and my best friend."

Molly, John's private nurse smiled with admiration. She could feel how much love they both had for each other but could tell that John's death was also a happy release.

Dorothy wiped her eyes with a clean white cotton handkerchief and smiled back at the nurse. "Thank you darling, he's gone to the rainbow bridge now."

She stood up and kissed John again, leaving him in peace. It dawned on her that she was alone, with no family of her own. All John's relatives were long gone and she didn't know any of hers, thus making it her mission to find out if she had any surviving relatives.

A few years later Dorothy was delighted when the two private detectives she'd hired found that she had family in Austin, Texas, Ontario, Canada and Auxerre in France.

She had managed to contact Annette's mother and father, Rose and Grant, both still living in Austin, and had tried to persuade them to join her at the charity ball but Dorothy infuriated them when she told them she was Rose's aunt and was trying to contact Annette.

"Who the hell is Annette? You mean Ella!" Rose shouted down the phone. "Ella is dead!"

She refused to talk to Dorothy anymore, slamming down the phone.

Dorothy also wrote to May, now living in Ontario. May must have held the same opinions as her mother and ignored Dorothy's letter.

At least Harvey and Florence were going to the ball.

Dorothy felt as though she had been hit by a freight train the morning of her charity ball. It was all she could do to muster up enough energy to get out of bed. Her illness was getting worse and finding strength to get through each day was becoming more and more difficult.

Popping her medication and drinking a half litre of spring water helped to pep her up, making her joints become more mobile. The effects of recent chemotherapy were dragging her down but Dorothy was a fighter and wouldn't let her cancer make her miserable. More importantly, she felt that she had to get to know her long-lost relatives before the inevitable happened.

Dorothy felt that she had handled everything badly. She drank tea with her old friend and neighbour Tom Salmon.

"Darling, how am I going to get them all to accept me before I die? It seems the root of the problem is Annette. I need to convince them that my intentions are purely for their good. I know that Harvey is a multi-millionaire and doesn't need an inheritance, but Rose, May and Florence would benefit tremendously! I'm going to leave them all shares in my will."

Tom sipped the tea, deep in thought. "I'm happy that you found them all Dorothy, really I am, but you are making life hard for yourself! You are ill and you shouldn't stress about things! Maybe you should let it go? Florence hasn't answered any of your calls, Harvey wasn't at all interested in getting to know Wren and fled when he realized that Florence was his half-sister. By my reckoning, it looked as though he wasn't attracted to my daughter but he was attracted to Florence! Poor man, what a shock!"

Dorothy played with the tea spoon on her saucer, dipping it in and out of the steaming hot cup of Earl Grey.

"Don't make me feel any worse than I do Tom! I honestly thought I was giving my great-niece the opportunity of a lifetime! She was very excited about the modelling contract. Heaven knows what must be going through her head at this moment in time! I truly wish that I could speak with her! I shall keep trying and trying. I'm not going to give up darling!"

Just then Dorothy's mobile phone rang "Dorothy Hamilton-Smythe speaking."

There was a muffled sound and a loud cough. "Oh bonjour madame! It is Florence speaking. I am very sorry that I did not return your calls. I hope that you understand, it was all a bit of a shock for me. I would like to meet with you and talk."

Dorothy held her hand over the phone. "It's Florence!"

Tom nodded approvingly, "Good."

"Darling Florence, thank you. I would love to meet you. I have so much to discuss with you!"

Florence fiddled with her hair. Twiddling it frantically through her fingers causing a tangled knot.

"That is good, when and where?"

"Come to dinner Darling! I'll have my chauffeur pick you up. Tomorrow night would be good with me, is that OK for you?"

Florence agreed and told Dorothy, she looked forward to it, before hanging up, then ringing straight back because they hadn't arranged a time.

"Darling, my chauffeur will collect you at seven."

Florence was already feeling nervous and later that evening whilst watching television with Lucy back at the flat, she hyperventilated at the possibility of terminating the contract with Silent Senses lingerie. Flo had time to think about it and came to the conclusion that her great-aunt had chosen her because she was her niece and felt she would have otherwise chosen a top model for the job had she not been so eager to introduce her to her half-brother.

"I cannot breathe – ugh, ugh, I, I, cannot breathe!!"

Flo was gasping for breath. Lucy rushed to the kitchen and produced a brown paper bag.

"Here, blow into this, breathe in… and out… In… and out. Now stop panicking! I'm sure she really does want you as her model Flo. Gosh Flo, great aunt, or not, I would've chosen you if I were her! God Flo you're drop-dead gorgeous! So, if she wasn't your long-lost aunt, and she'd discovered you just by say… bumping into you in the street, then offered you the job, would you have accepted the job? Plenty of modelling agencies discover their models whilst talent scouting on the streets of London. Are you absolutely sure that you don't want to do it? I mean, gosh! Look at the fabulous clothes and shoes you'll get to wear, and the exotic locations you'll get to visit!"

Flo carried on blowing in and out of the brown paper bag, listening all the while to what Lucy was saying.

Lucy snatched the bag from Flo's hand.

"That's enough. Take it from me, this is a great opportunity! You said my mother looked over the contract for you, it's all legit. It's only for a year! Look how quickly a year passes! If you don't like it, you will only have to suffer all that glamour for a year! I mean bloody hell, give me the chance and I'd do it! You only have to extend your career break for a little longer, you could always return to teaching afterwards."

Flo grabbed the bag back, splitting it in two. "I see your point, but I still need to meet with her, I want to know that she really thinks that I am worthy."

"Of course you are worthy Flo."

Lucy poured two glasses of merlot and handed one to Flo. "Now drink this, it'll help calm your nerves."

"Merci." Florence savoured a mouthful of the deep red wine. "Cheers, and thank you my best friend. What would I do without you?"

Lucy smiled. "Bottoms up! That's what friends are for! Fancy a chick flick? What shall we watch? Miss Congeniality? Again?"

The girls both giggled and searched for the film, then settled down with cheese and onion crisps, black olives, hummus and crackers, and a large box of Maltesers, just as they'd done many times before. Halfway through the film, both girls fell asleep, one upon each sofa, until Flo rolled over and fell with a loud clonk onto the floor, waking Lucy with a start!

"Come on! Bedtime!"

Lucy helped Flo up from between the sofa and the coffee table and they both retired to their rooms for the night.

The next day passed quickly. Flo began to get anxious again as the evening drew nearer. She made up her mind to carry on as Dorothy's model; Lucy had made her see sense, it was after all just for a year.

Florence put on white linen trousers with a pale green cotton blouse and white leather sandals. Lucy curled Flo's hair and added pale pink lipstick to her pout. Five minutes later the Bentley was tooting its horn from the road beneath the flat.

"Au revoir. Wish me luck!" Flo kissed Lucy on the cheek, grabbing her bag which was hanging on the coat rack in the hallway.

Lucy called out as she began loading the dishwasher. "Luck!"

The driver opened the car door and Flo slipped into the back seat. Feeling very small and vulnerable, she tried hard not to have another panic attack. She rummaged in her bag for her mobile and began to play a game until they pulled up outside a very grand row of townhouses.

Stumbling up a couple of the steps, Flo rang the doorbell. Dorothy greeted her with open arms.

"Darling! Welcome, do come in. Follow me."

Flo was close on Dorothy's heels, looking around in wonder at the beautiful works of art. There was a large white elegant marble statue of a nude man standing in one corner and a white marble jardinière holding large red open roses in the other.

Heading through to the dining room, there was an enormous oak dining table surrounded by twelve very regal looking chairs. Above it was an elaborate crystal chandelier, hanging low over the centre of the table which was laid for two, with silver chargers, linen napkins and crystal wine glasses.

"Darling, please sit."

A little dark-haired Spanish woman entered and poured the wine, then served them both French onion soup from a silver terrine.

Flo was frightened of making a mess with her soup and tucked her napkin into the neck of her blouse. She slurped the first mouthful of soup, and apologised, red-faced.

Dorothy felt amused. "Relax darling. Am I making you uncomfortable?"

Dorothy rang the bell, the made came in. "We'll have the rest of our meal in the snug. Bring it to us on trays please Martha."

Martha disappeared and Dorothy beckoned Flo to follow. "Bring your drink darling."

Flo followed through double doors, passing through a large

lounge with lavish furnishings, another set of doors and into a smaller lounge. They'd gone from walking on marble to the softness of a thick deep purple carpet. Dorothy headed towards the two pure white leather sofas facing each other, which were scattered with large deep purple flock cushions. The deep purple velvet curtains were drawn closed, making it feel intimate and cosy.

Dorothy smiled and beckoned Flo to sit. "Maybe you will feel more relaxed in here Florence. The dining room is really meant for lots of people, the two of us are a little lost in there."

Flo was relieved, and was beginning to warm to her host for being so considerate. Martha wheeled in a trolley with two trays containing battered cod, chips and peas, handing one each to Flo and Dorothy.

Dorothy smiled "I thought cod and chips would be comfort food for us. I hope you are hungry. We have a delicious desert to follow afterwards."

Florence tucked into her dinner, enjoying every mouthful. The wine flowed freely, loosening Flo's tongue.

"I intended to come here tonight and tell you that I wanted to back out of my contract."

"Really? Darling, if that's what you want, then it can be arranged, but I sincerely hope that you won't do that."

Flo smiled. "Lucy talked me into staying. She said that it is only for one year. I am happy with that. If I do not like it, I can terminate after the year."

Dorothy nodded, agreeing. "My darling, this is true, Lucy is very wise." Dorothy looked down.

Flo stopped eating and looked at her host with intrigue. Dorothy took a sip of wine. Before she could say anything else Flo asked.

"Have you a husband?"

Dorothy looked a little sad. "My lovely husband passed away a few years ago. My darling, I need to tell you something."

Flo noticed a photograph on the mantelpiece over the fireplace. "Is that him, in the photograph?"

"Yes, that's my John. He was the kindest man I have ever met. I miss him dreadfully."

Flo stood up and looked more closely at the photograph. "He has a kind look about him."

Dorothy took the frame from her. She kissed the photograph and gave it back. "I worked in the mailroom when we first met. He was older than me, but the age difference never mattered to either of us. We were devoted to each other. I was truly blessed to have him in my life. It's rare to find one's soulmate and be as happy us. I hope that you will find someone as kind as John."

Dorothy put her tray on the coffee table and pushed it away.

Flo looked at the almost full plate of fish and chips. "You have hardly eaten anything!"

Dorothy sighed. "I'm not hungry. You carry on darling. Don't let me stop you."

Flo ate a few more chips and put her tray beside Dorothy's. "Thank you, it was very nice but I am stuffed."

"Would you like some chocolate soufflé? I will ask Martha to bring you some."

Flo waved her hand. "No, no, thank you. I really could not eat any."

Dorothy fiddled with her wedding ring, and gazed up at John's photo.

"Darling, I feel bad. I have only just found you and now I have to tell you that I'm ill. I have cancer, I beat it once but it's back with a vengeance. I'm having treatment and I would dearly love to beat it again, but my surgeon has told me that isn't likely. I am a wealthy woman and now that I've found you, your aunt May, your half-brother Harvey and your grandparents Rose and Grant, I have a family to leave my fortune to. I would like to get to know you all but as yet, I have only persuaded you to give me a chance to explain. I meant it when I offered you the modelling contract. I hope that in the time I have left I can get to know you."

She turned and took hold of Flo's hand.

"I don't want to have to leave my fortune to strangers, which is what you are to me, and I am to you. Harvey doesn't need my money but I shall leave a share to him, and the others. They don't want anything to do with me, I only bring back painful memories of the pain that your mother caused when she left Harvey's father. I can't understand how they can be so unforgiving! There are usually two sides to every story, it surely wasn't all your mother's fault!"

Flo stood up. "It was not my father's fault, if that is what you are suggesting!"

Dorothy stood up. "Darling! I wasn't suggesting that at all! What I meant was, maybe it was Harvey's father's neglect that pushed your mother into the arms of another man. The arms of your father."

Flo nodded. "Look, you are most kind, I am happy with the modelling contract, but I really do not wish for you to leave me your fortune!"

Dorothy stood and held both Flo's hands. "But darling! Would you prefer that I leave it to some dog or cats home? You are my living family. It will be my pleasure to give you all some pleasure. You can spend it at your leisure! Have holidays, luxury holidays! You can buy yourself a house, help your father, buy a new car maybe? Please? I will leave it to you anyway! Like it or not, it will be yours to do as you please. I don't want to offend you... Any of you, I just think it's your legacy."

Flo squeezed her hands. "OK, if you put it like that. I understand... I would like to get to know you better, and my half-brother. I am going to get in touch with him and try and arrange something. If it is at all possible I would like two weeks to visit Texas. My friend Lucy needs a holiday and I would like to take her with me. If I were to arrange this would you also be able to come?"

Dorothy shook her head. "I'm sorry, the only way for me to be part of this is for Harvey to come to London. I'm having ongoing treatment, chemotherapy. I've been advised to take it easy."

Flo's mind was working overtime. "I will see what I can do. I would still like to take the two weeks' holiday before I start modelling, maybe in that time I could persuade Harvey to come back with us?"

Dorothy thought this was a great idea and nodded approvingly.

"Two weeks, yes darling that's fine with me. If you can persuade Harvey to come back with you, I would be more than happy for him to stay here with me, rather than book into a hotel. I would welcome the company. Your first photo shoot is scheduled for three weeks' time."

Flo nodded and smiled. "Yes I know. That is why I need to get in touch with Harvey and arrange our holiday. Even if he does not want to get to know me, I am still hoping to get away for a couple of weeks with my best friend Lucy and America seems as good a place as any."

Dorothy topped up the wine glasses before popping into the next room, returning with her designer handbag.

"Darling," she rummaged in her bag, taking out a cheque book and pen, "I want to pay for your trip. I won't take no for an answer. I didn't have any children it would give me the greatest pleasure if you would accept a cheque from me."

Dorothy scribbled words and figures on the cheque, signed it and handed it to Flo. She stood staring at the piece of paper, her mouth open and eyes open wide!

"Oh no! That is far too generous! I cannot accept." Flo quickly passed it back, knocking the wine bottle off the table, luckily it was empty.

"Oh mon Dieu! I am sorry!"

Dorothy picked the bottle up, and handed back the cheque.

"If you won't accept this as a gift please accept it as an advance. This should pay for a holiday for both you and Lucy."

Flo stared at the cheque for ten thousand pounds and imagined her delight at telling Lucy that she was treating her dear friend to an all-expenses-paid holiday. Lucy was an amazing person who had always been there for her. She could just imagine how excited they would both be on their trip!

"Thank you, if you are sure? An advance is fine. Merci, merci beaucoup."

Dorothy smiled a huge smile knowing that the cheque would be the first of many ways to treat her great niece to some of the lavish things that she would have showered upon a daughter, should she have had one of her own. It gave her the greatest pleasure.

"Wonderful darling! I'm so pleased! I'm sure you will both have a wonderful time! Have you ever been to the US before?"

Florence sat staring at the cheque, her stomach had butterflies, her hand was shaking with excitement, thinking of how to tell Lucy that she would be paying for their holiday.

"No, I have only ever been to Europe... Germany, Belgium, France and the UK. I have always wanted to visit America... New York, Florida, California maybe? But as Harvey lives in Texas, that is where I would like to visit. I am hoping that he will agree to meet us when we are there. If he will not, then we shall make the most of it and visit the local attractions. Lucy and I have watched every single episode of Dallas, therefore Southfork would be a great place to start." Dorothy was thrilled. "Dallas! Oh my goodness! I have seen every episode, I love Sue Ellen and JR, Bobby oh and Jock! I can't believe that you have seen them all too!"

Flo laughed with excitement at the thought of visiting the place where one of her favourite TV shows was filmed.

"Yes, old and new! We preferred the old Dallas to the new! How corny was it for Bobby to appear in the shower?"

Both ladies giggled and talked about how crafty JR was, and how handsome Bobby was.

"I haven't seen the new Dallas. I don't think I would want to. Sometimes you can spoil things by trying to remake them. I remember back in the seventies a show called Charlie's Angels. Farrah Fawcett-Majors had the most gorgeous hairstyle darling! I had my hairdresser style mine exactly the same. That was back in the day, when I had hair. My chemo has made all mine fall out."

Flo was fascinated at how fabulous her aunt looked studying her hair.

"I am sorry to stare, I thought that was your hair! It looks amazing. Very natural."

Dorothy played with her hair. "No darling, this is a very good wig. It's human hair."

Flo twiddled her own hair, feeling a little embarrassed.

"I think if I were to live again, I would choose the seventies. I love the fashion, the hairstyles, the music. Abba! I love Abba! I love the Stylistics, T. Rex, glam rock! Lucy and I are nuts about the seventies! Our all-time favourite chick flick is Mamma Mia. We know all the songs! Have you seen it?"

Dorothy was intoxicated by Flo's enthusiasm. It was exhilarating to have young company, making her feel alive.

"No I haven't seen that film. I'll take great pleasure in watching it, if it's one that you recommend."

"Oh yes! You have to have that one on your bucket list! Do you have a bucket list?"

Dorothy looked perplexed. "My darling, what is a bucket list?"

Flo felt awkward. "It is a number of experiences or achievements that a person hopes to have or accomplish before they... Um... Well, um, during their lifetime."

"Before they die, you mean?"

"Yes, I am sorry. You must have things that you would like to do? Things that you have never done before, like skydiving, bungee jumping, swimming with sharks, or simply dancing naked in the rain or even simpler, watching Mamma Mia? I would like to watch it with you! Do we have time tonight? Do you have Netflix on your TV? I can guarantee that you will feel happy and young again after you have seen it!"

Dorothy turned on the huge fifty inch television and

searched Netflix. To her delight the film was there. The two of them settled down to watch it.

Martha popped her head around the door.

"Do you require anything else, before I retire?"

"No thank you Martha, would you like anything Florence?"

"No thank you, I am fine."

Martha quietly closed the door and left the two ladies together, happily watching the television in the dimming light.

All through the film, Dorothy couldn't help but glance at Flo, admiring her new found relative. Her happiness was infectious and the songs in the film brought back happy memories of life in the seventies with her husband John, bringing a tear to her eye.

By the end of the film, tiredness had defeated Dorothy and when Flo turned to ask what she had thought of the film, she was fast asleep.

Not knowing if she should wake her host, Flo turned off the television and turned up the lights, instantly waking Dorothy, who sat up with a start!

"Darling, what time is it? I do apologise! I feel terribly rude!"

Flo looked at her watch, it was half past midnight. "I should get going! It is very late!"

"You are welcome to stay the night. I have plenty of spare

rooms."

"Merci, maybe another time. I shall call a cab."

"Nonsense darling! I have my chauffeur on standby. Just a quick call and he will bring the Bentley around for you."
Ten minutes later Dorothy was waving goodbye to Flo, as she clumsily stumbled down the steps. Flo thanked the chauffeur as he politely opened the car door.

Yawning all the way back to Lucy's flat, Flo sat in the back staring at the cheque as its value shone in the light of every passing car headlight.

Once home, Flo ran up the stairs, and burst through the front door. Lucy was just going to bed. Both girls came face-to-face, both girls jumped and screamed, then fell about laughing.

"Shhhhhh!" Lucy held her finger to her lip. "Have you enjoyed your evening?"

"Oh yes! Fabulous! My aunt is an amazing woman. Loooooooooook!"

Flo held out the cheque and waved it under Lucy's nose.

"This is for a holiday in Texas, would you come with me? There is just one condition. I have to go within the next couple of days. My photographic sessions start in three weeks. I therefore have to start my holiday as soon as I can get flights booked. Are you with me?"

The girls held hands and jumped around like children; Flo accidentally stamping on Lucy's bare foot.

"OUCH!!! Yes, yes, yes!!! Count me in! I would love to go on holiday with you!"

"Désolé, sorry, sorry! I am so excited! It is my treat! Dorothy has given an advanced payment, I do not want to go alone, you have said yes. I am paying... VOILÀ!"

Although both girls had been really tired, adrenaline woke them, and both sat at the laptop, searching for flights.

"I shall contact Harvey tomorrow and ask if we can meet up with him. I will have great difficulty sleeping tonight"

At two thirty both girls disappeared into their bedrooms.

Lucy lay awake thinking of seeing Harvey's handsome face again. Florence lay awake thinking of visiting Southfork Ranch in Dallas. Flo called out, "Night Lucy."

Lucy called back. "Night, John-Boy" and laughed knowing that Flo probably wouldn't get her reference to The Waltons.

Bright and early the next morning, showered and dressed, with scrambled eggs and toast plated and on the breakfast table, both girls sat together viewing images of Texas on Lucy's laptop.

Flo pointed to the screen. "That looks like a great place to visit! Ooh and look there! I expect Harvey will know of all the best places to go!"

"Yes, you'd best email him, or call him a little later to make sure he's going to be in the US. He's over here quite a lot, it would be a shame to go all that way and find he's not there!"

Lucy couldn't wait to see him again. Last night she'd dreamt about him. He was standing in a crisp white cotton shirt, dark blue jeans and brown leather cowboy boots. His face was obscured by his Stetson, just his smile and dimple shone out from under the rim. He beckoned Lucy and as she walked towards him he held out his hand, leading her towards a barn, where he pulled her close and was just about to kiss her, when she woke up!

Florence was really nervous at how Harvey would react and hoped that he had maybe warmed a little to the idea of a younger sister.

"I think that I shall email him. I do not wish to ring him, just in case he still does not want to talk to me."

She got straight onto it before she changed her mind.

Dear Harvey Dove,

My friend Lucy and I are due to land at Dallas/Fort Worth International airport on Friday at 9.15 p.m. We are holidaying for two weeks. Would you kindly recommend a good hotel please? We both look forward to seeing you again, if you are happy to meet with us.

Kindest regards
Florence x

"Should I end with a kiss?"

Lucy nodded, "Yes of course!"

Flo's finger anxiously hovered over the send button, then

quickly pressed it, before she could change her mind.

"There! It is done! I hope that he replies soon."

"Well I think you will have a while to wait, unless he is awake all night! There is a six hours time difference. He's probably tucked up in bed."

"Oh, of course! I do hope that he has calmed down since the ball. Dorothy is such a lovely lady, Harvey should take time to get to know know her while he can."

Lucy started clearing the table. "You are too Flo, you are his sister! He should get to get to know you. Think of all those wasted years? You all have a lot of lost time to make up!"

"At least Harvey and me have plenty of time to get to know each other. I am not sure how long Dorothy has, she didn't say, but I have a feeling she hasn't got that long!"

"Really? Poor woman, that's bloody awful Flo."

"I know! I feel deeply sorry for her. She has no one now except me, and my relatives who do not want to know her, I shall make it my mission to try and sort things out!"

Much later Florence received a message from Harvey.

Howdy Florence. You'll be pleased to know that I've calmed down since our last meeting! I realize that my resentment serves no purpose, it ain't no fault of yours or mine that my mother left my father to live with yours. Y'all can stay at our ranch in Dallas, we have plenty of room. I can even meet you at the airport. Please forward your flight details.

Best,
Harvey.

Flo and Lucy began to read the message with anticipation.

"There you go! I knew he was a decent guy! Nothing to get worked up about Flo."

"He did not end his message with a kiss! I should not have put a kiss, I knew it was a mistake, it was too forward Lucy!"

"Don't be daft, men aren't as free with kisses on emails! It means nothing! You worry about the silliest of things Flo."

"What do you think? It is nice of him to offer to put us up, but what about Ed? I think that he will feel a little awkward."

"Nonsense! Harvey couldn't possibly invite us to stay without asking his father first! It will be... Lovely! Say yes! He has horses! I expect we will be able to ride whilst we are there! Oh how wonderful!"

The girls hugged each other.

CHAPTER TWENTY

While Harvey was typing the message to Florence, he was thinking of a way to tell his father that Ella's daughter was coming to stay.

All through the night Harvey kept waking up. On the one hand he was still angry and on the other he felt sorry that he had fallen out with him and had actually hit him!

Harvey's train of thought was now that his father owed him. He'd deprived him of his mother's affections in the few years after she'd left and before she died. He couldn't object to Florence staying at the ranch. It was after all just as much his home as it was Ed's.

Ed entered the kitchen with a black eye, fat lip and bruised cheek. He looked far worse than Harvey had imagined.

He glanced at Harvey as he headed to the fridge for the orange juice carton.

"Mornin' Son."

"Mornin' Pa."

Hayley came in the back door. She was in her running gear, having been out for the past hour.

"Hey guys! I'm just gonna grab a shower. Ouch! That looks sore Ed!"

Ed sat down with Harvey at the large kitchen table.

"Wow Pa, I'm sorry. I must have been pretty dang riled up!"

"Son, it's fine."

"I flew off the handle!"

"Yeah I know Son. I feel bad for hidin' things from you."

"Well, I hope this bit of news won't rile you up too much Pa."

"News? What news is that?"

"My half-sister is coming to Dallas in a couple a days. She's bringing that artist with her, Lucy, the one that lives in London and painted the portrait that I wanted. Do ya know the one I'm talkin' 'bout?"

"Hang on Harv! Are you telling me she's gonna come to Dallas? Hell, where're they gonna stay?"

"I've asked the pair of them to stay with us. I wanna get to know my sister. I was bad to her before, what happened ain't her fault. See it from her point of view. She lost her mom too."

Ed slowly closed his eyes and put his head in his hands, grasping his hair he shouted, "Fuckin' hell Harvey! How dare you ask them before consultin' me first!" His face was bright red with anger.

"I feel like you owe me Pa, she' my flesh and blood, Momma's flesh and blood! Fuck Pa, don't forget, you hid all my mail, my gifts, and then you didn't tell me that my mom was dead!"

Jane walked into the kitchen, looking shocked at all the

shouting!

"Hey fellas, come on this is not like you two! What's all the dang shoutin' 'bout?"

Ed thumped the table! "He's gone and asked my ex-wife's daughter to stay at the ranch when she comes to Dallas!"

Jane looked stunned for a second or two, then thought about Harvey's situation. "OK, if it's a problem, they can stay here with Harvey."

Ed looked at Jane as if she was completely mad!

"What!!! Bless your heart but this is not your problem Jane! It's ours and we need to sort this out! I'm goin' for a walk, I wanna try and get my head 'round all this!"

Ed grabbed his white leather Stetson, and stormed out of the door, down the front steps and up the long driveway.

"I've never seen your pa so angry! Let him alone for a while, he will calm down, once he can get his head 'round it. If he can't come to terms with it, I meant what I said, she can stay with us."

Harvey sat silently, staring at his hands, then looked up at Jane.

"There are two of them, her friend Lucy is coming too... The artist from London, but it's all right Jane, I've invited them to stay with us and that is what they are gonna do!"

They sat and drank coffee and talked about Florence and the past. Hayley entered the kitchen with a pink towel wrapped around her head and joined them at the table for a coffee.

"So! What's all this about? Who's Lucy?"

Harvey explained everything. Then his feelings of anger subsided as he smelled Hayley's delicate perfume.

"You smell nice honey!"

"Thanks! I don't usually wear this perfume but I noticed that my wonderful ex-boyfriend Wayne, actually emptied all my perfume bottles! Sorry Mama, this is your perfume."
Jane was horrified.

"He did what? That guy is definitely two sandwiches short of a picnic. He's not right in the head! Why would he do that?" Harvey asked.

"Psycho, absolutely nuts!"

"He did it Mama, because if I smelled nice, I would attract other men. I'm beginning to find out just how warped his brain is!"

"Well I hope they lock him up for a long, long time hun."

Jane touched her daughter's hand then left them to fetch the eggs from the chicken coop.

Harvey was eager to ask, "So! Are you free for lunch or supper today?"

"Yep, you can take me for supper if you like."

"How about the steakhouse in town?"

"Great! Seven thirty?"

"Perfect! I'll order a cab so I can have a few drinks."

"Ok, well, I've got a client coming in ten minutes, so I gotta go hun."

Harvey admired his petite friend as she left him alone to go to her gym. Minutes later, Mitch returned from the top paddock.

"Where's ya pa?

Harvey had to explain things.

"Hell Harv! That's gonna be a hard pill for him to swallow! I don't think I could invite her to stay, if we were in the same situation."

"Well, what's done is done. It ain't my fault I got a half-sister and it ain't her fault she has me! I wanna get to know her Mitch."

"Your pa will understand, I'm sure once he's worked it all out in his mind, he's a good man."

Harvey managed to keep out of Ed's way all day. He had to return to the state police department to add a few things to his statement about the incident with Wayne the night before.

That evening, Harvey showered and put on the last clean shirt in his suitcase. He waited anxiously in the kitchen for Hayley. She appeared, looking gorgeous.

"Good Lord! You clean up real nice, you look amazing!"

Hayley smiled as she looked in the mirror and added some lip gloss.

"Thanks, not so bad yaself!"

Ed and Mitch were both on the porch drinking beer, Jane smiled approvingly at the handsome young couple as Harvey took Hayley's arm and walked her down the steps at the front of the ranch house, just in time for the cab to pull up to take them into town.

"My! I hope they have a nice time. It's been a long time comin', Harv has only just woken up to your daughter." Ed said as he sipped his beer.

Jane shook her head. "They make a lovely looking couple, but after Wayne, I don't think it's the right time to start a new relationship."

At the steakhouse, Harvey as usual was the perfect gentleman. They talked of times at the ranch when they were young and growing up together. Both avoided the subject of Wayne, instead music was the main point of discussion, they both loved country music. The steakhouse's theme was country and western, creating an atmosphere that appealed to them both, with pictures of John Wayne and Johnny Cash, Elvis, Dolly Parton, Tammy Wynette, Billy Jo Spears, Taylor Swift, Garth Brooks and Shania Twain, amongst a few of the different stars from past and present, hanging all around the walls.

Harvey told Hayley he was leaving in the morning to return to Dallas. He'd been to the state police earlier in the day, and they didn't need anything more from him.

"I still can't believe what you did Harv! Cheers, to you!"

She held up her glass and chinked it on Harvey's.

"Cheers darlin'."

The evening was going well, Harvey was convinced Hayley was interested in him and reached for her hand.

She retracted quickly and made an excuse to use the ladies. He ordered another Jack and coke, along with a large Merlot for Hayley.

When she returned she was open and honest with him.

"I don't know what you expect from me Harv, I really like you, I respect you, but I don't like you in that way. You are more like a big brother. I've grown up with you; I've seen your butt more times than I care to remember! We've shared baths and beds, camped under the stars, but as children Harv. That is all, I'm sorry honey. You're more like family to me than my own cousins are."

Harvey couldn't comprehend how she could so blunt about it. He was really attracted to her and didn't want to give up that easily.

"I've offended you haven't I, Harv?" Hayley cocked her head to one side.

Just then one of their favourite songs started, 'Crazy', by Patsy Cline. "Oh my! This brings back memories."

Others started to dance. Harvey pulled Hayley to her feet and guided her to the dance floor, then held her close as he started to move to the music.

She felt so small to him. He breathed in the scent of her hair and felt her tiny body close to his.

Hayley held her head against his chest; she could feel the sexual tension rising between them. She could feel his muscly chest and powerful arms as he held her.

Having drunk almost a full bottle of red wine she was beginning to feel differently about him. Harvey kissed her on top of her head.

"Mmm, this is nice."

Hayley looked up, she saw an extremely handsome man gazing down at her. Then she suddenly had a flashback of a young spotty-faced boy.

"No! This feels wrong! I can't, I'm sorry. Can we go now please?"

Hayley pulled away and rushed back to the table to fetch her bag. Sitting at the table with a huge smile on his face was Harvey's old best mate Joe.

"Fancy seeing you two here!"

"JOE! What a lovely surprise! How did you know that we were here?"

Hayley flung her arms around him and kissed him on the cheek, instantly snapping out of her mood.

"Good Lord Joe, we've not heard from you in years! Harv, look who's here!"

Harvey came back from the dance floor.

"Howdy fella I hardly recognized you! It must be ten years at least! But how did you know we'd be here?"

Joe pulled up a chair and sat down.

"I've just left the army bro; I'm free and looking for a job and somewhere to settle now. Just wanted a steak and a catch up with some of the old crew, didn't expect to see you both, and together! Erm, are you going out now?"

Hayley was quick to answer. "No! We are still just good friends. How about you? Are you still with Mel?"

"Hell no! She was hard work!"

Hayley had always liked Joe but never expected him to still be free and single after all this time. He had spent a lot of time with them when he was a child, and she had always had a soft spot for him.

"Treat 'em mean and keep 'em keen."

That was Joe's motto. He was certainly mean to Hayley when they were all together. He'd put worms in her shoes, whilst she paddled in the stream. He would tie her pig tails together, sit on her and make her eat grass, and once sneaked a frog into the house, leaving it in her bedroom. She knew it was Joe but was never able to prove it.

"How are Jane and Mitch, Hazie? And how's your pa Harv, did you ever hear from ya momma Harv?"

Hayley and Harv both answered at the same time.

"Good thanks."

"My momma is dead. Killed in a car crash."
Harvey beckoned a waiter to order Joe a drink.

"Same as always Joe?"

"You got it! Jack and Coke man. Hell I'm sorry about ya momma man. That's bad news. I remember it like it was yesterday when your pa picked you up from school and you came back to our house, the day your momma left you and your daddy. That was sad bro!"

Harvey swallowed his drink, emptying his glass.

"Another, Hayley?"

"No, I'm fine thanks Harv, I've still got some, shouldn't really have any more, I've an early start tomorrow."

The three reminisced about the good old days. Joe sat next to Hayley, he stretched out and casually put his arm around her.

"Hell Hazie, you're even better looking now than you were ten years ago!"

Hayley blushed, catching Harvey's look of distaste at Joe's ability to be so familiar and get away with it.

"Mama would love to see you again. She used to spoil you, didn't she?"

Joe laughed. "She sure did! She used to bake me those blueberry muffins every time I came to stay, and make those fuckin' huge piles of pancakes with maple syrup for breakfast!"

"Well I'll bet she still has the recipe for those muffins, and she'd bake them again if she knew you were coming over to visit!"

"Tell ya what! I'll stop by tomorrow! I'd love to see them again. Might just hang around for a while. My folks are in California now. I saw them for a coupla' days last year. Planning to get me a Harley and ride there someday."

Harvey and Joe drank far too many Jack and Coke's and both ended up very drunk. Hayley couldn't stop laughing at them, especially when they both got on the dance floor and danced to Achy Breaky Heart, both beckoning her to join in. Hayley couldn't refuse; they both looked like they needed a hand to stand up. All three danced to a few country songs and then Hayley left them to go and call a cab.

"Where are you staying Joe?"

"Not far, just around the corner. I'll stagger back now, and see you guys in the morning?"

Harvey shook Joe's hand, and Hayley kissed his cheek.

"I'm heading back to Dallas tomorrow with my Pa. Not sure what time we're leaving. If I'm gone by the time you get to Mitch's, I dare say I'll catch up again soon. Nice seeing ya dude!"

They stood outside the steakhouse and watched Joe swaying along the road, on his way back to bed. The cab pulled up and Harvey opened the rear door for Hayley, himself choosing to sit in the front with the driver. This time he'd got the message that she wasn't interested.

Back at the ranch, Hayley gave him a pat on the shoulder and headed to her room.

"Thanks Harvey, see you in the morning."

Ed was still out on the porch. "How'd it go, son?"

"It didn't Pa. But I had a good night. Joe's back in town! He's coming here tomorrow. Might see him before we leave."

"Jeez, that's great! He's a good guy!"

"Yeah, Hayley seems t'think so too! See you in the morning."

Off he went to bed. The following morning, Hayley was up and out before anyone else. Her focus was on her work. She needed to focus on that to rid herself of her thoughts and fears of Wayne. Jane was making a pot of coffee when Harvey appeared, bleary eyed and with a raging hangover.

"Mornin' Harv. Mitch tells me that you had a good night last night with Joe and Hayley!"

"Yep, good ole Joey's back in town."

"Do I sense a little sarcasm, Harvey Dove?"

"No, not really. I've missed him, but he's kinda stolen Hayley's heart and I wanted it."

"Trouble is Harv, she looks upon you as a big brother. I don't think she could imagine being with you romantically."

"Has she told you that, Jane?"

"To be frank… Yes!"

"Well that's it then, I give up! Joe will probably win her over. She always liked it when he was around."

"Harv, don't you think she needs to get her head straight first? She's been through a pretty traumatic time with Wayne!"

"Yes, you are right, of course. What am I thinking?! You must think I'm a selfish kinda guy!"

"Of course not! I've always thought of you as a son, I think that's why it's hard to get my head around you and Hayley being together!"

"I just don't understand what's wrong with me? My pa is the same! Are we destined to live a single life forever?"

"The trouble with the both of you is that you are both workaholics! Neither of you need to work half as hard as you do! You should slow down a bit, maybe sell one of the businesses, or give up the art side of things, then you can settle down, instead of jetting off here and there!"

"I would give it all up tomorrow for the love of a good woman. I certainly won't neglect her, once I find her, unlike my pa did with Momma."

"Don't lay all the blame on Ed. He was trying to build up a business and Ella was a bit of a recluse for a while. She was painfully shy you know! If she'd mixed a bit more, she wouldn't have been so lonely. It was a huge shock to us all when she left your pa. No one expected her, of all people, to up and leave without a trace!"

"I'm beginning to realize that now. I'm looking forward to seeing her letters when I get back to Dallas. Pa saved them all, they're stored away in the attic."

Just then, a cab pulled up outside. Joe tipped the driver, and took a large gym bag out of the trunk. Jane peered through the window, and watched him run up the front steps. She rushed to the kitchen door, opened it and flung her arms around his neck.

"Joey! You look fit and well! Let me look at you!"

She stepped away and smiled at the ex-soldier standing before her, remembering the skinny redheaded boy who was always playing pranks on everyone.

"You've lost your red hair!"

"Hell yeah, it's more a muddy blonde now! If I grow a beard it's auburn!"

Jane laughed. "You boys were my favorite. Little monsters, but I loved you for it!"

Joe shook Harvey's hand and sat beside him. Harvey poured a mug of coffee and handed it to Joe.

"Good times bro! This was our second home! Do you remember when we set one of the sheds on fire? Mitch wasn't pleased, I thought he was gonna ban us from coming again! Never seen him so angry!"

"Yes, he was mad! He only just put it out before the roof

set fire!"

Harvey pointed his finger at Joe. "That was your fault! You set fire to a lamp and knocked it over when you were waving that old baseball bat around."

Joe held his hands up. "Uh huh, I have to admit, it was me, I was so fucking scared of Mitch telling my pa that I let Harv take the blame."

Jane frowned. "Hmm, I wonder what else you did back then that you got away with?"

"That would be tellin' Janie, I wouldn't like to shatter the illusion of what a good young guy I was."

Jane laughed. "Pancakes? Or have you eaten?"

"I have eaten, but I saved room for your pancakes. Why do ya think I came so early? Where're Mitch, Ed and Hayley?"

"Hayley is at work, she has her own gym on the ranch."

Just then Mitch walked in and shook Joe's hand. "Howdy fella! Good to see you!"

Ed followed Mitch in, rubbing his wet hair with a towel.

"Joey, my boy! Long time since I've seen you!"

They all sat the table, ate stacks of pancakes, drank gallons of coffee and talked about life, until Ed stood up and suggested he and Harvey head back to Dallas.

Harvey was jealous about leaving Joe in the same vicinity as Hayley, but knew that he would have to accept that she wasn't interested in him.

When Harvey and Ed were ready to go, they stuck their heads around the door to the gym and waved goodbye to Hayley, who was busy leading a class of a couple of elderly ladies dressed in fluorescent gym clothes. They were dancing around to loud seventies disco music.

Hayley ran to the door and kissed them both, thanking Harvey once again for all that he'd done.

Ed drove back; Harvey avoided talking for most of the journey. He rested his head back, closed his eyes and listened to the country music playing on the radio.

Ed spoke first. "Son, I've thought long and hard about Florence. She's your flesh and blood, and I want you to know that I will be civil to her."

"OK Pa, gee thanks."

Ed couldn't make out if his answer was tinged with sarcasm, or whether he was grateful.

"The plane lands at nine fifteen p.m. I'm meeting them and bringing them straight back to the ranch. The spare room will be ready for them. I texted and asked Susan to give it the once over."

Then there was silence all the way home. Ed's mind working overtime, wondering how he was going to handle the next two weeks.

Lucy and Florence arrived at Fort Worth International airport, loaded with very loud hot pink and red spotty suitcases and even louder enthusiasm!

Harvey stood anxiously waiting to see their familiar faces. It wasn't long before he recognised the two beautiful young ladies amongst the sea of people all making their way through Arrivals. Lucy was pushing a cart laden with four suitcases, flight bags and duty free bags. Harvey did question in his mind just how long they were both staying. Florence was helping to guide the cart in a straight line when she spotted Harvey and swerved it in his direction, almost causing a multiple pile-up.

"I'm sorry, terribly sorry. Ooh so sorry! It's my fault, sorry!"

Florence kept apologising to everyone who was now stuck behind them, with scattered cases on the floor.

Harvey rushed to help everyone and silently hoped that Florence causing mayhem again was just a coincidence and not the norm!

"Bonjour!"

"Harvey! Hello!"

Both girls were buzzing with excitement, like two teenagers on their first girly holiday.

Harvey took charge of the luggage cart and guided the girls through and out to the car, where he lifted the heavy cases into the trunk, and made sure his guests were comfortable before setting off for home.

The girls giggled like children in the back of the car. Harvey interrupted. "How was the flight?"

They answered together. "Long!" Then giggled again.

Florence spoke first.

"Thank you very much for putting us up Harvey. It seems almost too much to expect, given the circumstances."

"It's quite OK. We have to accept what's happened and get over it. I would like to get to know you."

Lucy squeezed Flo's hand and let out a tiny squeal of excitement!

"What does your father have to say about me staying? I do not want to cause any trouble. It must be difficult, especially for him."

"We expressed our different opinions, but we're over that!"

Florence winced at the thought. Lucy felt awkward.

"Thank you for putting me up as well. I hope I won't be in the way."

"Nonsense, of course not. You are both welcome. I'm taking time out so I can show you some of the sights. Texas is a beautiful state."

Lucy clapped her hands together. "I would absolutely love to go to a rodeo!"

Harvey smiled to himself. "That can easily be arranged."

"Ooh fantastic! Imagine all that testosterone! And that's just the bulls! Ha ha!"

Harvey laughed at Lucy's comment.

"Believe me, there is a hell of a lot of testosterone at a rodeo and an awful lotta bulls and bull shit! I'll find out when the next rodeo is on. You can't visit Texas without the experience."

Lucy imagined all the strong cowboys in checked shirts and Stetsons, then focused on the handsome face reflected in the driver's mirror, as his dark brown eyes kept looking up to check the traffic behind.

Harvey every now and then noticed Lucy's face and flame red hair as she looked around at all the passing scenery.

"I sure hope that you gals like country music!"

"We do indeed! We are prepared for the whole country and western experience!"

"Mais bien sûr!"

"You'll have to translate that Florence. I don't speak French."

"Oui, sorry, I said but of course. Ha ha ha."

Florence and Lucy told Harvey about the places they were hoping to visit during their stay. He assured them that they wouldn't be disappointed, there was plenty to see and do in Dallas and the surrounding area. He was prepared to take them wherever they wanted to go.

As they pulled into the large white gates to the ranch, the girls squeezed hands again. Harvey drove down the long driveway and up to the ranch house. Florence got out of the air-conditioned car and the heat hit her as if opening an oven door. Lucy followed close behind, gasping at the sight of the multi-million dollar ranch house.

"Wow! This is beautiful!"

"Thanks hun. I'll give you both a tour tomorrow."

Harvey opened the front door and flicked on the polished brass light switch. The enormous crystal chandelier shone hundreds of bright rainbow facets around the pure white walls of the large square entrance.

"Wow! Breathtaking!"

Lucy loved sparkle and bling and was highly impressed.

"Follow me. I'll show you to your room, you can freshen up while I put the coffee on and find my pa. I thought you both would like to share a room? If not, there is another made up."

"Merci, we are very happy to share a room."

The floor was finished with large white marble tiles, then double doors lead into the long hallway, which had many polished oak doors leading off into different rooms. The girls kept stopping to admire some of the exquisite artwork and paintings as they followed Harvey.

Florence and Lucy entered the huge bedroom and smiled with approval at the two queen sized beds situated next to each other. The room was tastefully decorated with cream and pale champagne baroque patterned walls, with pale gold drapes and bed linen. The floor had the same white marble tiles as the hallway but with thick white shag pile rugs placed at the sides and ends of each bed. The wardrobes were wall to wall mirrors, which were dimly lit by a row of soft downlighters from the ceiling. The bedside tables both held heavy gold candlestick lamps which were finished with white silk lampshades and gold tassels. There was a forty-six-inch television upon the wall which was disguised with a gold ornate frame. They pulled back one of the curtains and peered outside. It was dimly lit with post lights all the way along the porch, which seemed to continue around the whole of the house. Beyond that it was pitch black.

Flo stood in awe, admiring the huge comfy beds. "Look at the size of those beds! I shall be lost in one of those!"

"Me too! I'm not sharing! Ha ha."

When they'd freshened up, they found their way to the living room. Harvey was perched on the arm of a large cream leather couch chatting to his father, Ed.

The men stood up.

"Pa, this is Florence, and this is Lucy... Girl's this is my pa, Ed."

Ed went over to the girls and shook their hands, "Pleased to meet you ladies."

He couldn't help noticing the striking resemblance Florence had to her mother, Ella, but decided not to make a statement.

"Please sit down, I bet you are both suffering with jet lag. If you need to lie in tomorrow, please feel free to."

Both girls sat on the other four-seater couch and admired yet another very tastefully decorated room. There was an enormous cream marble fireplace, which looked as though there should have been a painting or a mirror above, but there was just a faded rectangular mark left there instead.

Ed left the room and came back with a tray of drinks and some small bowls of snacks.

"Are you girls hungry? Harv and me were going to order you a pizza, if you'd like any?"

Both girls yawned at the same time and looked at each other.

"Thank you, I hope you don't think us rude, but I think all we would like is to go to bed after we've had a drink."

"Coffee or cider? It's our own make."

"Oh cider please!"

"Merci."

Ed poured a glass of their homebrewed cider for the girls to try, which they drank down approvingly. Then they said goodnight and retired to the bedroom for the night.

"Well, they both seem like decent sorta gals." Ed said to Harvey, who was a little shocked. He was expecting some sort of negativity, after all Florence was the daughter of his wife's lover.

"Yep, I'm glad you share my thoughts Pa. It must be difficult for you."

"She looks so much like your mother. Her hair, her smile, her eyes…"

"I know, she reminds me of Momma as well. I got an email from Dorothy today. She's shipped the painting, it will be here soon. The empty space over the fireplace is ready for that painting."

"I don't think it would be right to hang it there son. Do you? It'd be like hanging Ella up there again."

Harvey ignored the question.

"I've got a couple a' dozen paintings to choose from Pa, I'll let you choose."

Ed left the room, minutes later he returned, struggling with a large brown leather chest.

"I'm off to bed, I'll leave you with these and my apologies again son. We can't change the past but we can work on the present and the future."

Harvey poured himself a bourbon and stared at the chest. He wanted so badly to open it, yet felt he shouldn't for fear it might break him. He lay down; memories of his mother came flooding back. Her voice, her laugh, her smile... The way she always tied her apron strings twice around her tiny waist.

Harvey sat down and opened the lid with a mixture of trepidation and excitement. It was filled with memorabilia from his birth to teenage years. There were blue baby's booties, a little blue knitted cardigan, some tiny denim jeans, a silver trinket box with 'First Tooth' written on it, and a heart-shaped box with 'First Lock of Hair' printed on top, which Harvey opened to see inside a dark curl tied with a thin blue ribbon. There were letters and cards from both sets of his grandparents, and from his parents when they were together. The cards from Ed's parents had all been opened, he'd received them all on various birthdays up until his mother had left. At the bottom of the chest were letters and cards from Ella that he'd never seen before. His eyes filled with tears as he opened each one and saw the love which flowed from each handwritten page. Memories came flooding back, of happy days with her and his grandparents. His heart felt heavy. He mourned the loss of his precious mom.

Lucy had a headache, and despite feeling tired, couldn't sleep, so she got up and wandered down the hall to see if anyone was still awake. She stood in the doorway for a minute wondering what Harvey was looking at. He was sitting on the floor and had his back to her. His shoulders were shaking, Lucy could tell he was upset. Just as Lucy thought it best not to disturb him, Harvey turned and noticed her. He wiped the tears from his eyes.

"Sorry Harvey. I have a headache. I don't mean to intrude. What's wrong, anything I can do?"

Lucy walked over and looked down at the scattered contents of the chest, noticing the baby clothes and photographs. She knelt down next to him and gently stroked his shoulder.

"Hey, memories to be treasured eh Harvey?"

"From my momma, I haven't seen half of these. Please ignore me, I'm just feeling emotional right now."

Lucy picked up a photograph of Ella. "She looks the spitting image of Flo."

"Yeah, she sure does!"

He wiped his eyes again and started to sob as so many images of the past flashed through his mind.

Lucy wrapped her arms around him and tried to console him as he buried his head in her shoulder and cried. Harvey unashamedly let out all his pent-up emotions and did so in the solace of Lucy's arms.

"I'm sorry, I'm not usually this emotional. I guess it's been a long time coming."

Harvey went to stand up but Lucy held on to him.

"Don't apologise, it does one good to cry. It's not good to bottle up one's emotions."

Harvey's head was all over the place. He held her face in his hands and tenderly kissed her on the lips.

She pulled away, a little shocked at first, then kissed him back. Harvey stood up and pulled her up with him. He held her tenderly in his arms. Lucy looked into his tear-filled eyes and smiled.

"Come on Harvey Dove. I think emotions have got the better of us, don't you? I'm sure things will seem better for you in the morning after a good night's sleep."

Harvey felt embarrassed.

"Sorry. What must you think of me? Let me find you some pills and fetch you a glass of water."

He rushed passed Lucy and headed to the kitchen, Lucy

trailing behind him.

"Here, I hope these help your head."

"Thank you. I shall see you in the morning."

Lucy's heart was racing. From the first time she'd set eyes on Harvey, she had fancied him. To get that close to him and kiss him filled her with excitement but she didn't want to expose her feelings towards him yet. She left Harvey standing alone in the kitchen and headed back to the dimly lit bedroom. The sound of loud snoring was bellowing out of her best friend's mouth. She was sound asleep and sprawled out on her back lying sideways on top of the comforter with her head hanging over the side of the bed. Flo had started to dribble, which made her cough and splutter and then turn over, muttering something about a suitcase.

"Silence." Lucy whispered to herself and then climbed into bed hoping to dream of Harvey.

CHAPTER TWENTY-ONE

Meanwhile back in France Jack and Eloise made some big lifestyle changes in order to live together. Initially they were going to sell Jack's cottage but decided it might be better to rent it out instead, then they'd have a good income for however long they wanted, and Flo would get a nice inheritance in the end. Eloise didn't want the fact that she was marrying Flo's father to interfere with that.

Jack moved in above the shop and immediately started on repairs that were long overdue. He redecorated the kitchen and plumbed in a dishwasher, something Eloise had always wanted. He converted the back of the shop into a cosy little café and decorated it with white walls which were the perfect backdrop to proudly display his daughter's artwork.

Eloise eagerly awaited the delivery of four round black wooden tables and matching chairs. She had already taken delivery over the past week of red teapots, white cups and saucers and red gingham table cloths. She sat in the middle of the empty room and imagined her little tea room up and running. The French doors lead straight out into the small cottage garden, which was as pretty as a picture, with hanging baskets terracotta pots filled with fragrant flowers. They already had the four white ornate garden tables and chair sets set up outside on the decorative patio area.

Jack popped his head around the door and admired the sight of Eloise perched alone on the step ladder in the middle of the room.

"Excited ma chérie?"

"Just a little." She squealed.

Jack's phone received a message.

"Oh, it is Florence."

He read in silence, then his look changed from happiness to concern.

"What is wrong Jack?"

"She is going to America to stay with Annette's son, Harvey."

"I did not think that he wanted anything to do with her."

"That is what she said, but he has obviously changed his mind. She goes at the end of the week. She is taking Lucy with her. I suppose that is one consolation, she is not going all that way on her own."

"She is a big girl now my sweet man, she does not need a chaperone."

"Oh, but she does, this is Florence we are talking about!" They both chuckled.

"She will be fine. Lucy is a sensible girl and Harvey... Well let's face it, he is her brother."

"Yes, it is Ed that bothers me. I do hope that he won't hold a grudge."

"Are they staying in a hotel, or with Harvey and his father?"

"She just says she is going to stay with Harvey, so I imagine it is at his ranch. She's never been that far before."

Jack texted back.

"Let me know when you have arrived safely Flo, have a good time, take care. Je t'aime ma chérie. Love from Papa and Eloise. x x"

On Saturday afternoon, the café was all set up and ready for its first customers. Mme Henry and Mandy Dumont entered the elegant little room with delight, ordering homemade pain au chocolat, croisstants, éclairs and two coffees. Eloise was delighted to serve them, and as they were her very first customers their order was on the house.

Jack could be seen out back, watering the pots and hanging baskets. His mind was wandering, thinking about Florence and Lucy's flight and he kept checking his watch, wondering how far into their flight they were.

The café was a success, all seats were filled on and off for the rest of the day. Jack and Eloise took turns serving in the shop and the café. The ladies especially enjoyed Jack's gentlemanly attention.

At the end of the day, Eloise locked up and turned the 'Open' sign over to show 'Closed', whilst Jack fed the five hens some corn and shut them in their pen for the night, locking the French doors and turning out the lights in the café.

"Well, that all went very well."

He kissed Eloise on the cheek and followed her up the stairs, both taking up a tray full of crockery for the dishwasher.

"I shall cook dinner. You look exhausted ma chérie."

He made her sit down, then he loaded the dishwasher and prepared the onions, peppers, cheese and courgette for an omelette. Then he cut up an apple, a banana and some strawberries which he served with a large dollop of vanilla ice cream.

Eloise watched Jack as he busied himself in the kitchen. Life was simply bliss now that she had him to share it with.

"Shall we open a bottle of Shiraz?"

Jack was already on top of it, skilfully twisting the cork screw down into the cork.

They sat in front of the television with a tray each, watching the news, eating, drinking and discussing the day.

He felt so proud of today's achievement and overwhelmingly in love with his wife to be.

"Je t'aime."

"Je t'aime. Shall we have an early night?"

"Oui."

Eloise tickled Jack. She knew exactly where he was most sensitive, right in the nape of his neck and him goose bumps all over.

Jack laughed and laughed until he was out of breath. Eloise stopped and studied him, she loved his smiling face and his piercing blue eyes. They kissed with passion. Jack opened her blouse, undoing the buttons slowly one by one. Her heart was beating fast with excitement making her breathless. She slipped off her bra and Jack tenderly kissed her all over, admiring her body. His sensual touch made her weak at the knees. Despite being together as a couple for a while and sharing the same bed, it had been a while since they had shared such passion. Eloise had always been wary of Jack's heart condition but tonight she felt she had waited long enough and longed to make love to him. They ended up naked and exhausted on the sofa.

Jack joked "Not bad for a pair of oldies huh? What took us so long?"

"I have wanted that for a long time Jack but I was worried about your heart."

"Perhaps we can do it more often now that I have proved I am not going to drop down dead!"

She smacked him and laughed. "Je t'aime, even more than I ever thought humanly possible Jack Dubois."

"Ditto mon amour."

Early hours in the morning Jack's phone bleeped. He had been laying awake, thinking of how the day had panned out and worrying about his precious daughter.

Bleary eyed he viewed a text from Flo.

"*Bonjour Papa. Arrived safely. Harvey collected us from the airport and we are heading to the ranch. Au revoir. x x*"

Jack smiled and whispered. "Florence and Lucy made it!"

"That is good. I am very sure that she will have a wonderful time." Eloise whispered back.

CHAPTER TWENTY-TWO

The girls were woken by the housekeeper Susan gently tapping at the bedroom door and the sound of a rooster calling outside their bedroom window.

"Morning ladies. It's ten a.m. I made you some coffee."

She placed a tray with two mugs, a pot of coffee and a bowl of sugar on top of the chest of drawers, then drew back the curtains, instantly filling the room with Texas sunshine.

"Harvey is taking you on a tour of the ranch later. He told me to ask you to wear something casual."

"Ooh how utterly exciting! I'm so glad that we purchased cowboy boots!"

The girls quickly showered and dressed. Lucy wore faded skinny jeans and a plain white T-shirt. Florence wore red jeans and a white short sleeved blouse.

Florence made Ed and Harvey jump as she loudly entered the kitchen, accidentally knocking one of the coffee mugs on the floor as she carried the tray in from the bedroom. The mug miraculously bounced and Lucy caught it.

Ed clapped his hands.

"Lucky catch!"

Lucy gave Flo a sideways look. "Yes very lucky, eh Flo?"

"Sorry, I am so clumsy!"

"Don't worry, I'm here to try and keep her out of trouble!"

Lucy took the tray and safely placed it on the drainer. Ed was cooking ham and eggs.

"You gals want some? Ya gotta be hungry!"

"Golly gosh, I'm starving thank you!"

All through breakfast Ed couldn't help but stare at Florence. Every time she glanced at him, his eyes looked away, but Florence was too busy enjoying her breakfast to notice. Ed studied the silver heart locket around her neck and remembered that it was his very first gift to Ella. It stirred up memories of the magical night he spent with Ella on her nineteenth birthday. He just couldn't stand being in front of her any longer and stood up, making his excuses.

"I'll see you all later. I'm off out with the fellas. Someone's gotta do some work around here! I've had too much time off already. Jim said there are a coupla steers need attention."

"Right Pa, I'll be heading up that way later. I'm taking these girls out for a ride, assuming it's OK with you two?"

"Ooh yes! Yes! Yes! I haven't been on a horse for years!"

"Oui, that would be nice."

"Have you ridden before, Flo?" Lucy asked.

"Oui, but when I was a child."

Flo lied. She had never been on a horse in her life and knowing how accident prone she was, started to get sweaty palms at the thought.

Breakfast over; Susan was in the kitchen clearing away the breakfast things whilst Harvey took the girls outside for a walk to the stables. There were various hats hanging inside the stable. Harvey handed one to each of the girls.

"Here, put these on, you'll need these to protect you from the Texas sun." Harvey kissed his horse on the nose, "This is my boy, his name is Magic Boy. Hello fella, have you missed me?"

They walked along and looked in all the stables. There were some beautiful horses and a couple of ponies.

"I thought Silver Star would suit you Florence. She's a big old gal but she's a gentle one."

Flo looked at the size of her and gulped. "Bonjour Silver Star. I will be nice to you, if you are nice to me."

She nervously patted the white horse on the head; Silver Star snorted and made Flo jump and step back.

Harvey introduced Lucy to a large Arabian in the next stable.

"Lucy, I think Ranger is the horse for you. He's one of my favorites, we've had him around six years now."

"Great! Hello Ranger! You look a handsome chappie!"

Teddy, one of the hands, saddled the horses for them and led them all out so that they were ready to go.

Lucy mounted her horse with ease, followed by Harvey. They watched with amusement as Flo tried to mount Silver Star. She tried over and over but just couldn't quite get the hang of it.

"Do you have a step ladder I could use?"

"Ha, ha, ha! I thought you said that you'd ridden a horse before Flo?" Lucy laughed.

Harvey chuckled to himself but dismounted and gave Flo a leg up.

"Whoa! This is a little bit high up!" She felt a little dizzy.

"Are you going to be all right?" Harvey asked, feeling a bit concerned.

"I have a confession to make. I have never ridden before, I admit I am a little nervous!" Harvey patted Silver Star's nose.

"She'll be gentle with you, really she will. I'm sure you'll be fine. She will follow us. We'll take it slowly. Hold on tight!"

He mounted Magic Boy and walked on slowly. Flo's eyes nearly popped out of her head!

"Ooh. I really don't think that I like this!"

Lucy pulled back so that Flo was in the middle. She felt that she should really keep an eye on her, she could just imagine her horse bolting and Flo hanging on for dear life.

They had only gone a few yards when Flo had a panic attack. "Oh, I cannot breath!"

Lucy called to Harvey.

"Harvey, stop! Flo isn't feeling too good."

They stopped and helped Flo down from the horse; she took a minute to calm down.

"Please, you go ahead, I do not want to spoil your fun. I am happy to just sit on the porch and sunbathe. If that is all right with you both?"

"Sure! Susan will be there, if you want anything at all just ask. You'll find the pool around the back, have a swim, you'll need to use the pool to cool down. It's gonna get very hot today."

Harvey called Teddy to take Silver Star back and they waited to make sure Flo was happy, before setting off together.

They rode for a good twenty minutes before reaching some of the crew. Jim the head ranch hand was looking forward to meeting the girls, especially Harvey's sister.

"Hi there. You're missing one. What's happened?"

"Flo was a little nervous, she's never ridden before and thought it best to stay behind. This is Lucy."

"Maybe we will catch up with her later? Ed says we're having a cookout tonight."

"That will be smashing! It's very nice to meet you all. See you later."

Lucy and Harvey rode on. Harvey called out to Lucy. "I'm taking you up to see the orchard next!"

"OK."

Lucy wanted to show off and overtook Harvey. He watched as her long red hair flowed behind her in the breeze, and her bottom bounced up and down on the saddle. They rode on until they reached the orchard, then dismounted to give the horses a rest.

Lucy sat down under the shade of an apple tree. She leaned back on her elbows, pushed back the white cowboy hat and lifted her face to the sun. The sky was deep blue with the exception of two white fluffy clouds drifting high in the sky. She felt relaxed and happy. "Mmm, I could get used to this."

Harvey sat on the coarse tufted grass and watched Lucy close her eyes and soak up the sun, admiring her every curve and beautiful face.

"I'm sorry about last night."

Lucy opened her eyes wide. "There's nothing to apologise for. I can see how upsetting the contents of that chest must have been for you. I hope that it has helped you put some ghosts to rest now that you've caught up with your past."

"It has, kinda. I'm finding it difficult to forgive my pa though."

"I too have a lot of issues with my parents Harvey. They never had time for me. It felt as though I was just an inconvenience to them. Their careers always came before me. The only quality time I had with them was when we all went away on summer holidays. I was spoilt rotten and given everything I wanted but I needed love, and I only ever got it in measly amounts. Did you feel as though your father loved you?"

"Hell yes. He is a good father, but like you, I always felt that work came first. Look at him today! He could have taken time off but he chose to work instead! I spent most of my vacations with friends Mitch, Jane and Hayley and my best buddy Joe. You'll meet them all soon. We've asked them to come over next week. I'm not sure that Hayley will come though because I made a fool of myself thinking that she would fall for me. We've grown up together, she needed my help last week. I guess I was hoping that she would see me as her hero and take our friendship a step further. I got it all wrong, she didn't want to know."

"What? How?" Lucy was intrigued to find out all the details.

"It's a long story. Basically she was going to marry a psychopath!"

Harvey spent the next ten minutes filling Lucy in on all the details. Lucy studied his face all the while he was talking. She listened with great admiration at his braveness.

"We've both missed out on things in our childhood, maybe we should really forget the past. What's done is done. It's the future we should be concentrating on now. I'm sure that Hayley is highly grateful to you but I can see why she would find it difficult to be romantic with you; she thinks of you as a brother."

"Yep, I realize that now, and I know I've got to accept it and move on."

"Is that why you kissed me? Am I some sort of test, to see if you can move on?"

Harvey looked slightly shocked and moved to sit under the tree next to Lucy. He placed his hand on her knee and answered quietly.

"No. I felt an overwhelming need to kiss you last night. As I do now. If you'll let me."

Harvey took off his Stetson and leaned towards Lucy. They both looked into each other's eyes; Lucy hesitated for a moment then opened her mouth to enfold Harvey's lips. He teased her mouth with his tongue, making her body tingle. Lucy closed her mouth and let Harvey take control of the kiss, forcing her lips open, he explored her mouth with his tongue. She breathed heavily as his kiss excited her. He stroked her hair and her face while their kiss lingered.

Lucy stood up, remembering the promise to herself, not to make it too easy, even though she wanted him. Harvey stood up and pulled her close. She could feel how much he wanted her. He felt her breasts through her T-shirt, then sliding his hand underneath, he gently stroked her soft silky skin, making her shudder with pleasure. Lucy passionately kissed his lips, then pulled away again.

"What's wrong?"

Lucy wanted him more than ever but felt confused. "It's been a while."

She remembered the evening she returned home to find her lover in bed with an older woman.

"I'll be gentle with you."

"It's not that... the love of my life cheated on me with an

older woman. I never saw it coming. I thought I was going to spend the rest of my life with him, now I find it difficult to trust men."

"You can trust me Lucy, really you can."

Harvey held her close. She could hear his heart pounding with excitement as Lucy leaned into him for comfort.

He lifted her chin so that her blue eyes were looking into his. "Trust me."

He softly kissed her lips. Lucy responded by tenderly kissing his nose, then his cheeks, then his eyelids and finally landing on his ear, whispering softly,

"I'm yours if you want me."

Harvey held her hand and guided her further into the orchard, finding a more comfortable spot, he lay down with her. She leaned over and pulled him on top of her. Lucy took off her T shirt and undid Harvey's shirt and jeans. Then in the shade of a small apple tree, two became one. Their moans of pleasure drifted with the wind.

Afterwards, they lay in each other's arms. The feeling of freedom was exhilarating. The tree shaded them from the hot midday sun and a warm gentle breeze waved over their naked bodies.

"You're beautiful, Lucy."

"Thank you kind sir! You're beautiful too!"

"I guess we'd better leave this bliss and head back to my long-lost sister."

"Yes, and shall we should keep this as our secret."

"Yes, for now!"

They got dressed and headed back to the ranch to find Flo asleep by the swimming pool at the back of the house. She was flat out under a parasol, with her cowboy hat over her face which was muffling the sound of her snoring.

"There she is! Elegant as ever!"

They both laughed, waking Flo with a start, causing her to almost fall off of the chaise lounge.

"Oh, salut! Have you had a good ride?"

Harvey chuckled. "You could say that!"

Harvey, Lucy and Flo spent the afternoon getting to know more about each other. Flo told Harvey that Dorothy would have loved to visit but she was very ill and was hoping that he might visit her in London. Harvey said that he would consider it.

That evening Ed and Harvey lit the grill and laid the table with salad and potatoes Susan had prepared earlier. The ranch hands arrived to join them. Two of the younger lads were fascinated with the girls' foreign accents; laughing at the way they pronounced different words. Harvey took every opportunity to give a crafty wink to Lucy whenever he thought no one was looking. He and his father were noticeably a little off with one another and Ed was definitely very cool towards Florence, though she didn't notice, she'd had far too many cold beers and was decidedly happy. At bed time, Harvey waited until Flo had gone to bed and sneaked up on Lucy in the kitchen as she poured a glass of water. She felt two strong arms around her and turned to give him a passionate goodnight kiss.

"I want you Miss Bowes. When can I make your body shudder again?"

"You are now Mr Dove! Wait there!"

Lucy sneaked down the hall. Before she had reached the door to their room, she could hear the familiar sound of Flo's snores. She crept back to Harvey who was waiting by the back door.

"Let's skinny-dip!"

"What? That sounds dead exciting Mr Dove but supposing someone sees us?"

"No one will see. Everyone is asleep, the pool is at the back, only the office and my room are at the back."

He took her hand and they ran out like two naughty school children, giggling all the way. They stripped off and dove into the pool. Lucy felt liberated having the complete freedom of nudity. Harvey swam under water and popped up in front of her, making her squeal with excitement. They both dove under the water and enjoyed the sensual feeling and naughtiness of making out under the stars where they could so easily be caught out.

"Same again tomorrow, Miss Bowes?"

"Maybe? Mr Dove."

Lucy winked at him. She hurried back inside the ranch

house and to bed, Harvey admiring the rear view of her perfect figure.

Over the next week, Harvey took the girls to many interesting tourist attractions. Fort Worth Stockyards was a great day out; they watched a shoot out between a John Wayne look-alike and a couple of villains, dined on burgers and fries, walked around the museum and saw a cattle drive before taking a ride on the old steam train.

They enjoyed a stay in San Antonio and an historic visit to the Alamo and learned about its interesting history, and spent a whole day at the famous The River Walk, enjoying a boat trip, then an afternoon of shopping in the large centre, Harvey and Lucy sneaking a kiss and secretly holding hands whenever Flo wasn't looking.

Later in the week, back at the ranch, Lucy looked at Harvey and said "I can't believe that a week has gone already! I won't want to go home."

Flo nodded and agreed. "I definitely feel that I could stay here forever. It has been so nice of you to put us up Harvey, and also very generous of you to pay for everything! I would like to pay for dinner tonight."

"Well, it's cookout night tonight, Mitch, Jane, Joe and Hayley are all coming to stay. They're looking forward to meeting you gals. They'll be here in an hour or so."

The girls leapt up and offered their help in preparing the food.

"It's OK, Susan our housekeeper has it all under control. You girls go freshen up if ya like."

Later Ed and Harvey's guests arrived and introductions were made. They all sat down at the large table on the porch. Lucy couldn't help but feel a little resentment towards Hayley, after all, Harvey had tried to win her love.

Hayley sat in between Joe and Mitch, and strangely appeared to be taking an overenthusiastic interest in everything Harvey said and did. Joe didn't notice and seemed attracted to Lucy, throughout the evening making his intentions very obvious, which got Harvey's back up.

Joe was very attentive. "Can I get you another drink, Lucy?"

"No thank you, I'm fine."

"How about another steak?"

"Ooh no thanks, I've eaten half a cow already!"

Joe laughed. "So, what do you do for a living?"

"I'm an artist. How about you?"

"I've just left the army. Not sure what I'm gonna do yet. 'Been working for Mitch this week."

"You two live together?"

"No, Flo only lives with me when she's in London. We shared my flat when we were both at uni."

Harvey butted in, "You and Hayley, are you an item now?"

Joe nodded. "Yep, I think so."

Hayley tapped his knee. "What do ya mean ya think so? I

thought we were going out?"

"Just kidding hun."

As the evening continued, Joe took no notice of Hayley and concentrated his attention on Lucy, which aggravated Harvey no end.

Hayley felt jealous and noticed that Harvey couldn't take his eyes off Lucy, so she decided to play games.

"Harvey hun, would you mind if I speak to you in private, it's about Wayne."

"Sure 'nuff."

They both walked down the steps and along the wide dusty path, into the darkness. They walked in silence for a while, Harvey waiting for Hayley to speak.

"What's up hun?"

"Nothin'."

Hayley turned to Harvey, reached up and put her arms around his neck.

"I think I've made a mistake knocking you back Harv. Joe's not for me, you are."

She kissed his lips and opened them with her tongue. Totally not expecting this, Harvey kissed her back, then realising his mistake pushed her away, "Hang on just a minute! You can't play me like this!"

"Oh, I'm not playing! You are my hero Harv, you saved my

life! I do love you."

"I'm sorry Hayley, I just don't buy it! You had a big shock, I took advantage and for that I'm sorry. Joe's the guy for you, he always was."

"No, it's you I want."

She reached up and put her arms around his neck again, just as Joe came along to see where they were.

Joe pulled her off and punched Harvey straight on the nose, sending Harvey's Stetson flying in the air. Harvey was quick to punch him back, blacking Joe's eye. Hayley shouted at them to stop, but Joe swung another punch, this time in Harvey's stomach, making him double over and groan in agony. Harvey recovered quickly. Joe grabbed Hayley's arm and started to march her back up the pathway. Harvey grabbed Joe around the neck; they wrestled until they both looked up to see they had an audience of Mitch, Ed, Lucy and Flo.

Joe was first to shout accusations. "It seems Harvey can't keep his hands off my gal. I found them kissing."

Lucy turned away and stormed off, back to the house. "Wait, Lucy! It's not true! Hayley came onto me!"

Hayley smiled a sly smile; Harvey had just confirmed his feelings for Lucy.

Back at the house Lucy was nowhere to be seen, she'd taken herself off to bed. Flo went to find out why she'd stormed off.

"What is wrong Lucy? Why have you taken to your bed?"

"This may come as a shock to you Flo, I thought I'd found a man that I could finally trust but it appears that I was wrong. Your brother is no better than any other man!"

"Are you telling me that you and Harvey have been seeing each other, and I have not noticed?"

"Yes Flo, I've become more than just friends with your brother, at every opportunity!"

Flo then realised that she had noticed certain ways they'd been looking at each other, and even thought she had seen them holding hands a couple of times, but had dismissed her thoughts as just her imagination.

There was a knock at the door.

"Lucy, it's me. Please let me explain!"

"Go away! I don't want to talk to you!"

"But I want you to know that nothing happened! Hayley came on to me!"

"Go away!"

"Please Lucy!"

"I said go away!"

Back outside, Joe and Hayley were further along the road and could be heard having a heated argument. Mitch, Jane and Ed were discussing the situation, when Harvey returned and sat with them.

Jane was first to break the silence between them all.

"So, what's going on Harv? I thought you'd got the message. I thought you understood that Hayley wasn't interested!"

"You tell me Jane! I swear I didn't come on to her; she made a play for me! I dunno what she's playing at! I may as well tell you all that I have been seeing Lucy but I reckon that's all over now!"

Ed looked surprised. "Hell boy! You kept that quiet!"

"Yep, we wanted to see how things went, I told her she could trust me. I doubt that she does now!"

Hayley returned with Joe behind her. "Can we go now Mama?"

Joe had a very bruised face and swollen eye. He glanced at Harvey. "Fella, I'm sorry. It was all a misunderstanding."

"Try explaining that to my gal'."

Hayley looked angry. "So you and Lucy are together then!"

"Yep, I've fallen for her hook, line and sinker."

Hayley was overcome with jealousy. "Oh, so the fact that you are in love with me counts for nothing!"

"I'm not in love with you. I'm in love with Lucy."

Lucy heard the conversation from the kitchen. Her heart skipped a beat when she heard Harvey say that he loved her and she felt sure that Hayley was just jealous.

"You've always been in love with me. You told me back at our ranch, the night Wayne was there for the cookout."

"I may have thought I was Hayley but I think it was just infatuation, and a mixture of too many Jack and Coke's."

Hayley stormed off with Joe and sat in the car. Jane and Mitch apologised and said their goodbyes.

"I'm so sorry about our daughter. I think she has a problem. She's been deeply affected by what Wayne did to her. I'm gonna get her to see a doctor next week. You know our Hayley, she's never been like this before!"

Mitch, Jane, Hayley and Joe intended to stay the night but because of what happened they called a cab and booked into a nearby hotel, leaving Harvey and Ed sitting on the porch.

"Oh my! Are you sure you know what you're doing son?"

"What do you mean, Pa?"

"Are you sure this ain't no vacation romance?"

"No Pa, I've never felt like this about anyone before Lucy. I do love her, she's everything I want in a woman. She's intelligent, artistic, beautiful, good company and English."

"English?"

"Yes, I love her posh accent!"

"And what about your sister?"

"What about Florence?"

"How do you feel about her?"

"She's a great gal, she's funny, beautiful and artistic. You should get to know her Pa, you might find that you like her too! I've noticed that you can barely look at her!"

"What did you expect? It's hard for me!"

"Yeah, but her momma was called Annette. She was born to Annette, she didn't ask to be born! It's not her fault my momma left and changed her identity! None of this is her fault! Why won't you realize that?"

"I know, I just can't stop thinking about Ella again now!"

"Pa if you'd wanted to forget Ella, why did you keep her portrait over the fireplace for so long?"

"I guess that was for you."

"Don't lie Pa, you did it for both of us. You still love Momma, even though she left us."

Ed broke down. "It was my fault she left! Mine! If I had shown her more love, she would still be here!"

"No Pa, it wasn't all your fault. Jane explained to me that Momma was a loner, hard to reach, she didn't want friends, she just wanted you, and she wanted a daughter didn't she?"

"Yeah, I couldn't give her a daughter, that's another reason I'm finding it hard with Florence here, she's the daughter we never had!"

"So, get to know her! Alright, she may not be your flesh and blood, but she's mine and Ella's. Florence is a great gal once you get to know her!"

Ed rubbed his eyes. "I'm going to bed."

Lucy hurried back to her room, happy at what she had overheard.

Harvey and Ed both said goodnight and hugged before retiring to their rooms. Lucy waited until everything was quiet, then sneaked along the hall and into Harvey's room. She slipped her nightdress off and let it drop to the floor. Harvey was laying with his back to her. She slid under the sheet and wrapped her arm around his waist. She whispered in his ear.

"I love you, Mr Dove."

Harvey turned over and kissed her lips. "Does that mean that you understand what happened tonight wasn't my fault?"

"I heard your conversation with Ed. I understand."

Lucy stayed with him all night. The next day Ed decided to take the day off… Well sort of. It was Rodeo Day and he was taking a couple of his horses to compete that evening, so he wanted to make an effort and get to know Flo.

Florence couldn't believe the change in his attitude towards her; he sat next to her and chatted with her, asking about her past career as a teacher and her modelling. Ed couldn't believe how amusing she was and found that he really liked her.

Both girls were excited about going to watch their first rodeo. They spent the morning around the pool with Ed and Harvey and had a relaxing time, swimming and sunbathing.

Florence dived into the pool to cool off. They all heard a splash but then silence. It took a little while to notice that Florence hadn't surfaced.

Lucy screamed! "Flo, where's Flo?"

They all stood up, she was nowhere. Harvey ran along the side of the pool, Ed ran to the deep end.

"Fuck! She's on the bottom!"

He dived in and pulled her up. Harvey helped to drag her out, her body was floppy and lifeless, and her lips were blue. Lucy was frantic, waiving her arms in the air and running around in circles, screaming Flo's name.

Harvey called an ambulance, whilst Ed gave CPR. He pumped her chest until eventually Flo coughed and spluttered, spurting water and vomit everywhere.

Harvey held his sister closely.

"Oh thank God! Oh thank God! I thought we'd lost you!"

He pushed the hair from her face and kissed her forehead.

"Pa you saved her!"

Florence cried and hung onto her brother. Lucy cried with relief.

"Thank you! Thank you! You saved her life! What on earth happened Flo?"

"I do not know! I felt dizzy, I think I hit my head."

Lucy inspected her head. "Oh my! You have a nasty bump!"

Harvey looked worried. "An ambulance is on the way. You need to get checked out!"

That afternoon, Harvey, Ed and Lucy were still at the hospital waiting for news on Flo, when Ed dialled the number to his head ranch hand Jim.

"Jim, I'm tied up, can you take the horses to the rodeo please man?"

Harvey tapped his father's shoulder. "Pa, it's OK, you go, I'll stay here."

"No son, Jim can see to it. I'll stay here with you both."

The doctor came out of Florence's room. He had a smile on his face, which made them feel a little less anxious.

"You can go in and see her. We are just going to keep her in overnight to make sure she's OK. She swallowed a lot of water but her lungs seem clear, it's just the bump on the head we want to keep an eye on."

"Gee, thanks doc."

Florence was sitting up in bed. She looked pale but better than she had earlier. Harvey kissed his sister's cheek as did Ed, which pleased Harvey immensely. Lucy just winked at her best friend and smiled, knowing that Flo must be feeling ecstatic right now.

Flo felt her neck. "My locket! It has gone! It must have come undone at the pool."

Lucy assured Florence that they would look around the pool when they returned to the house.

Back at the ranch a UPS driver was delivering a package. Harvey undid it to reveal Flo's portrait, the note inside said.

"Dear Harvey, you have won this fair and square. By now you will have spent time with your sister and will have seen that she is beautiful inside and out.

Enjoy this painting with my best regards, Dorothy.

P.S. I hope that you will visit me next time you are back in London."

Ed studied the painting, noticing that Flo had the silver locket around her neck, reminding him to look for it.

"It looks as though it's the same size as your momma's portrait. Let's hang it there above the fireplace, it's almost like it's meant to be."

Harvey hugged his father, Ed hugged him back.

"There's something I've gotta do." he said, before disappearing around the back to the pool. He stripped down to his boxer shorts and dived into the warm water. He swam around and searched the bottom of the deep end and came up holding the silver locket. He climbed out and sat on the edge of the pool, with the locket in his hand and the chain dangling in the sunlight. Carefully he prised it open, inside was a picture of a young Harvey on one side and a baby Florence on the other. His heart felt heavy at the thought of all those wasted years, and how all that unhappiness could have been prevented. He had the chance to change now and that is what he intended to do from that moment on.

CHAPTER TWENTY-THREE

Harvey really wanted to take the girls to a rodeo before the end of their stay, so as soon as Flo was discharged from hospital he found the nearest one and booked in a couple of his own horses, so that he could enter himself and Ed to participate.

Flo and Lucy dressed appropriately in jeans, checked shirts and cowboy boots, looking quite the part and feeling excited about the forthcoming evening.

Ed drove the horsebox, whilst Harvey took the girls in the Range Rover. There were only a few people there when they first arrived, but soon the place was buzzing with excited people of all ages, all looking like they were on a western movie set.

Harvey and Ed tended to their horses and then took the girls on a guided tour around the arena. At the back were large pens with some huge, fierce-looking bulls. A couple of bulls were tied to the pens by their horns with ropes and the hands were teasing them, slapping their rumps, making them angry as hell so that they were ready to charge out into the ring. One enormous bull was snorting, foaming at the mouth, and scraping its foot in the sawdust, staring at Flo as she passed by.

"Oh my goodness! He is a very scary-looking animal!"

The loudspeakers blasted out country music which really added to the atmosphere, making the girls feel like proper Texan cowgirls. They settled down on the step of one of the raised wooden stands around the arena, sitting at the top so that they had a good view. A kind woman chatted to them, asking where they were from, offering them the use of her mosquito repellent spray.

"You'll need to use this; if not you'll get eat up by them skeeters!"

"Thank you very much." Flo replied, spraying the contents of the can up her arms and legs.

A Texan drawl bellowed from the loud speaker, announcing the first riders. Harvey and Ed appeared on horseback in full cowboy attire at the entrance gate to the arena. Flo and Lucy jumped up, waving and cheering along with the crowd. Harvey rode to the far end of the arena so that he was facing Ed. The music started and they galloped full pace at each other. On the ground were two large flags, as they both reached the centre of the arena, Harvey and Ed both hung on and slid sideways off their horses, reaching down to grab the flags, missing each other by inches. The crowd clapped and cheered as Harvey and Ed rode on, holding the large Texas flags above their heads, trailing in the wind behind them as they galloped full pelt twice around the arena. Then they rode towards each other and stopped dead so the horses were next to each other. The music changed and the horses began to dance, both making exactly the same moves. It was enchanting to watch such beautiful animals behave in such a controlled way. The music changed again, The Devil Went Down To Georgia played loudly as Harvey and Ed demonstrated their riding skills, fast and furiously going round and round the arena to the claps and cheers of the crowd. They both ended the routine, facing Flo and Lucy, with both the men and the horses giving a bow which made the girls cheer loudly with delight!

Next up were the youngsters. It was a race that Harvey had participated in many times in his youth. They each took turns riding out on the backs of large bucking sheep. The child who managed to stay on the longest was the winner. The girls both watched with admiration at the skills of some of the youngest riders, their names and ages announced each time, the youngest being only five years old, managing a few seconds on the back of his bucking sheep.

Next were the cowboys who came out in pairs, demonstrating their roping skills. The young steers were let out one at a time, whilst the cowboys rode around the ring twirling ropes in circles above their heads and then throwing them over the necks of the steers before quickly dismounting and bringing them to the ground, tying up their legs so that they were secure.

"Amazing!" Flo shouted! By the time Harvey and Ed returned with beers in hand for all four, the female riders had started bareback and saddle bronc riding, followed by some good looking cowboys riding the bucking broncos. It looked extremely dangerous; Flo watched, hiding her face behind her hands as several of the riders were thrown from their horses and nearly trampled on. Harvey laughed and wondered how Flo would react at the bulls which were on next!

Lucy hugged Harvey as he handed her a beer, "Well done you two! Pretty dangerous stuff!"

Harvey looked proud. "Wait until you see what the guys get up to next!"

Over by the tower, behind the entrance gate, an enormous jet black bull was tied up and waiting to enter the arena. Three hands were slapping its rear and geeing it on, making it snort and foam at the mouth in anger. The gate opened and out thundered the hefty bull which must have weighed a good sixteen hundred pounds. The rider was an experienced cowboy who managed to cling on for almost twelve seconds before the angry bull bucked him off, almost trampling on him as it kicked its way across the arena, staring angrily at the roaring crowd.

"Oh my goodness! That is so dangerous!" Flo exclaimed.

"This is so exciting! Thank you for bringing us!" Lucy shouted, clapping her hands and waving her arms along with the participating audience.

Harvey flashed his dimple as he smiled, admiring Lucy's enthusiasm, and shouted, "I'm glad you got to see a rodeo, it's a shame we couldn't get to the one at Bandera, you would have liked the diving mule. Maybe next time you visit Texas."

They all stood up, cheered and waved their hats as the last rider was bucked off a hefty white bull. Everyone gasped as the rider only just got out of the way, speedily jumping over the white fence as the bull narrowly missed his butt with its fierce looking horns.

The crowd all stood and cheered as the rodeo came to an end.

"What a brilliant night!" Flo said, as she danced around in circles like a child, then tripped and ended up on the ground in a cloud of dust and straw. They all rushed over to her together and picked her up, dusting her down. She laughed, exclaimed "Silly me!" and skipped all the way back to the car with Lucy, Ed and Harvey.

Ed jumped up into the driver's seat of the horsebox.

"Glad you enjoyed it. See you all back at the ranch."

In no time they were all home again. Ed put the horses away and headed back to the house to join the others who were gathered round the table on the porch. The girls were still buzzing with excitement.

Flo asked Ed and Harvey, "Have you ever ridden one of the bucking broncos or a bull?" They both laughed. Harvey was the first to answer.

"Yep, a horse though, not a bull. Pa would never let me, and I would never let Pa; neither of us are reckless enough, I used to lasso the steers when I was younger. The broncos are dangerous enough." Flo clapped her hands with excitement!

"Wow, you really are real cowboys aren't you?!"

"Ha ha yep, ya could say that!"

Ed tapped the top off another beer and sat reminiscing about the good old days, when he used to spend a lot of time at the rodeo. Then Ella sprang to mind, he remembered that it was at a rodeo that she met Flo's father, but instead of dwelling on it, he decided to change the subject.

"So, only a couple more days here and you gals fly back home. Where would you like to go tomorrow? I am taking the day off so that we can do something, if you'd like?"

Flo immediately shouted "Southfork! Ooh please could we go to Southfork? I would very much love to see where they filmed Dallas."

"Southfork it is then! Perhaps on Thursday we could take you to Austin and show you around. There's plenty to do there!"

Harvey was amazed at his father's new attitude but didn't complain, he just sat back and smiled happily at what had turned out to be the perfect end to a perfect evening.

As they all turned in for the night, Harvey noticed a message on his phone. It was Hayley.

"I'm sorry for the trouble I caused, I can't get you out of my head Harvey. I realise that you are the man for me. I want you and I will get you!"

Harvey was irritated by Hayley's attitude. She didn't want him until Lucy came along. He chose to ignore her text and went to bed, whispering to Lucy to sneak into his room once Flo had gone off to sleep.

Sure enough, ten minutes later, Lucy was sliding under the sheet next to him. He could feel her naked breasts pressing into his back. Her hand slid down under the sheet, she could feel how much Harvey wanted her. He turned over to face her, kissing her lips passionately, he slid on top, they locked together, thrusting in ecstasy. Through the moans of pleasure and in the height of passion Harvey's home phone rang. They tried to ignore it, but it kept ringing. It went to voice mail. Hayley spoke. "Harvey, are you there? I need you Harvey, I know you love me."

Lucy pushed Harvey off. "What's she doing? You told her you weren't interested! Why is she keeping on at you?"

Harvey sat up. "Hell honey, I know. She's sick Lucy. She

needs help!"

"I feel as though I can't compete with her Harv, you've known her all your life. I've only known you for a short while. Are you sure that you aren't really in love with her?"

Harvey looked Lucy straight in the eye and cupped her face in his hands.

"I'm telling you now Miss Bowes. I love you! I don't use those words lightly." He reached out and turned his cell phone phone to silent, then unplugged the home phone. "Now can we get back to what we were doing?"

Lucy disappeared under the sheet and showed Harvey what pleasure she could give her man. He lay there in ecstasy as Lucy took complete control. He pulled her up and she sat on him, he took her fast and furiously, both ending up feeling complete; they slept in each other's arms until sunrise.

Harvey was first in the shower, leaving Lucy stretched out on the bed. She reached over and glanced at Harvey's phone. There were four missed calls, all from Hayley.

"This has got to stop." thought Lucy.

She texted Hayley.

"I thought we had established that Harvey isn't interested in you. He is with me now, so leave him alone. Lucy."

When Harvey returned, rubbing his wet hair with a towel. Lucy confessed to him that she had just sent Hayley a message from his phone.

"OK. I hope she will be OK with that. She seems a bit unhinged at the moment. She really isn't that sort of person. I've never known her to behave like this before! Wayne has messed with her head."

"Oh! You hope that she'll be OK with that! What about us? Do we really have to put up with her behaviour? Imagine how I feel right now? I fly back to the UK in a couple of days! I'll be wondering if she's around here as soon as I'm gone!"

"I can assure you that will not happen Lucy!"

"Well, Hayley was quick to kiss you before and that was when I was here!"

"I've told you. She's not right, she needs to see someone and get her head sorted out."

Lucy grabbed her robe and left the room. Flo was dressed and brushing her hair when Lucy stormed into the bedroom.

"Hey!"

"Hey, what is wrong?"

"Nothing! Well yes something! Hayley keeps ringing your brother. I'm worried she'll get her claws into him after we leave here."

"I am sure that will not happen my friend! My brother seems a pretty decent man. He will not betray you."

"Hmm, we shall see! I don't think any man is fully trustworthy!"

Lucy showered and when she met up with the others in the kitchen the atmosphere was decidedly frosty between her and Harvey, until Flo changed the mood with her enthusiasm for the forthcoming events of the day.

As the four of them pulled into the driveway of Southfork, Flo giggled with delight.

"It is not as big as it looks on the television."

After they all got out of the car, they headed for the entrance where they were ushered into a small conference room, which quickly filled up with people. The elderly gentleman waited until the seats were filled and then introduced himself before asking everyone where they were all from. Flo was the only person from France, there were a couple of Brits, Scots and Germans, and everyone else was from the US. The talk started by asking which series the public preferred, the old Dallas or the new. There were mixed reactions, Flo declaring that she loved the old series. The guide then explained that "The show first started as a miniseries of five episodes premiering on April 2, 1978, but was so popular that they made thirteen full seasons from September 23, 1978, until May 3, 1991, fourteen seasons in total including the miniseries." He then went on to talk about the characters and the ranch itself, before inviting everyone to explore the house and the grounds.

Harvey grabbed Lucy's hand and they all wandered around, heading for the kitchen first, up to the bedroom overlooking the swimming pool, took a tour of the grounds and finally entered a large conference centre which was a museum with lots of exhibits including JR's gold Rolls Royce. The gift shop had a good stock of memorabilia, Flo picked up a couple of fridge magnets. "I must take one back for Dorothy, she loves Dallas!"

The day was a success and everyone was in high spirits as they headed back home. Just as they pulled up to the house, Harvey and Ed noticed a familiar car parked in the driveway.

"Oh no." Harvey sighed. His face dropped.

Flo peered out of the window as they pulled around next to the car.

"What is the matter?"

Harvey held Lucy's hand. "Don't worry."

Lucy looked angry. "It's Hayley isn't it!"

"Yes, but don't worry, I told you I'll handle it."

Lucy threw open the car door and stormed up to the car. Hayley was looking in the driver's mirror and applying her lipstick. Lucy banged on the window. Harvey grabbed her around the waist and pulled her away. Hayley got out and swayed up to Harvey.

"Hello handsome."

"Hayley you're drunk!"

"Yes, I am!"

"What are you doing here, please tell me you haven't just driven from Austin ?"

"No, I've been staying in a hotel and now I've come to get

you!"

Ed took Hayley's hand and led her up the steps to the house.

"Come on young lady. This isn't like you! What has gotten into you? Let's get you some coffee."

"I don't need coffee, I need your son! He can make me better."

Meanwhile Harvey checked in Hayley's car and found an empty bottle of vodka. Lucy was fuming!

"Trust her to turn up and spoil everything!"

Harvey picked up the empty bottle and pointed to the house. "This is not like her! I've never seen her get drunk like this! She has to be sick, I know she is."

They headed inside to find Flo making coffee and Ed with his arm around Hayley, who was waving her arms around and crying very loudly.

"I'm sorry! I made a huge mistake! My life is just one big mess now! I have no one, I need you, Harvey!"

"Pa, she's drunk a bottle of vodka, she doesn't know what she's saying! We need to sober her up!"

Lucy stormed off down the hallway feeling foolishly jealous but just couldn't help shouting, "She needs a good slap!"

Ed sat up with Hayley all night, whilst Harvey slept alone and Lucy and Flo had a sleepless night. The morning came too soon. Lucy wandered out of the bedroom to find Ed asleep on one couch and Hayley asleep on the other. She headed back passing Harvey's room just as he opened the door.

"Hey honey! I had a crap night's sleep. How did you sleep?"

"Dreadfully, no thanks to her in there!" Lucy replied, pointing to the living room.

"You've nothing to worry about hun, I promise you. Come here." He pulled Lucy towards him but she was cold to his affections.

"I'm going start packing my things."

"Honey, don't be like this, it's our last day together."

"Yes, I know, and I'm sorry. I can't get my head around all of this. I guess I'm just a jealous bitch!"

Both girls packed their cases in silence, then made their way to the kitchen where Ed was rustling up pancakes and coffee.

Hayley was sitting at the table looking decidedly dishevelled. Her usually perfectly kept hair was hanging limply in her face. Her eyes were bleary and her makeup was smudged from the night before. She glanced up at Lucy and Flo.

"Guys! I'm sorry, what more can I say?" Lucy sat in front of her.

"Just say that you aren't going to steal Harvey from me the moment I go back to England."

Hayley looked up at Harvey with doe eyes. "I'll try my best

not to."

"You'd better try damned hard! I want a promise!"

"OK, OK, you win Lucy! I promise! Does that make you feel better?"

"No, not really. You could make a play as soon as I'm gone. How do I know that you will keep your promise?"

"Because I'm going to get help. I need help!"

Harvey pulled up a chair and sat next to Hayley. "Your ma and pa have spoken to a doctor and they are going with you to see him."

Hayley reached in her purse for a tissue, tears streaming down her face. Lucy felt sorry for her and felt ashamed at the way she had spoken to her. She took hold of her hand.

"We are on your side. You have been through a lot Hayley."

Ed dished up the pancakes and they ate in gloomy silence. It was the last day in Texas for the girls. Ed had grown fond of them and felt as though he'd found a way to unwind and have some fun, just as they were about to leave. Harvey felt sad for Hayley and Hayley felt confused by everything.

Ed spoke up. "What is everyone doing today then?"

Hayley looked at him. "I'll be out of your way soon."

"No rush hun."

"You gonna be OK driving back?" Harvey asked, sipping

his coffee.

"Yep, I'll be fine. I should think the gallons of coffee I've drunk have replaced all the alcohol by now!"

Lucy glanced at Hayley with a look of concern.

"Are you sure? Maybe you shouldn't drive?"

"Honestly, I'll be fine."

When breakfast was finished Harvey walked to the car with Hayley. He opened the door and watched her tiny frame get behind the steering wheel.

"Take care hun. Make sure you do as the doctor tells you and before you know it, you'll be back being your gorgeous self again."

Hayley looked up at him. "Don't talk kindly to me Harv. It makes me want you all the more."

"Hun, you don't really mean that."

"But I do, Harv."

"Come on, you made Lucy a promise."

"Yes I did, I'll leave it, but I do love you."

"Yes and I love you too hun, but as a friend, that's all."

Harvey closed the door and watched as she drove away, waving his hand in the air. When he returned to the house, Lucy was waiting in the kitchen. "Gosh, I hope she gets home safely!"

"Yes. She's sobered up, she's a mess but her mom and pop will help her through this."

Harvey put his arms around Lucy and kissed her hard on her lips.

"Let's just enjoy our last day together hun."

Ed and Flo bounced into the kitchen laughing their heads off, as if they had known each other all their lives. All of Ed's resentment had dwindled away.

"Right," said Ed. "let's go to Austin! Where the music plays all day, where the shops are plenty and where we find the bat bridge!"

Flo looked puzzled. "The bat bridge?"

"Yes, I'll explain on the way."

Just then high in the sky and circling above they saw a helicopter which lowered down and landed before them in the next feild. The whirring blades blowing a haze of straw and dust everywhere.

"Come!" Ed beckoned as he ran towards it, "This is our ride to Austin ladies!" Ed proudly shouted above the noise of the rotating arms.

"Oh wow! I've never been in a helicopter!" Lucy exclaimed.

They all ran over and climbed inside. The ride to Austin was fabulous as they looked down on all the scenery, the pilot pointing out all the landmarks, eventually landing safely much to Flo's relief.

They all had a fabulous last day together, eating, drinking, sightseeing and shopping, before returning home again in the helicopter with plenty of designer bags and lots of talk about what a day they'd all had.

Flo followed Ed into the house, followed by Lucy and Harvey who were hand in hand.

"Wow! What a totally fantastic time we've had! Thank you so much Ed for absolutely everything! It's been splendid!" Lucy exclaimed as she planted a huge kiss on Ed's cheek.

Ed looked rather pleased with himself. He'd actually enjoyed taking time off work.

"You're welcome, anytime. I mean that!" he said, looking at Lucy and Flo. "Hey and maybe you can even teach us some French?"

"Oui! It would be my pleasure." Flo smiled happily, and then looked glum before confessing. "I am very sorry for breaking the soap dish last night."

"Soap dish?" Ed asked.

"Erm oui, I dropped it, it did bounce and I caught it, but it jumped out of my hands and broke." She fished around in one of her shopping bags and produced a replacement.

They all laughed and retired to the living room where they all happily relaxed and watched TV for a couple of hours before Harvey and Lucy made their excuses and went off to bed.

As Lucy appeared from the bathroom, Harvey was standing

with his hands behind his back.

"Honey, close your eyes and open your hands."

Lucy did as he asked and felt him place a small box in her hands. She opened it to see a beautiful pendant on a white gold chain.

"Oh my gosh! It's beautiful! I didn't see you buy this!"

"I quickly bought it when you and Flo went along to the handbag store."

Harvey undid the clasp and hung it around her neck. Lucy felt it and admired it in the mirror. She let her towel drop to the floor and stood naked before him. Then she undid Harvey's shirt and helped him out of it, kissing his broad shoulders and teasing him with her tongue.

"I love you." she said, as she undid his belt buckle and slid her hand inside his jeans.

Harvey caressed her naked body, gently and slowly from her lips to her toes. Lucy watched in the mirror as he did so, making her want him completely. She ran her fingers through his dark curly hair and gasped as he made her body shudder with his tongue. He picked her up and laid her on the bed, making love hard and strong, Lucy cried with pleasure as they made love over and over.

The next day after breakfast, the ranch hands all stopped by to say goodbye to the girls. Susan gave them both a kiss on cheek.

"It's been nice to have you gals around. I'll miss you."

They in turn thanked Susan for all the delicious meals she had cooked throughout their stay.

Harvey, Ed, Flo and Lucy loaded the trunk with luggage and headed off to the airport. Lucy sat in the back with Harvey and held his hand all the way. Flo talked the whole length of the journey, hardly taking a breath between each sentence. Ed was intoxicated by her enthusiasm for life, which was notably different to her mother's.

Ed and Harvey stayed with the girls in the airport, making sure they knew where to go and then bid a sad farewell.

Ed hung his arm around his son's neck. "She's the one then son?"

"Yes Pa, she's the one."

"Great choice. I approve."

"You also approve of Florence, don't you, Pa?"

"Yes I do. She's a great gal. She's nothing like Ella, except for her looks, that smile and those eyes, but her personality is totally different!"

They drove back to the ranch talking about both girls and how they had changed their lives in the past fortnight, both admitting that they couldn't wait to see them again.

"Tell you what son! Let's call in at the bar and raise a few beers to Flo and Lucy! Come on son, it'll do us good, last day of our vacation!"

"Fine by me Pa, I could really do with a beer. I miss them already!"

The bar was busy, Harvey looked around and waved at a few of his fellow rodeo buddies. Jed, an old drinking partner from way back came up behind him, patted him on the back and handed him a beer.

"Here ya go Harv, have this one, I'll grab another, Ed? Beer too?"

"Hey Jed, great thanks." Ed replied firmly, shaking his hand. "Long time since I last bumped into you fella! How's the family?"

"Good, all good man, expectin' another one in a coupla months."

"Whoa! You don't hang around do ya fella! That's munchkin number four isn't it?"

"Yep! Love kids man! 'Bout time you settled down Harv. How's that gorgeous gal you used to hang around with? Hayley?"

"She's OK. She's not my gal though. I'm with an English beauty, her name's Lucy, we've just dropped her at the airport. That's why we're here, drowning our sorrows."

"Good man, good. 'Bout time you found someone to share ya millions with!" Jed joked.

They chatted for about an hour, then Ed decided to make a move. "You coming, Harv?"

"No, you go on ahead Pa, I'm gonna have a Jack Daniels or two and get a cab back."

Ed said farewell to everyone and head home to a dark, empty ranch house.

Jed and Harvey carried on drinking until Harvey got up to go the bar and almost fell over.

"Jeez Harv, I think you've had one too many! Let me call you a cab?" Jed laughed; he'd never seen Harvey so drunk. He helped his pal to the door and into the cab, shaking hands and vowing to keep in touch more, shoving his business card into Harvey's shirt pocket before closing the cab door and thinking "Someone is gonna have a massive hangover in the mornin'."

Harvey fell out of the cab door, paid the driver far too much, then staggered up the steps, making several attempts to fit the key in the kitchen door. He poured a glass of water and stood swaying from side to side whilst he downed the refreshing drink. Stumbling along the hallway to his room, he noisily entered, holding his finger to his lips and whispering to himself, "Shhhhhh". He sat on the bed and as he helplessly tried to remove his boots, he heard a noise which came from his bathroom.

"Hello? Someone in there? Pa, is that you?"

Ed could hear a lot of clambering about and popped a sleepy head around Harvey's door to make sure his son was alright.

"Hell boy! You've had a few too many!"

"I'm OK Pa... Night, see you in the morning." Harvey chuckled.

"OK, I'll see you in the morning... Night Harv." Ed said,

giving his son a pat on the back.

Harvey struggled to get undressed. He stripped off to his boxers and turned on the bathroom light. He jumped!

"Hayley! Man, you made me jump! What the hell are you doin' here? How did you get in?"

Hayley was provocatively sitting on the white linen basket, her head tilted to one side, her legs crossed and her arms folded. She was wearing a white lace basque, stockings and garters.

"Hey handsome!"

As cool as a cucumber, she seductively stood in front of him, running her fingers through her hair, licking her lips and giving him a sexy wink.

"What? How?" Before he could splutter any more words, Hayley grabbed hold of his hair, pulled his head down and kissed him hard on the lips, then she hung on his shoulders and wrapped her legs around his waist.

Her lips were full of passion. Harvey tried to hold back, but Hayley wasn't letting him. She took him completely by surprise. With her athletic legs wrapped tightly around him, she hung onto Harvey's hair with both hands. It was pleasantly painful. Harvey was so drunk he couldn't resist. Hayley kissed his mouth with forceful passion, trying to open Harvey's tight lips with her tongue.

"Relax Harv. I'm gonna show you what good sex is!"

Harvey couldn't help himself and gave in, exploring her tongue with his. She still had a tight grip on his hair, and dug her long nails into his scalp. Harvey winced with pleasure and pain; it made him feel shamefully sexy. He grabbed her bottom tightly; his large hands covering her tight buttocks. He slid his hands up and down her back, whilst responding passionately to her kisses.

"Mmm, Harvey, give it to me!" Hayley loosened her legs and slid her body down until she was level with his bulge.

"Mmm, that's what I'm taking about!" She let go of his hair and leaned back, hanging on by her legs. Harvey swayed from side to side, losing his balance, and they both fell to the floor, Harvey landing on top of her in a drunken mess. As she struggled to push him off, he giggled like a naughty school boy. Hayley turned him over and sat on him.

"Hey gorgeous man, look at what I have to offer!" She seductively writhed around on his stomach, Harvey could do nothing but lay there smiling, and admiring her sexy body. He reached up, pulled her head down and kissed her and promptly passed out. Hayley slapped his face and tried to wake him, but he didn't move. She stroked his handsome face, "Poor baby, so drunk, wanting me so much, my one big chance to prove my love for you and you go and pass out on me. Wake up you idiot!"

Hayley put a wet washcloth on his face but Harvey was in a deep slumber. She took the sheet from his bed and placed it over him, then lifted his head and placed a pillow beneath, lying down beside him and falling asleep with her arm and leg wrapped around him.

Morning came; Harvey woke with a pounding head, a dry mouth and a massive surprise to find himself on the bathroom floor with Hayley asleep next to him. He sat bolt upright. Looking around him, he couldn't work out how he had ended up on the floor, let alone why Hayley was there! She stretched her arms and yawned.

"Hey handsome! Thank you for a wonderful night of passion!"

Harvey got to his feet. He held his sore head and looked at her with disgust!

"What do you mean?"

"You were everything I thought you'd be, and more!"

"I don't remember anything Hayley." He ran his fingers through his hair, looking puzzled, trying to remember what had happened.

"Mmm, best night of my life!" Hayley said with a sensual voice.

Harvey couldn't believe that he could betray Lucy. What had he done?"

"No, no way! I wouldn't do that to Lucy! I just wouldn't!

CHAPTER TWENTY-FOUR

The pilot announced that it was raining in London as the plane descended into Heathrow Airport. Both girls had hardly spoken on the long-haul flight home, mainly because they were feeling down after such a wonderful holiday. As they waited for their cases to head towards them on the conveyor belt, they stood arm in arm looking sad.

An old lady couldn't help but remark "Holiday blues ladies? Must have been a pretty good one, or else you've come home to some bad news?"

They both answered, "Brilliant holiday, unfortunately back to reality, and the British weather!"

"Ah yes, I know the feeling, I've been staying with my sister for four months. I didn't want to come home."

"Ooh our cases, excuse us please!"

They both grabbed their cases and made their way out of the airport. Back home, they clambered out of the taxi and got soaked in the pouring rain.

"Get the kettle on, Flo."

Lucy turned the central heating on. "Reality with a bump eh?"

Flo started to unpack. "What is this?"

"Huh, what is what?" Lucy asked inquisitively.

"This!"

She took out a tiny box, inside was a wedding band, and a note from Ed.

"This was your mother's. I would like you to have it. Love Ed."

Flo couldn't help but get emotional. "How wonderful!"

She placed it upon the middle finger of her right hand.

"It fits this finger. What do you think?" she asked, showing Lucy her hand.

"Perfect, I'd say!"

"Fancy Ed keeping it all those years! I must say I am a little surprised!" Flo exclaimed.

"How thoughtful!" Lucy remarked, giving Flo a quick hug. "Such a nice man. You are very lucky to have Ed and Harvey in your life."

"Yes you are too. Who knows, maybe one day my best friend will become my sister-in-law?"

They both smiled at the thought, and carried on unpacking before heading to bed. Flo texted Jack to tell him she had arrived back home safely.

The next morning the girls woke to loud claps of thunder and bright flashes of lightening. They both sat at the breakfast table listening to the torrential rain hitting the kitchen window.

Lucy grabbed her phone to check for messages and got excited when she noticed one from Harvey. A picture flashed up, it was a selfie of Hayley which looked as though she was in bed with her man. She had an evil smile upon her face.

Lucy burst into tears of rage, "Fucking bitch!!!"

"What is wrong?"

"Look!"

"Oh my goodness! I do not believe it!"

"How could they!"

"Maybe it is not as it seems?" Flo said, trying to sound positive.

Lucy grappled with her phone and tapped a message saying… "*I knew it!*"

When Harvey received the message and was horrified!

He typed back "*This isn't how it looks! I'm going to call you hun.*"

Lucy was fuming and dismissed his message, rushing into her bedroom in floods of tears. She got dressed and threw on her raincoat. "I'm going out; tell that pig that I don't want to talk to him!"

Florence sat in silence, waiting for the phone to ring. When it did it made her jump. She dubiously picked up the receiver. "Bonjour."

"Flo, it's Harvey. Can I speak with Lucy please?"

"She is not here. She has gone out, she is very upset!"

"Rightly so but that picture is not what it looks like. Hayley forced herself on me. I was drunk! I passed out and she slept next to me all night. Nothing happened! At least I don't think anything happened." Harvey's voice deepened. "I wouldn't do anything to hurt Lucy. You have to believe me. Can you tell her, explain to her please?"

"I will try. She has to calm down first. She is very angry!"

"Ugh, everything is such a dang mess! I feel helpless, I'm so far away! All I want to do is hold her and tell her nothing has changed between us. My Pa will assure you! He knows what happened!"

"I will try and calm her when she gets home." Flo asked to speak to Ed.

"Bonjour Ed, I just wanted to thank you for giving me my mother's wedding band."

"You are welcome Flo, it rightfully belongs to you. I'm just glad that I kept it, I almost threw it away when Ella left me."

"Thank you, and thank you again for having Lucy and me to stay with you. We had a wonderful time. Lucy has gone out, has Harvey told you what happened?"

"Yes, Lucy has nothing to worry about. Harvey loves her, he's not interested in Hayley."

"I hope that I can get her to believe that! I will try my very best Ed, au revoir, take care."

"Goodbye darlin'."

Flo put down the phone and sat by the window, staring out at the heavy rain. She decided to call Dorothy. The phone rang and rang. Eventually an out-of-breath Dorothy answered.

"Hello, Dorothy Hamilton-Smythe."

"Bonjour Dorothy. It is me, Florence. How are you?"

"Florence, my darling girl! How lovely to hear from you! Did you have a nice time in the US?"

"Oui, it was wonderful, merci. I have so much to tell you! I am also looking forward to starting my first modelling assignment."

"Good darling!"

Dorothy coughed. The phone went quiet.

"Are you still there Dorothy?"

Dorothy coughed again.

"Dorothy?" Flo asked, feeling concerned.

"Oh my darling, I'm sorry about that! I'm a little under the weather at the moment. I have John's nurse here looking after me."

Flo was worried. "Can I come and visit you?"

"Yes, it would be nice to see you. When would you like to come round?"

"I would not want to tire you out, I will just stop by to

discuss a couple of things, tell you about Dallas, and give you a couple of small souvenirs, if I may?"

"Of course, I would love to see you! I will send Richard to collect you at say... Twelve o'clock?"

"Perfection! See you later. Au revoir."

Flo was excited to see Dorothy again. As the morning wore on, she became anxious as to where Lucy may have gone. Despite ringing and texting, Lucy wouldn't answer. Flo could only assume that she had gone to the café. She scribbled a note saying that she was visiting Dorothy, and wasn't sure when she would be home, also mentioning that Harvey had rung and Ed had spoken to her, backing Harvey's story. She signed it Flo with two kisses and a sad face, followed by a *"P.S. Harvey has not done anything wrong"*, adding another two kisses and a heart with an arrow through it.

Flo opened her umbrella as she stumbled out the front door and into the street to greet Richard who was opening the passenger door to the Bentley.

"Good day, Madam."

Flo grappled with the flimsy umbrella "Here, let me help." He closed it with ease, and Flo climbed into the front seat.

"Merci, Richard."

In no time they arrived at Dorothy's. Despite Richard explaining that her health had taken a turn for the worse, Florence was shocked when she saw Dorothy who looked pale and drawn.

"Darling! Come in!"

Florence followed her into the lounge and sat down, looking around at the beautiful room, which appeared even more stunning in the daytime.

They talked about Dallas and all the places Flo had visited. She told Dorothy about how Ed had saved her life when she sank to the bottom of the swimming pool. Then she produced a fridge magnet, a souvenir from Southfork, a small bear wearing cowboy attire, and half a dozen postcards of pictures of the characters from the TV programme Dallas.

Dorothy was so happy that Flo had been thoughtful enough to bring home these little gifts for her, and got up to give her a kiss. Dorothy felt dizzy and swayed slightly, then stumbled.

"Ooh!"

"Shall I call your nurse?" Flo asked grabbing Dorothy's arm to steady her.

"I got up too quickly. Thank you darling, besides, I gave my nurse the afternoon off."

Dorothy and Flo sat and chatted and didn't notice the time, until Dorothy glanced at her watch.

"Oh my! Are you hungry darling? The day has slipped by so quickly! It's been such a lovely afternoon I do so enjoy your company! Would you consider moving in with me for a couple of weeks? I could show you everything there is to know about Silent Senses and you would be such a tonic for my health!"

"Moi? A tonic? Really?"

"Yes darling! You are like a breath of fresh air!"

"I would love to stay here but I must warn you, I am more than a little accident prone. I can't help but break things! I would worry that I would ruin some of your precious antiques."

"Oh my goodness!" Dorothy chuckled. "Don't worry about that! I'll soon be long gone and I can't take them with me! Anyway, if they get broken, we can always glue them back together!"

Flo looked at Dorothy with admiration and held her hand. She could see how Dorothy's health had deteriorated.

"I will have to run it past Lucy. She may need me at the moment though. She is having boyfriend trouble. My brother Harvey and her are an item now but there is someone else who is trying to make trouble for them." Flo smiled at Dorothy. "It is a long story."

"Would you like something to eat, Florence?"

Flo looked at her watch. "I really should go now, thank you very much for a nice afternoon. I will let you know when I can move in. I am sure that Lucy will not mind."

Dorothy called Richard who waited for Flo with the car.

"Thank you for my souvenirs!" Dorothy waved and called out as the car pulled away. Flo gave an enthusiastic wave and blew a kiss.

"She's a nice lady."

Richard smiled. "Yes she is. She's one of the best."

The rain had stopped by the time they reached Lucy's flat.

"Thank you Richard. I am hoping to move in with Dorothy soon, so I will no doubt see you more often."

"That's nice. I hope to see you soon Florence. Goodbye for now."

Lucy was home and called out as Flo entered the flat.

"Hi Flo."

"Hello my friend!"

Flo popped her head around the bedroom door. Lucy was sitting cross-legged on her bed, flicking through the photographs on her phone.

"Bloody men! Why did I have to go and fall in love?"

"I have something important to run past you." Flo said excitedly as she plonked herself down next to Lucy.

"What's that?" Lucy asked, concentrating on her phone.

"Dorothy has asked me to move in with her, but I guess you need me?"

Lucy yawned. "If you want to stay with her, please don't let me hold you back."

Flo put her arm around Lucy. "Have you spoken to my

brother yet? Have you been drinking?" Flo asked, sniffing her friend's breath and detecting a strong smell of alcohol.

"Yes I have. I needed a little Dutch courage to telephone your brother and tell him where to get off!"

"You did not! Did you?" Flo asked looking shocked.

"Oh I did! Indeed I did!" Lucy started to cry.

"I told him, I didn't believe him. I told him that I knew he would end up with Hayley as soon as I boarded the plane."

"What did he say to that?"

"He denied it! Am I being stupid Flo? I can't trust a man. Why do I always have doubts?"

"It is understandable that you have doubts after what happened to you! But not every man is a liar and a cheat. I am sure that Harvey is telling the truth."

"Well, I have told him that I don't want to see him ever again!" Lucy flopped back onto her bed. "God! I feel like a teenager again! What the hell is wrong with me?"

"I shall make you some coffee. Then we shall talk." Flo marched off to the kitchen. Then she appeared five minutes later with two mugs of coffee and the biscuit tin.

"The trouble is, my brother lives too far away! It is not something you can resolve over the telephone."

"Tell me about it! I should have known that a long distance relationship wouldn't work! It's for the best that I finished it. I shall just put it down as a holiday romance." Lucy burst into tears again.

"Do you want to know what I think? I think that you really do love Harvey!"

Lucy wailed. "I do!"

"Then maybe you should believe what he has told you?"

"Nope! It's for the best! Anyway, who knows when we will see each other again!"

Flo couldn't help but feel slightly annoyed. They were perfect for each other.

"I am hungry, I am going to make a sandwich, have you eaten?"

Lucy wailed again. "Yes!"

All the while Flo was in the kitchen making a cheese sandwich, she could hear Lucy's drunken wails. She sat on her own at the table, Lucy went quiet. When Flo checked in on her Lucy was sprawled out and sound asleep. Flo covered her with the duvet and left her to sleep, muttering "My silly Lucy. You are making a big mistake!"

CHAPTER TWENTY-FIVE

Weeks soon passed and Flo was enjoying her modelling career far more than she had ever imagined. Dorothy was impressed by Flo's ability to work with the photographers, she was a natural.

They spent almost every day together and Flo enjoyed the company of her aunt in the evenings. It was true, she was a good tonic; Dorothy's health had shown a great improvement.

Harvey had spoken to Flo every week, even chatting to Dorothy. He had a heavy workload and wasn't able to visit the UK, though he promised to make time soon. Truth be known, he was avoiding Lucy, since she refused to speak to him.

It was Saturday morning, a week since Lucy had heard from Flo. She had to call her.
Flo's phone buzzed on the bedside table. She picked it up bleary-eyed.

"Bonjour Lucy! Do you missing me? I am missing you! I have so very much to tell you!"

"Hello Flo. I need to talk to you! Can I see you later?" Lucy asked firmly.

"Oui, shall I meet you at the café?"

"No, can you come to the flat?"
Flo propped herself up on one elbow, glancing at the alarm clock, which showed seven thirty.

"It is only half past seven, it is Saturday is it not? This

sounds important my friend!"

"It is!"

"Ok, I shall see you at around nine thirty. Au revoir."

Flo flew out of bed and into the shower. She felt excited, imagining that Lucy was going to tell her that she was back with Harvey again.
Dorothy was sitting at the table in her spacious pure white kitchen, reading the newspaper. Flo kissed her aunt's cheek and poured a mug of coffee.

"How are you feeling today?"

Dorothy smiled, "Not too bad darling. How are you?"

"I'm excited! I think Lucy is back with my brother! She wants me to go to the flat so that she can tell me!"

"Oh that's good! Have some breakfast first darling."

"I will just have some cereal thanks."

Flo poured some cornflakes into her bowl, which came out a little too fast and ended up overflowing all over the table.

"Oops!" She picked up handfuls of flakes and crammed them back into the box.

"Pardon, I am so clumsy!" Dorothy chuckled.

"For a minute I thought it was because you were feeling very hungry! Ha ha!"

After breakfast, Flo telephoned her father and filled him in on all the details of her eventful week, making sure that her precious papa was happy and well. Since his engagement to Eloise, Flo contacted him just once a week instead of every day. She knew that he was being taken good care of, and happy that he was deeply in love with his fiancée.

"I've been on two photo shoots, visited the perfume factory and had dinner with a couple of television stars. Papa, life is such fun! I am loving every minute! Every second! Dorothy is such a lovely person. You shall have to meet her!"

Jack listened with wonder as his daughter babbled with excitement about all the events of her week.

"That sounds good Flo, I am so glad that you are enjoying your new life! Have a quick word with Eloise."

Flo happily chatted to her, then promised to send some photos.

"Au revoir Papa." Dorothy smiled. She listened to a one-sided phone conversation in English and French and gathered that her great niece was entirely happy.

"I am off now." Flo kissed Dorothy's cheek, rang for Richard, and was gone.

Dorothy muttered to herself. "Like a whirlwind that girl! Like a whirlwind…"

Flo burst through the door of Lucy's flat, making her usual noisy entrance.

"Yoo-hoo! C'est moi!"

Lucy emerged, still in her pyjamas.

"Hey!"

"Hey" Flo studied her friend before giving her a kiss.

"You look rough. Are you ill?"

"No, I'm not ill. I'm pregnant!"

Lucy rushed to the loo and threw up.

Florence stood in a daze! Lucy's news came as a complete shock! She hurried to the kitchen, poured a glass of water and took it to Lucy, who was standing in the bathroom looking pale and vulnerable.

"Drink!"

"Thank you."

"Does Harvey know?"

"No!"

"Why not?"

"Because I'm not talking to him!"

"He should know! What are you going to do?"
Lucy held her head. "I don't know! I only did the test yesterday!"

"You did it yesterday and you only just told me today?"

"It was a shock! I did another test to double check, and then a third, they were all positive!" Lucy pointed to the bin.

"Well, come on, I'll make you some tea and we can talk." Flo said putting her arm through Lucy's.

"No tea! I can't drink tea any more. A glass of milk will suffice."

"Come on then. Milk it is!"

Flo made herself some tea, poured Lucy some milk and made her a slice of toast. They sat in deep thought.

"I don't want Harvey to know. Not until I've decided what to do."

"What do you mean, until you have decided what to do? You are surely not thinking of...?"

"No, I could never do that! You should know me better than that Flo!"

"Yes, I am sorry."

"I meant... I don't know if I really want him to know."

"But he's the father, he has a right to know, does he not?"

"It was a holiday romance he hasn't contacted me since I told him to get lost!"

"I think that you will find, he thought of you as more than a holiday romance!"

"I thought that too, when we were in Texas, but looking back, was it more? As soon as my back was turned, Hayley was in bed with him!"

"That was not so! She came onto him. He was drunk, she took advantage, he told me what happened. Hayley is a little minx, she set him up to make it look like they had slept together."

"They did sleep together! All night apparently!"

"But Harvey knew nothing about it! He passed out! He was drunk! As far as Harvey knows, all they did was sleep next to each other, rather than sleep together."

"Oh I don't know what to believe. It all looked rather suspicious! Why hasn't he been in touch then?"

"Because you, my dear friend, are stubborn, and told him to get lost!!!"

Lucy put her head in her hands. "How can I bring up a child on my own?"

"Tell Harvey! Then you won't have to!"

"Oh I can just imagine the conversation! Hi Harvey, it's Lucy! I didn't mean to tell you to get lost! Could we get back together, because... Hey! I'm having your baby!"

"Well, if you put it like that!" Flo grabbed hold of Lucy's hand. "He has been in touch with me. He asks after you every time we speak! He is a good man, I'm sure he will stand by you. Do you love him?"

"Love! What is love? I loved Roy! Look what he did to me, he shattered my faith in men. I came home early to hear laughter coming from our bedroom. He was in our bed with that woman. I will never get that image out of my head!"

"Put it this way, would you like to trust Harvey?"

"Of course! I slept with him! I don't sleep around I must have felt something for him! I'm so bloody confused! If Hayley wasn't on the scene my mind would be a lot clearer! Oh gosh, what should I do?"

Flo shook her head. "I do not know. Perhaps you should give him a call? Maybe not mention the baby yet, but just talk?"

"Yes, you're right. I can't ignore the fact that he told me that he loved me when we were together. I did feel strongly for him. I want to trust him, I really do! Maybe if I break the ice by at least speaking to him."

"Great! You do that ma chérie."

"I will! It's settled! I shall call him later and just talk to him."

"Have you told your parents yet?"

"Gosh no! They are the last people I need right now!"

"But you will of course have to tell them soon, how many weeks are you exactly?"
"Work it out Flo. It's not rocket science! I'm sorry, that was uncalled for, when I missed my first period, I thought it was because I was on antibiotics for that throat infection, but when I missed the second one and kept feeling sick, I realised that I might be pregnant!"

"Hey! Do you feel like a little retail therapy?" Flo jumped up from her chair, hoping Lucy would agree.

"Why not? I'll get dressed and we'll pop into town."

The two girls hadn't seen each other for a few weeks due to Flo's new work schedule. It was nice to spend some time together. They popped in and out of the clothes shops, picking up the odd bargain, then they passed a shop window showcasing prams and baby clothes.

"Oh, très agréable. Très mignon."

"Yes, very cute!" Lucy dragged Flo passed the shop window. "I don't want to start looking at baby clothes, it will make it all too real."

They stopped at the café for lunch.

"I think that you have to avoid certain foods like pâté, and brie, is this so?"

Lucy looked thoughtfully at the menu. "Yes, I believe you're right. I'd better stick to a cheese toasty."

They sat in their favourite window seats and watched as people went by. One young woman passed with four children and a baby in a pram.

"Poor love! She looks exhausted! I couldn't imagine having five kids! One is going to be hard enough!"

"You will be a great mother! I am slightly envious of you. I do not know when I will ever settle down with a steady boyfriend, let alone a family."

"You my French friend are drop-dead gorgeous! You will find someone soon."

"Well, I do not know when this will happen. My life is jam-packed with everything else at the moment."

After lunch, they kissed cheeks, hugged and went their separate ways.

"I'll call you and let you know how it goes when I've spoken to Harvey!" Lucy called out.
Florence waved.

Back at the flat, Lucy sat on her own in her quiet kitchen. She really missed Flo. The silence was too much to bear. She headed to her studio and prepared her paints in order to complete a commissioned canvas for a wealthy business man who wanted some artwork for his office in town. Harvey was on her mind. She reached into her bag and glanced at her phone. There were texts from Harvey!

"Hey hun, how are you? I know that you told me to get lost but I can't x x!"

Her heart skipped with excitement! Just when she needed reassurance there it was! She opened the next text.

"Honey, please don't ignore me! I'm coming to London again next week. I need to see you x x."

Lucy, felt a mixture of emotions, happiness and panic! If he saw her next week he would be able to tell that she didn't look right and she'd have to tell him about the pregnancy. Her phone buzzed again.

"I am booking into a hotel, I really want to see you, are you free to meet up when I come to London? X"

Her phone buzzed again and again.

She was bombarded with texts, one after the other, then there was one from Flo.

"Just had a text from my brother. He is coming to London next week. He wants to see you! He is coming here to meet with Dorothy and me too. I told you he is a good guy x x"

Lucy texted back.

"I'm suspicious, you haven't told him have you? X"

"NO WAY! x"

"Ok x"

"Dorothy has asked Harvey to stay here x"

"What did he say? x"

"Yes x"

Lucy texted Harvey.

"I'm happy to see you. To talk. Lucy x x"

Lucy felt a little happier and painted with ease, singing loudly to the Abba tunes blasting from her stereo.

CHAPTER TWENTY-SIX

Hayley's mind was totally mixed up, she'd never felt so lost and out of control. Depression set in every time her thoughts wandered back to Wayne. She stood before Ed feeling ashamed and confused at the way she was behaving but she simply couldn't help herself.

Ed called Mitch and Jane and told them that their daughter was at the ranch.

"Cover yourself up young lady!" Ed demanded, handing her a robe. "Have you got any clothes with you?"

He looked at the girl standing before him, hair bedraggled, makeup smudged, body barely covered with a see-through basque.

"Have you no shame?"

Hayley looked pathetic. "I'm sorry Ed, I was drunk! Harvey took advantage of me!"

"I don't believe that! I saw the state my son was in last night! He wouldn't have been capable of taking advantage, anyway what were you doing here in the first place? How the hell did you get in?"

"I have a key!"

"You've changed Hayley! You aren't the sweet girl you used to be! Wayne has messed with your mind, you need help!"

"I'll get dressed and get out of your hair."

She made her way to the bathroom, passing Harvey in the

hallway. He barged past her, not even glancing her way.

When Hayley appeared again, her hair was brushed and put up in pigtails, her face clean and innocent looking with no trace of makeup. Ed and Harvey both looked at the tiny young woman standing in the doorway. She looked like the child they used to know. Both men felt sadness as memories flooded into their minds of the sweet, fun-loving child she used to be.

"I'll go now then. I'm sorry Harvey." She stood on tiptoe to kiss his cheek, Harvey pulled back, dodging her. She shrugged her shoulders, pouted her lips and kissed Ed's cheek.

"Go and see a doctor Hayley, he'll help you to get Wayne out of your head!"

"I can't, he nearly killed me, how will I ever forget that?" She snapped.

"Yes but a shrink will help you! Listen to what I'm saying and accept help. Please?"

Hayley grabbed her bag and was gone, slamming the kitchen door, and speeding off in her car, leaving behind a cloud of dust.
Both men heaved a sigh of relief.

"The trouble she's caused! How am I ever going to get Lucy to believe that nothing happened? She told me to get lost! She doesn't want to see me again!"

"Well if there is anything I can do to help, I will Harv."

Over the next few weeks Harvey contacted Florence and

always asked after Lucy. The longer he was away from her the more he missed her. Every day he looked at the photographs on his phone, and longed to hold her again.

Finally he decided to book a flight to London. He had waited long enough. He didn't want Lucy to meet someone else, he had to see her. He texted her and Flo to tell them he would be visiting. Florence was over the moon, she told Dorothy that her brother was coming to London again and Dorothy insisted that he stay with them instead of booking himself into a hotel. Harvey texted Lucy and told her of his plans, she agreed to meet up and talk, but as she didn't suggest that he stay with her he accepted Dorothy's kind offer, thinking it would be a good way of getting to know his great-aunt.

Things went quiet with regards to Hayley until the day after Harvey had booked his flight to London when he received a text from her.

"Harv, I need to talk. There's something I must tell you. It's really important! x x"

Harvey's heart sank. He couldn't think what could be so important but he wasn't in the mood for any more of Hayley's tricks.

"What is so important?"

"I can't explain by phone or text, I need to see you. Can I come over today? x x"

"No, I will come and meet you halfway. Let's meet in Waco in that little bar we used to drink in.

"Ok, shall we say 2.00ish? x x"

"*Yep.*"

Ed had gone out with the ranch hands up to the creek for a day of fishing. He texted his father saying that he was going into town, but didn't mention Hayley.

Harvey arrived at the saloon bar later that day, and waited for Hayley to arrive. He felt anxious and swallowed down a Jack and Coke for Dutch courage.

Hayley waltzed in wearing pink jeans, white cowboy boots, and a white open shirt over a white vest.

"Howdy cowboy!" She boldly cried as she sat down next to him.

"Get to the point Hayley! I'm not here to mess about!"

"Are you gonna offer me a drink?"

"What would you like?"

"Just an orange juice."

Harvey looked at her in disbelief. "An orange juice?"

"Yep, I am a reformed woman!"

Harvey ordered her drink and sat down, waiting for her to speak.

"I'll cut to the chase, I'm having your baby Harv."

"What?!"

"Yes, your baby!"

"Ha, ha, ha, you have got to be kidding me!"

"What's so funny honey?"

"Well, aside from the fact that I've never laid a finger on you, I think it's quite funny, don't you?"

"Ah yes, but you did! You made love to me all night when you were drunk!"

"Hell no! I passed out!"

"You passed out after we made love, over and over and over again! Like I said, it was the best night of my life! Stud!"

"I don't believe you!"

"Well, you had better! It's your baby I'm carrying in here." She felt her stomach.

"How many weeks are you?"

"Ten"

Harvey thought back to the night he ended up on the bathroom floor. He remembered being really turned on by Hayley, but that was all he could remember.

"Hell honey, you gotta be jokin'. I'm not the father!"

"Oh yes you are!" She dug around in her bag and found her phone. She had photographs of her and Harvey on the bathroom floor. One she had managed to take of herself sitting on him, and one which looked as though he was on top of her."

Harvey's stomach churned. His eyes dropped and he stared at his empty glass.

"What do you want from me?"

"I have my scan in a couple of weeks. We can take it from there."

"So you're keepin' it?"

"What do you mean, I'm keeping it? Of course I'm frickin' keepin' it! It's a baby, not a doll!"

"Sorry, sorry, of course you are. Have you told Jane and Mitch yet?"

"No one else knows."

"Hang on a minute! Word has it that you've been heavily drinking lately! Isn't that harmful to a baby?"

"Yes, but I've only just found out I'm pregnant! That's why I can't wait for my scan, just to make sure that everything is OK."

"And if it's not?"

"Well, if it's not, I... We will have to deal with it."

Hayley got up and put her chair next to Harvey's. She put her head on his shoulder. "You and me, Mom and Dad, who'd 'a' thought eh?"

Harvey stood. "I gotta go. Let me know how the scan goes. I'll be in London on business."

Hayley looked angry. "You're going to see her aren't you?"

"Well, she is my girlfriend!"

"Really! I thought she didn't want anything to do with you?"

"That's my business."

"She won't want you back if she hears that we are having a baby!" Hayley grinned.

"Don't you dare contact Lucy! If what you are saying is true, it'll be me that tells her. I want proof that the baby is mine before you wreck our lives!"

"So, will you make an honest woman of me?"

"You're not listening! It's not you I want to marry! I will make sure that I'm there for the child, if I really am the father, but that's all."

Hayley glared at him. Her plan wasn't working! Maybe he just needed some time for the news to sink in.

She put her arms around him, "Honey, we've known each other for a long time! Let's not fall out! I love you!"

Harvey pushed her away. "I liked the old you Hayley. I really don't like the new you! Send me a picture of the scan, and promise me that you won't tell Lucy?"

"I don't know if I can promise Harvey, I'll try and keep it a secret, if that's the way you want it?"

She made it sound so sordid, Harvey felt disgusted with her and himself, what a mess! He said goodbye and left her standing in the middle of the bar with a smirk on her face. Right there and then he despised her!

Back at the ranch Harvey sat by the pool, drinking a beer and staring at the clear water, thinking of his red-headed beauty and himself, skinny-dipping. The sound of her laughter and her naked body was a happy memory. Why did he have to get so drunk the night she left for London?

Just then Susan called out to him. "Bye Harvey, see you tomorrow!"

"Bye Susan, thanks hun, see you tomorrow!"

He sat alone, looking around at the beautiful surroundings, listening to the gentle breeze rustling the leaves on the trees, the distant sound of his horses neighing, and the hens clucking. He thought to himself, "I have everything I want and need, except for the one person who I should be with, but now everything is about to change forever." He couldn't wait for his father to return from his fishing trip, so that he could share his burden and ask his advice.

Back in London Lucy was excited at the prospect of seeing Harvey again. She kept rehearsing how she was going to tell Harvey her news.

"Harvey, I have something to tell you... Harv, hun, I have some important news..! Harvey I have something important to say, you are going to be a dad... Harvey? How do you feel about babies...? Hun, you and me... Oh gosh! How the hell do I tell him?"

Lucy downed a glass of ice-cold milk. She stared at herself in the mirror, she was showing already. She checked her diary for the date and time of her scan, as she'd done on numerous occasions before. She desperately missed Flo. Feeling all alone she decided to text Harvey.

Harvey's phone buzzed. He woke from his daydream, and smiled with delight to see a text from Lucy.

"Hello Harv, how are things? I'm looking forward to you coming to London."

He texted back. *"Good to hear from you baby I am missing you like crazy! X"*

Lucy's emotions were all over the place; she was really hormonal and needed a hug.

"I'm missing you too. X"

Harvey felt so much better, now that Lucy was missing him. Somehow, some way he had to prove to her that he loved her.

"Not long now until I can hold you in my arms again."

"I can't wait."

He felt so happy at that moment, then he remembered Hayley and her news. His world crashed again with a bump. Maybe she had tricked him... but her photographs looked pretty convincing.

He lay on a chaise lounge and closed his eyes, imagining that he was holding Lucy in his arms. He could smell her perfume, feel her soft naked skin. Her face was so beautiful, her smile enchanting, her voice so posh and English, her laugh captivating and infectious. She had to be the one for him, nothing was going to get in the way, he just had to convince Lucy that Hayley had manipulated him into sleeping with her and that everything was just a big mistake. He was sickened by what Hayley said they did. How the hell was he going to get her to believe him?

Harvey went for a run, the day was drawing to an end and he needed to clear his head. He ran for three miles, thoughts racing through his mind, it suddenly dawned on him; he needed to check the dates of the scan. If what Hayley claimed was true, she would be roughly twelve weeks at the scan, any more than that and the baby was Joe's or even Wayne's! The trouble was, she was having the scan while he was in London. He felt a little optimistic on his return to the ranch. Ed was back and was surprised to find that Harvey had been running.

"Hey Son! Something troubling you? You usually only run when there's something on ya mind!"

"Yes Pa, there is. I'll fill you in over dinner. Susan has prepared a casserole for us. I'll just shower and change."
Ed was intrigued to find out what was going on, suspecting that it had something to do with Hayley.

They sat at the table eating and drinking beer. Ed cut large chunks of crusty bread to accompany their delicious chicken casserole.

"So Harv, what's eatin' ya?"

"I've booked a flight to London. Lucy and I are talking again. She's agreed to see me, even told me that she misses

me. Dorothy has asked me to stay with her." He paused for thought. "But... I had to meet Hayley today, she said she had something important to tell me..."
d waited.

"Yeah?"

"Pa she reckons she's pregnant, and the baby is mine!"

"Jeez boy! No way!"

"Pa she has these pictures on her phone and they look as though I'm... I'm, well you know!"

"Do you think they are for real?"

"They look real enough but they could be quite innocent! I truly think she's trying to mess with me! She's having a scan when I'm in London. I need to know how far gone she is. I think it's Joe's, or it could even be Wayne's!"

"So how are you gonna find out the truth?"

"Maybe Jane would tell us?"

"Does Jane even know?"

"That's just it! I'm the only other person that knows!"

"Hell, we'll have to get hold of the scan results Harv."

"How are we gonna do that? I won't even be here!"

"Find out the date and time of her appointment, then leave it with me."

Harvey was uneasy, but felt that a little skulduggery was needed.

CHAPTER TWENTY-SEVEN

Harvey made his way out of the airport and was greeted by Richard, Dorothy's driver, who was holding a piece of white card with Harvey Dove written boldly on it.

The two men vigorously shook hands and talked along the way about the weather and the flight, until they reached the car park.

Back at Dorothy's house, Florence bounced up to Harvey and greeted him with a large kiss on both cheeks, followed by Dorothy who made a shaky entrance holding on to her walking stick. Harvey couldn't help but notice how frail she had become.

"How are you?" Harvey inquired sympathetically.

"I am fine thank you, how about you?" Dorothy replied, slightly out of breath.

Florence was highly excited! "There is someone waiting in the lounge to see you!" She pointed the way, and headed into the kitchen with Dorothy.

Harvey opened the lounge door to find Lucy standing before him with a beautiful smile on her face.

"Hey!"

"Hey!"

"Come here." Harvey rushed towards her and embraced her with open arms.

Lucy buried her face in his shoulder. His familiar smell of

aftershave took her back to Dallas.

"Gosh, I've missed you!"

Harvey felt happy.

"Lucy, I've missed you too. How have you been? Have you had a lot of work?"

"I have been busy I've also had time to think about us. I'm not going to let Hayley come between our happiness. I can see that she needs help Harv, she needs to see a shrink so that she can get her head sorted. Do you agree?"

Harvey felt sick at the thought of Hayley.

"I do hun, she is sick. She never used to be like that! She was always a bit overdramatic, but she never lied... Speaking of lies..."

Just then, Flo burst through the door, beaming from ear to ear at seeing them both in each other's arms.

"Je suis très heureux."

Harvey didn't know what Flo had said but kind of got the gist.

"Group hug darlings." Dorothy announced as she held her arms open and pulled them all together. "Now then, who would like a glass of champagne?"

Flo answered "Moi, s'il vous plait."

Harvey needed a glass.

"Not for me thanks, could I have a glass of milk please?" Lucy asked, feeling a little awkward.

"No champagne? Darling, I have a nice red, if you prefer, or maybe a spirit?"

"No, just milk please?" Feeling and looking very awkward, Lucy excused herself and asked where the bathroom was, leaving Harvey a little puzzled, for he knew that Lucy loved a glass of champagne. He looked at Florence and asked, "Is Lucy ill?"

"No, she is not ill."

Florence coloured up and hurried after Lucy, leaving Harvey and Dorothy in the lounge. They both shrugged their shoulders, and looked at each other with puzzled expressions.

Flo whispered to Lucy, "How are you going to get through this without being obvious?"
Lucy looked decidedly flustered, "Oh gosh! I shall just tell them that I can't drink alcohol because I'm on antibiotics."

"That is a good idea!"

When they both returned to the lounge Harvey lovingly put his arm around Lucy's waist. "Not like you to refuse a glass of bubbly Hun!"

"Yes, I'm taking pills for a throat infection."

"I thought you looked a little peaky!"

They all sat together and enjoyed a hearty meal cooked by Martha.

"I thought a typical English meal would be a good idea. Nothing like roast beef eh?" Dorothy declared, looking deliriously happy to be spending time with her family. Every time Flo glanced at her aunt, she was smiling or laughing. Harvey felt at ease and forgot his troubles back home. Lucy felt nothing but love for him, he was so handsome and charming, and he was being so attentive towards her. Flo noticed that Harvey gently touched her at every opportunity.

"This has been so wonderful darlings!" Dorothy said with a yawn. "I'm exhausted now, would you excuse me please, I need my sleep. Lucy you are welcome to stay tonight. Harvey, Martha has taken your case to your room. Flo will show you where you are sleeping."

"Thank you for your hospitality, it's been awesome." Harvey said as he pulled out her chair and kissed her on the cheek. "You look done in."

Dorothy leaned heavily on her walking stick and made her way to bed.

Lucy was worn out and didn't relish the thought of being the only one to leave the house to go home to an empty flat, even though Richard was on hand to drive her.

"Stay?" Flo asked.

"I could come back to the flat with you, if you don't want to stay." Harvey suggested. "If I'm not being too presumptuous."

Lucy was too tired to think about going home. "I think I'd like to stay here Harvey."

"Good, you look plumb tuckered out."

Lucy kissed him on the lips, a soft gentle kiss which told him that she was still very much in love with him. Her feelings for him were even stronger now that she'd seen his gorgeous face again. He reciprocated her kiss with tenderness in his lips and longing in his eyes. Flo could feel the warmth was back in their relationship and felt happy for her best friend.

"Come on you two! I'll show you where your room is." She leapt up enthusiastically from her chair and beckoned excitedly for them to follow her up the large winding staircase, feeling like the lady of the manor, and proud that she lived with Dorothy in such an amazing house.

Harvey lay in bed and waited for Lucy, who appeared in the doorway dressed in pale pink silk and lace pyjama's borrowed from Dorothy. The silky fabric draped softly over the contours of her perfect breasts. She slid next to him under the warm duvet, the silk seductively touching his naked body. He reached over and touched her cheek. Then leaned over and kissed her eyelids.

"Don't."

"Huh?"

"Please don't Harv. I'm so tired, I just need sleep."

Harvey's thoughts were muddled. "Maybe she won't let me near her because of Hayley. She must still believe the texts.

"Please love, Hayley manipulated me! You have to trust me on that! I was so drunk and I didn't know what I was doing!"

"I just need sleep Harv." Lucy turned her back on him. She was afraid to tell him that she was pregnant. Her heart was pounding; she wanted him so much but was afraid to make love, in case he suspected what she was hiding from him.

Harvey lay wide awake, staring at the ceiling. Lucy lay beside him also wide awake, watching the digital alarm clock. Sleep wouldn't come for either of them; they both had so much on their minds.

"Are you awake?" Harvey whispered.

Lucy ignored him and lay still.

"I just want to say that I've never felt like this about anyone else Lucy. Life has been kind to me, but I've never been happier than I am when I'm with you."

Lucy wanted to turn over and hold him but she remained still. They both eventually drifted off to sleep.

Reality woke Harvey from a pleasant dream about Lucy and himself stacking firewood into an inglenook fireplace in a huge English country mansion. Instantly Hayley was on his mind. He sat up, Lucy wasn't next to him, but he could hear her retching in the en-suite. Throwing back the duvet and leaping from the bed, he knocked gently on the bathroom door.

"Lucy, are you ill?"

There was no answer, Lucy went silent, his unexpected knock on the door bringing an abrupt silence to her morning sickness.

"Hun, I thought I heard you throwing up?"

"I'm fine, thank you!" Lucy just wanted him to leave her alone.

"If there's anything you need, just shout!"

"I will." Lucy was sick again. This time Harvey was really concerned.

"Let me in hun."

"No, I'm alright, I think I must have a reaction to the antibiotics. I'll come out in a bit, when I've stopped being sick."

Harvey sat on the bed and waited. When Lucy emerged from the bathroom, she looked pale and drawn.

"We should get you to a doctor, if those pills are making you sick you should get a different prescription, come here, sit here."

He patted the bed and Lucy sat beside him. She rested her head on his shoulder; a tear trickled down her cheek and fell on her satin pyjamas.

"What's wrong? Why are you crying?" he asked, taking her chin in his hand and facing her, looking into her eyes for an explanation.

"Harvey, I don't know how to tell you."

He jumped up, fearing bad news! "Oh jeez! What?"

"It's nothing bad! At least not for me… Harvey… I'm having your baby!"

Harvey stood and stared at her.

"I can't hide it! I have such bad morning sickness; I'm not really on antibiotics."

She looked at him. He seemed confused, worried even.

"Say something?!"

Harvey's mind went into overdrive, he thought "Now, of all the times in my life. I should be over the moon at this news but it's the worst timing ever! Could he be Father to two women's babies at the same time?"

Lucy sat on the bed waiting for him to say something.

"Any reaction would be good! Are you angry? Happy? Disappointed? What?" She asked with a shaky voice.

He still just stood there, unable to utter a word.

Lucy grabbed the dressing gown hanging on the door and rushed out, slamming the door behind her.

Flo was on her way down the stairs.

"Attendez! What is wrong?" Lucy was in tears.

"I've just told your brother that I'm having his baby. No reaction! None, nada, nil, nothing! Bloody nothing!"

"Perhaps it was a shock!"

"I expect it was but I gave him the chance to say something and he just stood there!"

Harvey rushed out behind her and hugged her tightly.

"I'm sorry, I really am! I'm happy! Really I am! I'm so happy!" He had a huge grin on his face. Inside he was feeling a mixture of happiness and fear.

"Congratulations to you both! I am bursting with excitement!" Flo exclaimed, jumping up and down and clapping loudly.
"What's all this?" Dorothy asked as she entered the kitchen.

Harvey placed his hand on Lucy's stomach. He was surprised at the size of the bump.

"We are expecting!"

"Congratulations my darlings!"

Lucy smiled and said "I wasn't going to tell anyone until after my scan but it's a little hard to hide, especially as I can't drink and I can't stop being sick!"

Harvey kissed her cheek. "When is the scan?"

"On Monday. Will you come with me?"

"Try and stop me!"

Harvey thought about Hayley, her scan was also on Monday. What an impossible situation he was in. Happy about becoming a father to the woman he loves, and scared in case he is the father to another baby at the same time!

"I'll have to phone Pa and tell him!"

"Can you wait until we've had the scan? Only a couple of days."

"Sure hun." He wrapped his arms around her and rested his hands on her belly.
Dorothy sat down suddenly, feeling hot and looking pale.

"You look peaky, are you feeling poorly today?" Lucy asked. "Can I get you a glass of water?"

"Thank you darling, yes please, I'm feeling poorly today. I might go back to bed for a while."

Lucy handed her a glass and watched with concern as Dorothy drank. Her hands were shaking and she looked very frail, unlike the first time she met her, when she looked bold and glamorous.

"Darling would you help me up the stairs?" She asked, grabbing hold of Flo's arm.

When they left the room, Lucy looked at Harvey solemnly. "I don't think she has much longer on this earth."

"She is very ill isn't she! Poor woman, at least she's spent some time with Flo and got to know her."

"Yes, I think it's Flo who's kept her going! I'm going to have a shower." Lucy kissed his cheek and went upstairs, leaving Harvey alone at the kitchen table. He texted his father.

"Pa let me know the minute you find out anything about Hayley's scan."

CHAPTER TWENTY-EIGHT

Monday at the hospital was exciting. Harvey and Lucy sat in the waiting room holding hands. Flo sat beside them, equally as excited as they were. The sonographer called Harvey and Lucy into the room and helped Lucy onto the bed. Flo remained in the waiting room and nervously flicked through a couple of magazines, thrilled to see herself in one, advertising Silent Senses.

"Right Miss Bowes, this will feel cold," she said squirting ultrasound jelly all over her tummy.

Harvey squeezed Lucy's hand. The sonographer moved the wand over her swelling stomach and they all watched the screen with excited anticipation.

"There's baby, looking fit and well. Let's listen to the heartbeat."

Harvey smiled with pride as they listened to the boom, boom of the baby's heart.

"Hang on... We have another heartbeat!" She moved the wand around. "You have twins!"

"What!" Lucy sat up in disbelief, and stared at the screen.

"Yes, definitely twins, little one was hiding behind the other."

"Gosh! Twins! Gosh!" Lucy didn't know what else to say, she looked at Harvey who was beaming with pride!

"Instant family honey! That explains why your bump is showing already!"

"Oh gosh! I can't wait to tell Flo."

They found Flo in the waiting room, on all fours looking for her ring. She had apparently been playing with the ring on her finger, when it flew off and bounced underneath the chairs.

"Found it!" She declared, noticing that everyone was staring at her.

Back in Texas, Hayley went into the room by herself. The nurse checked her details and began the scan.

"Why have you only just come along for a scan? This is your first, right?" She questioned Hayley looking puzzled.

"Yes, it's my first scan why? Is there something wrong?"

"You are twenty-one weeks!"

"Twenty-one?"

"Maybe twenty-two!"

Hayley was shocked. "Are you sure?"

"Positive. Didn't you know?"

"I thought I was around twelve weeks. I've only missed two periods."

Hayley knew she was pregnant and had convinced herself it was Joe's. That way she could trick Harvey into believing it was his.

"Do you drink or smoke?"

"Well, I didn't know that I was pregnant and I did drink. I downed almost a bottle of vodka a few weeks ago! Have I harmed my baby?" Hayley asked in a panic.

The sonographer took her time scanning. "Everything looks OK. You must take more care of yourself from now on."

Hayley felt awful. All alone, pregnant with a baby who was obviously Wayne's. Her plan to trick Harvey had taken a turn for the worse. Her mind was racing, could she make out that the baby was premature perhaps? But then it might be a large baby. Hell, now what was she going to do?

The nurse gave her a handful of leaflets to read and a form to complete for a blood test.

Ed was hiding down the corridor. He watched Hayley head in the opposite direction and then nipped into the room.

The nurse looked up from her paperwork.
"Can I help you?"

"I need the results of the scan you've just done."

"I'm sorry, that's patient confidentiality. I'll have to ask you to leave."

"It's really important. She's trying to trick my son into believing that he's the father. All I need is the date it's due!"

"No, I'm sorry; you will have to ask her."

Ed produced a wad of money. "There's five hundred dollars here, cash. All I need is a date."

"I can't."

"Take it!" He said waving the money under her nose.

The nurse hesitated then pointed to the screen, it still had the picture of Hayley's scan with all the details upon it. She took the money, then turned her back on Ed.

"I can't see you, that's her scan."

Ed took out his phone and photographed the screen, then looked up and down the corridor before exiting the room, feeling elated, the dates proved that his son wasn't the father.

Back at the ranch, he printed off the scan picture and hid it in the safe. Then he texted Harvey.

"Son, she's five months pregnant. Not yours. Had to bribe the nurse. Hayley doesn't know that I have seen her scan. If she gets in touch, don't say anything."

Later Harvey read the text and breathed a sigh.

"Thank the Lord!"

He texted his father back. *"Pa, I'll call you tomorrow."*

The next day Ed's phone rang.

"Hey!"

"Hey Pa. Guess what?"

"You're happy?"

"I'm with Lucy. You need to sit down, I have some news for you... We are having twins!"

Ed sat down with a bump. "Twins? Boy! That's cause for celebration! When are they due?"

"We are twelve weeks! They're due in March."

"Son, that's great news!"
"I know! We're so happy!"

Harvey walked away from Lucy who was telling Flo all about her plans.

"Pa thanks for what you've done. I can't tell you how happy I am that everything has worked out. I knew Hayley was trying to trick me. I knew I was too drunk that night. If she's that far gone the baby must be Wayne's. How's she gonna deal with that? How are Miss Jane and Mitch gonna feel about it?"

"Well that's not our problem, but I feel for them all, knowing that psycho is the father. He hasn't even had his trial yet."

"Poor Hayley, I genuinely feel sorry for her. She must be due in January."

"I'll get in touch with her, see if she 'fesses up Harv."

"Is that wise? You don't want her to find out that you've got her scan results."

"No I don't but she might be thinking differently now that she knows she's five months gone, it'll be harder to pretend you're involved."

"Maybe I should get in touch?"

"Shall I leave it to you then son?"

"Yep, I'll do it later today Pa. Hey! On second thoughts, why don't you call Mitch and tell him about our news, tell him we are expecting twins, then he will tell Hayley and she might just drop all her accusations!"

"Good plan. I'll call him. I am going to be a grandpappy after all! I wanna share my news!"

"Bye for now Pa."

"Bye son."

When Harvey got back to Lucy and Flo they looked like two school girls chatting and giggling together.

"Come on my lovely ladies. I'm taking you to lunch!"

"Ooh great! I'm starving!" Lucy declared, rubbing her tummy.

"Me too!" Flo said and hooked her arm in Lucy's.

After lunch they all went back to Dorothy's. Her nurse came down the stairs, with Dorothy's doctor looking grim.

Flo put her hand to her forehead in a panic. "Is she...?"

"She's comfortable. She would like you all to go up and see

her."

As they entered Dorothy's bedroom, she managed to raise her hand and beckon them all to her bedside.

"Sit darlings." She said in a faint whisper. "How did the scan go?"

"We are having twins!" Lucy said, taking Dorothy's hand.

"Wonderful. Two little darlings to leave some inheritance to."

Flo started to weep. "Dorothy!"

"Goodbye my lovelies, I'm so pleased to have met you all."

She closed her eyes and fell into a deep sleep. Flo hysterically called down to the doctor, who rushed upstairs with the nurse. He took her pulse and listened to her heart, then shook his head.

"Nurse Moore." He nodded at her.

"I'm so sorry, she's gone. Gone to the Rainbow Bridge to be with her John. They are together now. I was with her husband when he died many years ago." She affectionately kissed her cheek.

They all kissed her and sadly went down the stairs. Harvey found Richard who wanted to see her so that he could say goodbye to her. He stood by her bed, bent down and gently kissed her forehead.

"Goodbye ma'am. I shall miss you more than you will ever know."

They couldn't console Flo, she was sobbing. "This should have been such a happy day, finding out that I will be auntie to twins. Poor Dorothy, I loved her, she was a wonderful woman!"

Harvey put a comforting arm around his little sister and pulled her close, he couldn't help but feel remorse for all the lost years.

"She has brought us all together, for that I will always be grateful."

CHAPTER TWENTY-NINE

Ed telephoned Mitch. Jane answered the phone.

"Hi Ed." She recognized his number.

"Howdy Janie! How y'all doing?"

"We are all fine thanks honey, how about you?"

"Well Janie, that's why I'm calling, I have some lovely news! Harvey and Lucy are making me a grandpappy."

"That's awesome!"

"That's not all. They are having twins!"

"Even more awesome!" She called out to Mitch. "Hey, Mitch, listen to this!"

She handed him the phone. "It's Ed, he's got something important to tell you."

"Hey Ed."

"Hey Mitch. I've just told Jane I'm going to be a grandpappy to twins!"

"Awesome news! Twins, lucky man, two at once!"

Hayley entered the kitchen and heard her father's side of the conversation. Looking puzzled she asked, "Twins? Who's having twins?"

Mitch put his hand over the mouthpiece. "Harvey."

Hayley sat down heavily on the chair. She went white and shaky. Jane rushed to her side. "Hun, what's wrong?"

Hayley knew that there was absolutely no way of ever winning Harvey now, she had to face the truth.

"Ma and Pa, just hold the line a minute will you please?"

"Ed, can you hang on a sec? What's up honey?"

"You are going to be grandparents too! I had my scan yesterday." She broke down. "It's Wayne's."

Jane put her hand to her mouth in shock! "Oh my God! How far gone are you?"

"Five months at least! I didn't know, I had no idea! It's his though Mama."

"Ed, can I call you back? Hayley isn't feeling so good."

"Sure Mitch." Ed imagined what Hayley's reaction to Harvey's news would be, and could only hope that she would confess to her parents about her pregnancy.

"Honey, we are here for you. You are having a baby, that's wonderful. It doesn't matter that Wayne's the father we can bring that baby up! You have our full support."

"My mind is all over the place Mama. I've been an absolute bitch to Harvey! He has always been so good to me and yet I've treated him like dirt! What's wrong with me?"

"I expect your hormones have been all over the place and what with Wayne causing all that pain and heartache, it's no wonder you haven't been yourself! I'll come with you to see

Dr Harper. I'll make the appointment straight away."

"Thank you Mama."

Mitch cuddled his daughter. "I'd never have guessed, where are you hiding the baby bump?"

"I have my scan picture to prove it, but my bump is so tiny, I am still in the same sized clothes!" She produced the ultrasound photo and they all studied it.

"My grandchild... I must phone Ed and tell him." Mitch called Ed back. "Hey Ed. Sorry about before. Hayley had something to tell us. It appears that we are going to be grandparents before you!"

Ed made out this was new to him. "Awesome! I bet you are pleased!" He chose his words carefully.

"Yes, we are!"

"When is it due?"

"January 6th." Mitch tried hard to hide his disappointment about Wayne being the father, and avoided any more questions by cutting short the conversation. "I'll call you later in the week fella to arrange a few celebratory beers. Bye for now!"

"Hmm, short and sweet! Ed said to himself placing the phone down. He called Harvey straight away.

"Hi Son. I got some great news!"

"Hey Pa, before your good news, I have some sad news. Dorothy has passed away." Ed could hear Flo sobbing in the background.

"Jeez son, I'm sorry to hear that."

"What about you?"

"I've just spoken to Mitch. He told me that Hayley is having a baby in January. You are off the hook son!"

It felt so good to hear his father's news. "I hope so Pa. I'll wait until I hear from Hayley."

"There's no way she can say that baby is yours! Just relax now and enjoy your time in London."

"I will Pa, thanks. I guess I'll be helping Flo arrange a funeral now though."

He walked away from everyone and spoke quietly to his father. "Do you think Mitch and Miss Jane know who the father is?"

"Well, she's told them it's due in January, so they must know it's Wayne's. Poor kid, you have to feel for her."

"I'm gonna call her later. I feel bad, I treated her like crap when I saw her last. She must be feelin' pretty damned low right now Pa."

"You're a good man Harv, but I'd wait until she phones you, she owes you an apology."

"Yeah, maybe you're right. I'll leave it for her to get in touch."

Later that day Harvey noticed a text from Hayley. It simply

read,

"*Sorry Harv. How can you ever forgive me for the way that I've been? I'm five months pregnant. Not yours, it's Wayne's. Congratulations to you and Lucy. X*"

Harvey texted back. "*Thank you. I do forgive you.*"

A few days later Ed called Harvey. "Son, I had a drink with Mitch last night. Hayley is in hospital she's had a bit of a breakdown. She's having some counselling. The sentencing is tomorrow. I was shocked at all the evidence, what a complete bastard, a sexual predator, I doubt he'll be out for a very long time! That poor girl, he has really messed her life up! She can't handle her business anymore. Let's hope they manage to make her better before she has the baby."

"I hope she accepts the baby, knowing that he's the father, it wouldn't surprise me if she doesn't."

"Yeah, it's a bit of a worry for them all. Hayley's lawyer has been representing her as she's in hospital. Jane and Mitch have attended every day and will be there for the sentencing."

"I hope they lock him up for good."

"They frickin' should do!"

"That'll make Hayley feel safer, knowing that psycho is locked up."

"Anyway son, I'll let you know how it goes. Hope the funeral goes well. Give my best to everyone."

Two weeks later Wayne was sentenced to ten years in prison. Mitch punched the air with delight. The same day in London, Dorothy's funeral was being held at the crematorium at one o'clock. It was a cold wet, miserable day. Harvey was staying at Lucy's flat, and woke to find himself in bed alone. Lucy was sitting in her kitchen drinking a glass of milk and eating a digestive biscuit.

"Hey my gorgeous mama-to-be, how are you feeling today? Any sickness this morning?"

"I'm trying not to think about it, so I'm starting the day with a dry biscuit and my craving... milk."

Harvey pictured her as a permanent fixture in his life. He had finally found 'the one'. She was the warmest, most genuine person he had ever met. Harvey wrapped his arms around Lucy and turned her around to face him.

"I'm so happy that you are having my babies Lucy Bowes."

Lucy kissed him. "Mr Dove, you are a very special man and I am also happy that I'm having your babies!"

"I'm dang glad you said that Miss Bowes, because I would love you to become Mrs Dove, before you actually have our baby Doves."

Lucy looked surprised as Harvey reached into his back pocket and produced a small red ring box. He placed it in her hand.

"Open it Miss Bowes."

Lucy removed the lid to reveal a sparkling platinum diamond solitaire ring.

"Oh my goodness! Oh my gosh! It is amazing!"

Harvey placed it on her finger. "Will you marry me Miss Bowes?"

Lucy kissed his lips as a single happy tear fell onto her cheek. "Yes... Yes, of course I will, I love you Mr Dove. Mmm, Lucy Dove... that sounds fab!"

Harvey held her hand and looked at the engagement ring. "Are you alright to take it off for now and keep it in the box until after the funeral, Flo knows nothing about this. We can both tell her later."

Lucy held out her hand and gazed at the beautiful ring.

"I really don't want to take it off but I do understand. Eek! I could burst with happiness!"

CHAPTER THIRTY

Before she passed, Florence had moved in with Dorothy and had become part of the household. She was popular with all of Dorothy's friends and staff, taking good care of her aunt in her final days. Together Harvey and Flo had made all the funeral arrangements. They all gathered at Dorothy's house and waited for the hearse to arrive. Florence was a gibbering wreck. She had become so attached to Dorothy and felt such deep sadness at losing such a wonderful woman.

"It's here!"

They all gathered outside with Tom and Wren Salmon. Richard, the chauffeur pulled the Bentley around to meet them. He was looking down and shuffling from foot to foot, trying hard to keep his emotions from showing but in the end they got the better of him and he broke down when he saw the beautiful flowers and Dorothy's coffin.

Harvey patted him on the back. "Are you OK to drive Richard? I can do it if you like?"

"Yes sir, please get in. I shall compose myself."

The Bentley followed behind the hearse all the way to the crematorium, which was packed with people from all walks of life. They were a mixture of VIP's and celebrities and all of Dorothy's employees from both her houses and businesses. There were also a few surprise guests who were unidentified at first and it wasn't until everyone gathered at Claridge's for the wake, that they introduced themselves.

An old white-haired couple stood before Harvey and Florence, who were talking about their great aunt.

"Harvey? And you must be Florence? You both look like your mother."

Harvey and Florence both stopped and looked in silence.

"Grandma Rose? Grandpa Grant?" Harvey studied them, as old memories came flooding back. He was so full of emotion, as he choked back his tears and hugged them both.

"Good Lord! What a surprise! Good to see you both! How have you been keeping? My... You haven't changed!"

Rose ruffled his hair and smiled, a single tear trickled down her right cheek.

"You are still my handsome boy, just taller! A lot taller! I'm saddened that we have missed so many years, I'm so sorry for the way things worked out. Hopefully we can change things now and make up for lost time."

Harvey produced a white handkerchief and wiped his Grandma's tears before introducing his sister who was standing next to him, eagerly waiting for an introduction.

Flo, these are your grandparents. Grandma, Grandpa, meet Florence!"

They all hugged and kissed, Lucy watched from the other side of the room, until Harvey beckoned to her. He proudly put his arm around her.

"Lucy, these are my grandparents. This is my gal Lucy!"

Rose, interrupted, gesturing to the people standing beside

her, "Nice to meet you Lucy. Harvey and Florence, this is your mother's sister May and her family, her husband Ben, son George and her two daughter's Bethany and Ella."

Harvey hugged them one by one.

"Ella? You named her after Momma?"

"Yes I did."

Harvey looked surprised.

They all had so much catching up to do. Harvey was so happy to see his grandparents after such a long time.

"I know it will be difficult to ever forgive my pa for preventing you from keeping in touch, but there was so much bitterness back then. He's a changed man these days. There will be another two good reasons, actually three good reasons, for us all to meet up in the near future."

Flo held her breath in excitement. He held Lucy's hand.

"This may not be the right occasion to announce it, he reached into his pocket and placed the ring on Lucy's finger again. This morning I asked Lucy to marry me and she said yes!"

Tears of joy fell down Flo's face.

"Am I to be your chief bridesmaid?"

"Of course you are! Who else?"

Rose smiled, "And the other two reasons?"

"Well Grandma, we are having twins!"

"Wow! Congratulations! I'm so glad that we are all reunited! What a lovely family! Your children are going to be stunning if they look like their parents!"

Lucy instantly warmed to her newly found family. Florence was appointed executor of Dorothy's will. She was overwhelmed by her great aunt's generosity. She was now a very wealthy young woman who owned two houses. Dorothy also left large amounts to Rose, Grant and May, all her staff, and various charities. She knew that Harvey didn't need her money, so her secret gift to him was to guarantee that his grandparents and family would be at her funeral, paying for their flights and accommodation. She also left him four paintings which were locked in a vault in her cellar, knowing that he would appreciate them far more than anyone she knew. Her ever faithful chauffeur Richard was guaranteed a job, as Flo's driver. She was very fond of him and happy to keep him on, along with Martha and Dorothy's other staff.

Rose, Grant, May, Ben the three children, Harvey, Lucy and Florence all raised a glass.

"To Dorothy!"

Then Harvey raised his glass higher.

"To Florence, my little sister and our beautiful French connection!"

ABOUT THE AUTHOR

Having been a cake maker for thirty years a change of career was much needed. Enjoying my daily solitude apart from the company of two beloved dogs, there was plenty of time to pursue an interest in writing, computers making life much easier than back in the days of pen and paper.

As a child I would make up stories at bedtime and amuse my two sisters Jan and Lynne, often getting told off because of the roars of laughter that would erupt from our shared bedroom.

Hating school with a passion, I couldn't wait to leave...my biggest ever regret in life! With no qualifications, having sat no exams, I ended up leaving school to work on a checkout at a supermarket. Drifting from one mindless job to another, I struggled to stay in the same employment until I married and settled comfortably into motherhood, giving me a newly found purpose in life.

Two daughters and five grandchildren later, now is my time to finally try writing. This is my second book, the first a short story aimed at young teenage girls.

23960341R00195

Printed in Poland
by Amazon Fulfillment
Poland Sp. z o.o., Wrocław